The

SONG

of the

BEES

KRISTIN GLEESON

An Tig
Beag
Press

LISTEN TO THE MUSIC CONNECTED TO THE BOOKS

Go to www.krisgleeson.com/music

Receive a FREE novelette prequel, *A Treasure Beyond Worth*,
and *Along the Far Shores*

When you sign up for my mailing list www.krisgleeson.com

GLOSSARY & PRONUNCIATION (Munster)

PRONUNCIATION OF NAMES:

Meadbh – Mave

Diarmuid – Deermud (sometimes spelled Diarmaid)

Máire – Maura

Feardorcha – Fahr door ka

Sadbh – Sive

Síle – Sheila

Derbhla – Derv la

Ita – Eeta

Eoin – Owen

Aedh – A (like letter)

Sean – Shawn

Devorgilla – Deh vor gil ah

Gormlaigh – Gorm la

Domhnall – Though nall (tongue behind top teeth)

Gofraidh – Jo fra (Geoffrey)

Cearbhall – Ker rool

Mairgreg – Mar greg

Bebhinn – Bevine

Una – Oonah

Eithne – Ethnuh

Turlough – Ter lock

Cobhlaigh – Cove la

FAMILY NAMES

Clan heads were known just by their surname. Example: O'Mathghamhna is the chief of that clan. Ui Fhlionn is the head of the Ui Fhlionn clan.

Ui vs. O. The Ua/Ui (meaning 'of' or 'from' – as in son, grandson of/from) – 'O' came into use about a hundred years before this novel. There was a bit of an overlap and I chose to use 'Ui' for Meadbh's father because they were so proud of their heritage.

Mac Carthaigh – MacCarthy – Muck Car Hig
    O'Dálaigh – O'Daly – Oh Dahl ig
    O'Mhaithghmhna – O'Mahony – Oh Mah GOWN nah
    Ui Fhlionn – O'Flynn

IRISH WORDS (Meaning and pronunciation)

A thiarna – oh Lord (ah HEER nuh)
    Banóircindeach – abbess – formal term (ban OR kin dech)
    Banrían – queen (BAN REE un)
    Bantiarna – lady (BAN TEER nuh)
    Bawn – grounds of castle enclosure
    Beach, beacha – bee, bees (BACH kuh)
    Bean – woman (BAN)
    Brat – rectangular wool length of cloth, sometimes big enough to wrap around the body five times.
    Breitheamh – judge (Breh hiv)
    Caoine – lament – Both a song poem and later anglicized to 'keening' (Kwee nuh)
    Chara (mo chara) – my friend (KAH ruh)
    Cabaicc – The talkative (Conor Caibaicc mac Dermod – literally Conor the talkative son of
    Dermod) (Kuh back)
    Ceann Fine – head of land owning clan (Kee owhn Fee nuh)

Ceann Cuibhrinn – sub chief (Kee owhn Cuv rinn)

Ceithearn Tigh – household troop (Keh urn Tig)

Ciúnas – calm (kune iss)

Clairsach – harp (Clar shuck)

Clairseoir – harper (Clar shure)

Cochall – short, hooded cloak (cluck ull)

Corcaigh – Cork (Cor cig)

Cráinbheach – queen bee (Krahn vack)

Cuid Oidche (Cuddies) – Entertainment for a night for lord and attendants at houses of

various gentry of 'country (kwid Ee huh)

Dia duit – God be with you (Dee ah gut)

Duthaidh – sometimes used for territory (tuath obsolete) (Doo uh)

Fallaing – poncho type cloak (Fall ang)

Fili/ollamh – poet, fieadha/file was more than composer of verse – a sacred personage, almost a priest or magician. Would speak versified curses if threatened. (Fill Uh/ O lahve)

Galloglach – galloglass – mercenary soldiers with distinctive weapon and way of fighting- spar or Galloglass axe. Originally Scottish. (Gallo glahk)

Ighean (medieval) – daughter – used in giving surnames shortened later to ní or nín (Ee un)

Ionar – tunic worn over léine, usually by men (un er)

Léine/léinte – shirt(s) Made of linen, usually ankle length. (LAY nuh)

Lorica – protection prayer, with roots in pre-Christian times (Lor i kah)

Máthairab – name to address the abbess (MAH her ab)

mo crioí, mo leanbh. Is do mháthair mé. My heart, my baby.

- It's your mother/I am your mother (mo kree, mo lan uv, iss the va her may)

Ogham – symbols like hash marks on a staff that signify letters and words. (Oh um, sometimes ahg um)

Oireacht – lordship (iraght – anglicization) (I rackt)

Ollamh – professor, scholar, highest level, usually given to a poet formally schooled. (Oh Luve)

Ráth – ringfort – early dwelling for more well to do. (RAW - rhymes with awe)

Reacaire – professional reciter – often accompanied by a harper (Ra car uh)

Scológ mhaith – well to do farmer. (Skul ohg vah)

Sin é – that's it (shin EH)

Sliocht – later medieval word for clan, literally 'section', later shortened to 'sept' (Sh luckt)

Suantraí – soothing music, lullaby (Shawn tree)

Tá bron orm – I'm sorry (Taw brohn or um)

Taoiseach – chief (THEE shuck)- tongue back of top teeth

Truibhas – loose hose-like trousers made of wool (Tru uss)

Tuirseach – tired (tir shuck)

Note: In this novel I used the contemporary names for Anglo Irish – GAILLS (pronounced 'gall'), for the native Irish, 'GAELS' and for the English, 'SAXAIN'.

Chapter One

P rime. The First Hour. The bells have tolled. A precious candle lit.

The murmur of women's voices echoes off the church's stone walls and floor, creating an intentional harmony. Their tone varies, their words smooth, vowels rounded with practice that stretches back through time. Each word forms a phrase that creates an intention, a supplication, a hope, but only Meadbh can detect a trace of desperation that their sore knees, stiff backs, and chafed skin hidden beneath their habits affirm.

1

Meadbh's voice doesn't join the others. Not because she isn't one of them, or not quite, they being now ten and she soon to make it eleven, but because the words, the sounds are stuck somewhere deep in her throat. They choke her. They are a great wedge of cloth in her mouth, gagging her, so that it leaves her almost breathless.

Her pain comes not from her sore knees, chapped skin or stiff back. She's young, and although she feels the discomfort, it annoys her more than anything. She wants to roar. Roar her pain. Roar her anger. She needs to tell the *beacha*.

The air is soft, damp webs cling to the furze bushes outside the church and glisten in the early morning light. In the distance, beyond the valley, the hills line up against the sky, the russet colours ceding to the verdant greens of spring. Cattle low in a nearby field. Meadbh takes this in, her glance hooked like a sheep in a herder's crook, even as she follows the nuns back to their quarters, Máthairab at their head.

She breathes deeply, the cool air loosens the tightness in her chest, washes over her. The light, which had seemed almost too bright initially, now soothes her after the darkness of the church's interior. This she can manage, appreciate the details, both small and large, of the land around her. They are blessings she can count, to balance those details that aren't blessings.

The land slopes gently away from her, drawing Meadbh forward, towards the faint hum below which begins to vibrate inside her. It speaks of rightness, belonging, her own community, where fellowship is more intimate and intense than any she has experienced inside the walls of the church.

The hum intensifies as she draws nearer, corresponding to the growing lightness of her step. She stops beside the first hives. She pauses and drapes the loosely woven linen cloth over her head. Máthairab insists she wear the face covering as well as the gloves, although they're unnecessary. The *beacha* know her. She would call them her *beacha*, but in truth she is theirs. She is part of them, as much as they are part of her. Their hum is her heartbeat. Their honey is her blood. Any sting is carefully placed to make a point, to instruct her, and she never fails to understand.

Today they are unsettled. She frowns, wonders about the cause. She sings to them, her breath inhabiting each note, a song she made inside her, the hum guiding her, her own hum, her own language that she shares with them. It's always a precious moment when they share their hums. But today, there is no soothing response. They haven't settled.

She listens intently for a moment, then slowly lifts the lid of the circular woven mass of stripped briars that shield the *beacha* from the weather. The hum grows, the sound carrying a dissonance she hasn't heard before. The hive beside it responds with its own hum and she considers this, just as the next three hives raise their own voices in agreement.

She lifts her head, scans the field near her and the one beyond. A figure catches her eye, the sinewed muscles of his back glistening in the weak spring sun that's climbing the sky as he wields the hoe. She watches, mesmerised, as she has been many times before in the months since he has joined this community as a labourer. His dark hair is damp with sweat and he straightens a moment, draws the back of his arm across his brow. It's then he turns to her, his eyes fix on her, penetrating, discerning, even though it's impossible that he would see what she's thinking at this distance, through the opacity of the linen cloth. Her breath catches.

"Siúr!"

Meabh purses her lips when she hears that call. She isn't a sister. She has no sisters. And this place has yet to formally make her so, even in the religious sense.

She turns and sees Siúr Máire standing at some distance from her, her face fearful, her voice tentative. Siúr Máire doesn't like *beacha*. She labels them noisy, her voice awash with disdain when she says it. Meadbh knows her dislike stems from her fear of them. Ironic that someone with such a holy name would dislike or fear creatures as wondrous as *beacha*, thinks Meadbh.

Meadbh regards the woman, noting the too thin frame and hollowed eyes, dark against the white headcovering that surrounds her face and swallows her neck. She knows that beneath that veil is a mass of golden hair that is nearly as fair as Meabh's own now shorn close to Siúr Máire's head. Even with the spare rations, the self-deprivation, Siúr Máire, can't rid herself of such beauty.

"You must come," Siúr Máire says. "Máthairab would speak with you."

Meabh sighs, gives a nod.

Meadbh stands in front of Máthairab, her hands folded, a picture of solemnity and obedience. Late morning light pours through the small window of this room that acts as a sleeping and receiving chamber, illuminating Máthairab, as if to emphasise this woman's holiness. But even as the light casts holy aspirations, the gloom of the damp patches on the lime washed stone walls and thatched ceiling create a devil's war with it.

Inside, Meadbh fights her own holy war of sighs and impatience as she lets her mind wander back to her *beacha* and puzzles their agitated state. She hadn't had enough time with them to understand the cause. She knows, though, she must return as soon as possible. Their hum is already filling her head, coursing through her blood. She thinks of the man, standing in the field, regarding her, grasping the hoe as if it were a weapon and he ready for battle. She knows nothing about him, not even his name, yet. She halts at the "yet" and pushes it aside, focusing once again on the woman before her. Máthairab. The woman's large frame fills the chair she sits on, a small psalter resting on the lap of her coarse grey wool habit. The psalter came from France, Meadbh knows. Máthairab has told her that numerous times, pointing out the fine quality of the scanty illuminations, though Meadbh thinks them ugly and ill-formed.

This woman reminds Meadbh of her own mother, although that reminder brings no fond memories. Even the snub nose, ruddy cheeks and full lips, now brought into a small pout, that are nothing like Meadbh's own mother's features, can't seem to dispel that feeling. It's other things, things that include the gesture she makes to Meadbh at this moment to indicate that Meadbh take the seat on the low stool that's placed at Máthairab's feet. The way she fixes Meadbh with a steely look, her grey eyes hard, knowing. The way she pulls Meadbh's chin up so that she can peer into Meabh's face, to loom large, to impose her will.

"*Inion,*" Máthairab begins. Even though Meabh isn't her daughter, and she really has no right or family tie to do so. Even though Meadbh flinches every time this woman calls her such. Máthairab takes pleasure in Meadbh's flinch. Meadbh is certain of that much.

Máthairab calls her daughter again and Meadbh forces herself to remain still, to provide no reaction to this woman who peers into her face.

"I've had word from your family. I'm afraid the news isn't good."

Meadbh stills at the word "family". Clan. There is so much attached to this word. Mother, father, brothers, sisters, aunts, uncles, cousins and cousins and cousins, until there is no end of cousins, that made up her *sliocht* – unless the name goes, and with it, all of them.

"Is it my mother?" Meadbh asks, more from obligation, though any obligation seems far afield from this place, from her, Meadbh.

Máthairab tilts her head, regarding Meadbh carefully. Assessing her distress, maintaining sufficient tension, so that when she does deliver the news, Meadbh will be suitably desperate to pray, to ask the others to pray? Meadbh thinks of her *beacha*, wills them to calm her so that not even the merest flicker of anger will show. Calm. She repeats the word three more times, focusing on each syllable. *Ciúnus*.

"It's your father." Again the searching eyes, seeking out some small sign. Máthairab frowns. She sits back in her chair. "He's ill. You'll have to go to him."

Meadbh feels her throat tighten. She blinks. Yet the burning comes, the sign of tears. Máthairab wins.

Chapter Two

She stands in front of Máthairab, this time, one hand clutching a sack, the other holding her mantle. Beside Máthairab is Siúr Eithne, her thick, sturdy frame too much for her lame leg, so that she, too, has a chair to sit upon and regard Meadbh. Siúr Eithne acts in Máthairab's stead when needed and oversees the daily details of the convent. It allows Máthairab to contemplate the psalter that came from France, to trace her fingers over the figures that depict every kind of sin, in order to best instruct her charges.

Siúr Eithne gives Meadbh a tight smile and gestures her to set down her bundle. The sighs and impatience rise up in Meadbh once more. She's at once anxious and fearful to be gone, though she strives to keep all of this to herself. She won't let this woman draw anything more from her than she's prepared to give. And she's prepared to give nothing.

"My *beacha*," Meadbh says. Her tone is firm and flat and that pleases her, though she regrets the slip of her tongue that tells them how much the *beacha* mean to her.

Máthairab purses her lips, her eyes narrowing just enough to show her disapproval. "The *beacha* will be well cared for. Siúr Bríd will personally look after them."

Meadbh fixes her gaze on the pig-shaped damp patch on the wall behind Máthairab, suppressing the anger that rises at the thought of Siúr Bríd tending them, with her stubby fingers that chop, stir, boil and slice with little understanding or care for the food that's in her charge. Meadbh wants to go to *beacha*, explain, apologise and make promises that she knows she can't keep, but still wishes could be met.

"Diarmuid will accompany you. You may use one of our precious horses."

Máthairab makes this statement as a form of benediction, a sign of her munificence, how she cares for her flock, though Meadbh can imagine the horse that will carry her on her journey. But that thought is brief, because it's the name that really catches her attention, a man's name that has no more familiarity to her than true munificence from Máthairab. Meadbh frowns, staring still at the pig-shaped stain.

"*Inion*," says Máthairab, her voice cool. "As much as it pains me, I must make it clear, that since we don't know the nature of your father's illness, and given the current circumstances every-where, we can only assume the worst."

Meadbh turns her gaze back to Máthairab. "The pestilence."

Máthairab winces as if the mere utterance of the word would bring it down upon them all. But that would negate the power of their prayers. The power of the purity, the goodness of Teampall Gobnatán and all who reside here. For God only punishes the sinners.

A moment later, Máthairab forces a nod. "Exactly. And you can be sure that we'll pray most fervently for you and for your father, and all of your *sliocht*, that the pestilence has not yet touched them. God in his infinite wisdom and mercy has left us so far untouched and we must do everything to ensure his blessing continues."

Máthairab's meaning is clear. She must not return to Team-pall Gobnatán. Meadbh allows herself to raise one brow.

Wide-eyed, she takes in the scene front of her as she approaches the clearing outside the small cramped building that functions as the sleeping quarters for all but Máthairab. Behind her, the *beacha* remain as agitated as she feels now, their message as clear as her own rapidly beating heart. Even though she just left them, she glances once more to the hives, seeking reassurance or comfort. Perhaps both. Her mind is confused. The relief of the knowledge that once she leaves she won't return has now given way to mixed emotions about what she faces. Her father, her mother, if she arrives without mishap at her old childhood home. What she feels about returning to a place that held both pain, anger and only the occasional comfort, is something she has chosen not to think about.

Up ahead, in that clearing, stands a horse and a man. A man with sinewed arms and dark curls. A man she's watched, studied as he wields a hoe, chops the wood, gathers the cattle into the pen.

He ties Meadbh's sack to the other one by his side and flings it over the horse so that it straddles the animal's flanks. His movements are deft, efficient and speak of ease of purpose, the muscles of his back under his *léine* are like a breeze on water. The horse's mane hangs loose and free of any burs or tangles. Even so, it doesn't hide the slight bow to its back. His back. No man would ride a mare, so Meadbh has no doubt about the gender of this horse, despite the curved back and the paucity of flesh that hangs on his frame. His thinness is no fault to Máthairab, or anyone at the nunnery, but the famine that has intermittently occurred in the past several years, that has driven livestock, as well as people, to suffer, some to die. Its toll evident even in the dwindling numbers of her community. Even with the blessed St Gobnait, their founder and personal intercessor to hear their prayers, the community has suffered. Although Máthairab would remind her that their most treasured saint has protected them from the terrible death that is the pestilence.

She thinks these things, all the while knowing it's a distraction. A distraction from every thought and observation that she has had about this man. Even as she stands before him, clutching tightly her loosely woven frieze mantle, the tufts woven through it already damp from the morning mist, and while he stands large in a *léine, ionar, truibhas* and boots, a roughly woven *brat* draped around his shoulders. Even in his *truibhas* she can see the outline of his leg muscles. She blushes thinking about them. Their strength. The *ionar* fits him well across the chest, and the arms of his *léine* can't disguise the well-shaped limbs underneath. She knows she should take it upon herself to take the lead, introduce herself so that she can establish her authority. Máthairab, true to form, has left her to it, remaining in her chamber after Meadbh took her leave, no other person to bid Meadbh farewell on her journey. Or smooth over the introductions and instructions to this man who is to take her to her home place. *A bhaile.*

"I'm called Diarmuid," says the man, interrupting her thoughts.

Meadbh nods, deciding at the last minute to say as few words as possible. It's pure whim, a whim she refuses to dissect. Before she can change her mind, he grasps her waist and swings her up on the horse. She handles the action clumsily and tries to seat herself more comfortably on the padded cushion. She rarely rides now. A journey to the market or visiting the ill comprise the infrequent occasions she'd ride. The market visits are conducted by Siur Bríd with the cart and one of the labourers to assist.

Diarmuid swings up behind her, startling her, his body right up against her, against the cushion. She thought, assumed, presumed and any other phrase that would have crossed her mind, that he would lead the horse and leave her to ride alone.

She finds her voice. "Will the horse not suffer with two of us on his back?" She wishes she hadn't made it a question. That makes her sound tentative. She isn't tentative.

11

"Looks can be deceiving. He's sturdy, so he is. With a loyal heart. He'll manage fine."

The words were spoken low but firmly into her ear. She feels them in her chest. She nods. "Fine, so." She keeps her reply economical, her tone clipped. So.

He slips his arms around her waist. She stiffens on her cushion.

Her back is starting to ache. Meadbh stretches carefully, conscious of Diarmuid's arms around her, the hands that hold the reins with ease just at her waist, yet still keep her firmly fixed in place. He shows no sign of discomfort and she's almost annoyed that he should find this so easy. They've been travelling for hours and her body is protesting. She notes each tree she sees in the wood that borders the track they follow. Oak, ash, willow, alder, whitethorn. All showing buds, catkins and other indications that life is springing forth. In the distance, she thinks she hears the warbling of a capercaillie sending out a mating call. A deer has already fled across their path, startled by their presence. It had been grazing right by the track. She can see that the track isn't as worn as it was in past times. Too few footfalls.

The moment the thought fills her mind she spots a few boats on the river, though, and one she's certain carries a merchant, his wooden crates and barrels stacked neatly near him. She doesn't know if she should take comfort in the merchant's presence, and what it might indicate about the pestilence's progress.

"Some merchants are still trading then," says Diarmuid. "Perhaps all will be well."

His words ring in her ear, echo in her chest, and something

about them irritates her, though she refuses to look any closer at the reason.

"Have you ever seen anyone fall ill with this pestilence?" she asks.

Her voice startles her, not just because it's the first time she's spoken since the journey began, but because the words tumbled from her mouth before she knew she would speak them. Her tone is curious, but the irritation she feels must have bled through, because he gives a brief snort.

"I have not been that far afield since the onset of this plague, siúr," he says.

She stiffens. "Don't call me siúr. I'm a postulant nun. I'm not yet pledged."

"What shall I call you then?"

Her response had been an impulsive reaction to the word that carried so much weight, so much meaning. A length of thick chain that would entangle her soon. But would it now? Suddenly she feels light at the thought. Giddy.

"Call me Meadbh," she says, the giddiness fuelling her impulse.

"Meadbh," he says, his voice soft.

Chapter Three

A man approaches them on the track. He wears a *cochall*, the hood pulled up against the cool breeze blowing off the river. Underneath hangs his *léine*, but it only reaches mid-calf and he's wearing *triubhas* that disappear into his sturdy boots. He has a small sack slung on his back and he carries a staff. His hair is long, flowing, and the sight of it gives her heart. A Gael. It isn't until he draws closer that she can see he's beardless. A Gael who lives among the Gaills then, perhaps, his clothes and style a mixture of the two. A skilled man, carrying the tools of his trade on his back. They are only guesses, but it occupies her mind.

Diarmuid slows the horse as they near the man and greets him. "*Dia dhuit.*"

Meadbh dismounts, her body stiff. If not for Diarmuid's hands around her waist as he helped her down, she would have stumbled. With effort she regains her balance. She refuses to let him see the toll the journey has taken on her body. Her mind, however is taken up with the thoughts that have filled them since their brief conversation after spotting the merchant on the river. The thoughts bite at her still, like a swarm of midges at the height of summer. It's only one merchant, not several. They'd encountered no other person since, except one lone man on the track. He'd worn the mantle of a Gaill, but his saffron *léine* and bare feet had marked him as a Gael, though his haste was hardly the manner of a Gael.

It was his manner that worried her. Diarmuid had said that he probably feared they might be carrying it, though it was clear they weren't. It was the miasma that carried the pestilence, he'd added. A miasma that could enter through any orifice. He'd paused a moment and added that a cloth across the face might be wise. To prevent the miasma's entry.

Any sense of ease she might have felt in the freedom of the open track, endless scrub and scattered stands of trees, had fled with the sight of that man's haste.

Now she faces another man and tenses against the news he might have, the threat he might pose.

The man nods to Diarmuid, hesitating. The hesitation is only momentary, because he can't seem to refuse his inbred compulsion for hospitality, so he greets Diarmuid in return. Still, he eyes the two of them warily and stands at a distance.

"Is all well with you?" asks Diarmuid, his tone equable. "Have you come far?"

"Not so far," says the man. He glances around him as if someone might appear, or perhaps the sickness. "I'm headed towards Borneach, to kin. And to Teampall Gobnatán. To do the rounds, in hopes the prayers will provide protection." He crosses himself.

Diarmuid nods. "We've just come from that direction. All is grand there, *buíochas le Día*."

The man's eyes brighten. "*Buíochas le Día*." He crosses himself again, then nods his head in the direction from which he came. "Sadly, all is not well beyond."

"The pestilence?" asks Diarmuid with a hint of tension.

"The pestilence. But only as you draw near *Corcaigh*," he says. "Though each day there are more and more reports of it further afield." He nods ahead of him. "So I'm headed as far away as I can manage. To kin."

Meadbh's heart lurches at those words and feels a sudden rage grow within her. The rage is not to be reasoned with. She knows her mother shares no blame in the sudden arrival of this pestilence, or its deadly effects, but she can't help but blame her mother, that after forcing Meadbh out of the world, she should draw Meadbh back into it again, only to ensure that she won't have an opportunity to enjoy it.

She stuffs these feelings away. They're unhelpful and feck-less. But hadn't her mother called her that countless times?

The man stares at her and she finds herself flushing. Had she uttered the words aloud? She glances at Diarmuid but he only shifts his position so that she's half obscured from the man.

From a distance all seems well. The clearing is small but sufficient. Blackbirds sing from the alder and ash, still bare of any growth, though the oak in the distance hints at green buds. The oak would most likely be out before the ash, she thinks. Sign of a good summer. The thought comes to her from her distant past, when she'd hide behind the stone shed that housed the pigs, to avoid her mother's needlework instruction and listen to the labourers talk among themselves.

A weak sun is breaking through the overcast sky and casts its light on the spot where they now stand beside the horse. Meadbh is glad to be standing once again and not mounted on the poor animal's back, as much for the horse's sake as her own. In her mind she's named him Fintan, like the shape changer of the tales she'd heard as a child at the feet of the servant Eithne who cooked the meals. Fintan, because this horse had changed from a worn, faltering beast, to a sturdy, brave animal who would bear them both to her home. He deserves a name, and most especially a name such as this, no matter that the nuns said the animals should have no name, but should only be the brown horse with the white star, the brown cow with the twitch, the black pig with the spotted ear, for they were God's beasts and possessed no soul.

Meadbh reaches out to pat Fintan, murmuring sweet soothing sounds and praises. Beside her, she can hear the small noise of amusement emanating from Diarmuid. She eyes him carefully, still stroking Fintan. He's removing one of the sacks, the strong muscles of his fingers working the knots, seemingly intent on his task, but there's a tell-tale quirk to his mouth. She frowns and decides to ignore it.

"Will I put the blanket down over there?" she asks. No words have been exchanged to confirm they're breaking for a meal, but it seems unnecessary once he's starting to untie the sack. Though the bell no longer structures her day or prayers, the sun is well past midday, and her stomach tells her that it's more than time to put some food in there.

"That would be very kind of you, siúr," Diarmuid says, his tone formal.

He hands her the blanket and she takes it from him, wondering if she should correct him again. Would it reveal too much about her abhorrence of becoming a nun, to be known as a *siúr*? To have the other idea of "sister" taken from her, this time not even in past tense? No, she won't be this kind of sister, this "siúr" kind, not even in the future.

"Call me Meadbh," she reminds him.

He looks at her, a flicker of something crossing his face before it resumes its passive expression once more. He gives a quick nod.

The food will be plain. Meadbh knows this, but she's used to it, and she has no doubt that as only a labourer, Diarmuid is too. Though his manner of expressing himself marks him for something more, and again she tries to puzzle him out as she unfolds the cloth containing a large portion of oatcake and spreads it out on the blanket where she kneels. His hands, finely tapered, yet carrying strength, are work roughened and a nail is chipped. The muscles under his léine and those that shape his thighs are hardened and speak of labour, or, she thinks, recalling her father's *ceithearn tigh*, perhaps battle training. She remembers how she felt so compelled to watch his fluid movement, the ease that held her for a length of time she knows better than to count. Is his muscled shape from battle practice? This thought only occurs to her as an off chance and it surprises her. She considers Diarmuid in a different light and sees the possibilities of her thought. Although he carries himself upright and proud, his manner is of service, and she knows that a man trained for battle wouldn't be tending fields for a nunnery.

The other question, related to this one, is why he'd agreed to accompany her on this journey that had all the potential of danger at best, and mortality at worst. The land is rife with battles among the Gaels and with the Gaills, fighting over territory in the face of the English king's loosening hold. And now this pestilence. She thinks again of the cloths covering the mouths of the merchant and the craftsman. Sitting there now, Diarmuid seems calm, unafraid, and the only emotion that seems to fill him is interest in the food that he's unfolding from the cloth. Oatcakes and a small pot of honey. Precious, healing honey, not for consumption, a thought she ignores.

As if sensing her regard, he looks over at her and Meadbh thinks she detects a hint of amusement. She looks away. A moment later he hands her another cloth bundle. She takes it with a nod, unfolding it, and adds the chunk of cheese it contains to the spread in silence. It's a silence that seems to sit more comfortably on him. She represses an inward sigh. She should be used to the silences, living at the nunnery for so long. Too long. Perhaps it's the promise of conversation that has her on edge.

Diarmuid moves around the horse, taking its reins, startling her from her thoughts. "I'll just take the horse over to the river beyond the trees. It should be shallow enough there."

She stares at his retreating back, the horse ambling beside

him, haunches swaying slowly, suddenly wishing for the silence that moments ago sat so heavily upon her.

The sound of the horse's hooves and the rustle of leaves signal their return a short while later. Relief washes over Meadbh and she realises how tense she's been while he was away. She shakes herself from such a repulsive dependent notion and frowns at him to disguise any relief that might show. His own concerned expression releases her from that effort.

"What is it?" she asks, forcing down the alarm.

He glances over at her, his blue eyes darkening for a moment. He forces a smile. "Nothing, I'm sure."

"Nothing didn't cause that expression." Her words take her by surprise, though she's certain that Máthairab would have found little surprising about them.

Rather than a dark look or a deepening frown, his smile widens a little, a touch of humour reaching his eyes. "There are a few animals loose, drinking at the river."

"Wild animals?"

"Cows."

The word is given reluctantly. It takes her a moment to understand the reason. She's spent too many years in the confines of Teampall Gobnatán, in the company of her *beacha*, with only occasional healing visits, to immediately remember the value of cows. Cows are payment. Cows are dowries, cows are life and death. Cows are taken before any gold in some places. Cows unattended seem impossible in the light of that knowledge.

"There's probably an innocent explanation," she says with

deliberate calm. She hands him a chunk of cheese and some oatcakes.

"Yes," says Diarmuid, his tone neutral. He remains standing, takes the proffered food, but doesn't eat it.

She can read the message in his stance, in his refusal to eat, and is suddenly angry, resisting the message, refusing it. She's risking enough, and though she might feel some joy at being released from her pledge, albeit unofficially, she knows there's a price to pay. A price that might be too much in the end, so why hasten it?

He crouches beside her and starts to pack up the small spread of food. She stares at him for a moment and then helps. Around her the wind soughs through the trees, sending a few birds into flight.

Chapter Four

The cattle owners' dwelling is moderately sized, sitting there in its weathered yard. Instead of the rounded walls of clay, this dwelling is squared off, clay filling the space between the branches, with a roof recently thatched topping it. A small *baile* squats nearby, empty of any animals, the woven branches of the enclosure sagging in places, the makeshift gate trampled.

If not for the *baile*, Meadbh would have found nothing remarkable about the scene before her. Behind her, the lowing of cows fills the air as they make their way up the path behind her. Diarmuid shoos them, his voice firm and persuasive. She stands beside Fintan, their old horse, reins in her hand and finds she can go not further. The cows ignore her and filter past her to the pen, bellies full of grass and water, but ready for the security of their familiar enclosure, now that they've been directed properly.

A hand rests on her shoulder. She turns, even though she knows who it is. The gesture goes some way towards calming her, easing some of the dread she feels at the sight before her. Of what awaits her behind the door to the dwelling in front of her.

"Stay here," says Diarmuid.

His instruction, given with the same firm tone he used on the cows not moments ago, annoys her. Now she has a strong desire to stalk past him up to the door and fling it open. To confront whatever might lie inside, if indeed anything does. Instead, she frowns at his back, drops the reins and follows slowly behind him.

A short distance before the door he stops, and she has to catch herself so that she doesn't stumble into him. He lifts up the neck of his *ionar* over his nose, mouth and ears and moves forward. Meadbh seeing its sense, copies his gesture and holds the cloth of her headcovering over her own nose and mouth. Her ears are already covered. She squints, hoping that might help.

When he reaches the threshold she's not far behind. It's then the odour reaches her. Putrefaction. She gags and forces herself forward. Diarmuid turns, his face darkened with anger.

"Go back to the horse," he says in a forceful voice that will brook no disobedience.

23

"No," she says. Her tone is more like a petulant child than a woman who is in control of her situation.

It's then she remember what she is. Who she is. "I'm a healer. I must see if there's anything I can do."

"There's nothing to be done. They're all dead."

She wants to ask him how he possesses such knowledge. Does he have powers that extend beyond the norm? But the impulse to say those words still has the air of the petulant child. Besides, she knows that odour. It takes no special powers to understand its message of death.

"There might be someone still alive, though."

He looks at her, a flash of something crossing his face, but a curt nod and a firm finger pointing to her chest tells her that she has won a small concession and so she remains in place as his finger indicates while he enters the dwelling, his *ionar* firmly covering his nose and mouth.

A moment later he returns. "No one is alive."

She'd expected the words but hearing them still takes her aback. She stands a moment and tries to take it in. To understand it.

"Is it..." she lets the words tail off, because uttering that final terrible word somehow seems too much for her.

"Perhaps. Probably. I've not seen the evidence of the pestilence myself before, but from the accounts I've heard it seems so."

She nods. "I have to see." The words are uttered and though her mind screams "fool" she knows she must. "I need to view the bodies for myself so that I may recognise the pestilence in the future. For the sake of my father," she adds in a softer voice.

He studies her carefully and she bears his scrutiny, trying to appear calm, determined. After a moment he sighs and moves aside. "Just go to the door. You'll see enough from there."

This dwelling is small, rude. The clay is thin, broken through in places, a home for an outcast perhaps, or a temporary shelter, unlike that dwelling they'd left just after midday. That dwelling's inhabitants had possessed a small degree of wealth, as evidenced by their clothes and surroundings. But that wealth had proved useless against the plague. Here, in this dwelling, though it was roughly made and even now beginning to fall apart, its very rude emptiness gives Meadbh a reassurance that would have surprised her just days ago.

She dismounts slowly with a grunt, ignoring Diarmuid's outstretched hand. At least he hadn't attempted to grab her at the waist, she'd been too quick for that. He makes no comment and goes about unfastening the bundles from the back of the horse. Already the name she'd given the horse is gone from her mind, lost in the hours of plodding along and the images of the dwelling's interior. The makeshift pallets on the floor containing the discoloured bodies, hair wild or plastered to each skull, their *léine* stained with blood and vomit. Six of them in all. Three of them children. And the fingers, blackened as if they'd been burnt. She shudders at the image, just as she shuddered all the other times they came to her mind.

A hand rests on her shoulder and she jumps. "Come," says Diarmuid. "Will we go and eat, take our rest now?"

His tone is gentle and he phrases his words as a question, but she knows that he's the one in charge. He'll give the direction, the instruction, she no longer has any illusions about that.

She's hopeless, useless in the face of this land and everything it contains now. Her incarceration all these years has seen to that. Though she has no desire to return to the nunnery, she knows now that she has little chance of surviving long outside of the nunnery without the aid of someone like Diarmuid. It's a conclusion that's little to her liking, but there's no help for it. Despite that knowledge, she still feels resentment simmering in her belly. Unreasonable, but there it is. She misses her *beacha*, even now understanding that they'd been telling her this all along. After all, she and the *beacha* worked together.

Diarmuid's hand presses into her back, urging her forward to the rude dwelling with its sagging roof of fir branches.

Although they sit in the relative darkness, Diarmuid unwilling to light anything more than a small fire, Meadbh can hear the rats scurrying along the branches overhead. It's not an unfamiliar noise, but when the only other noise is the feeble hum and crackle of the pitiful fire she's huddled by, it seems overly disturbing. Diarmuid has said little to her, communicating only necessary instructions and questions to establish the fire, set out the food, or to offer the small ale contained in the stoppered leather gourd. The words are uttered frequently enough though, that it distracts her, just as her thoughts fill with the awful images still swirling around in her mind, looking for any opportunity to descend on her like a dark cloud.

"Your family are situated at Raithlinn, is that so?" asks Diarmuid.

She gives him a puzzled look. "Did Máitharab not tell you?"

Diarmuid cocks his head. "She directed me where to take

you, but she didn't explain anything more. I was just confirming that it's to your family I'm taking you."

Meadbh stares at him, absorbing his words and their implication. "She told you no more than that?"

Diarmuid shrugs. "Just that your journey is urgent and I'm to do my best by you."

"And on that alone you agreed to go?" Meadbh finds it difficult to believe. Certainly, it's considered an honour of sorts to assist and work for any of the religious houses, a method of absolution, but for him, a virtual stranger to the area, with no ties or affiliation to St Gobnait, or the community at large, to make such an open agreement puzzles her.

"I had no objection to leaving," he says. "And to escorting you as a way of thanks to them for taking me in."

She opens her mouth to speak, to state the words that hang so readily in the air. The words that would add an extra burden to her of an innocent man offering assistance without full knowledge of what it meant. But something holds her back. Something that has fear, need and pragmatism in its quiver. And those bolts, those arrows that are an unwanted part of the arsenal with which she had to navigate the world, this world, refuses to be shot.

"My father requires my help," are the words that she manages to issue. They're words of compromise and she blushes at their prevaricating qualities.

"And he's in Raithlinn?"

"He is."

"And your mother, your siblings?"

She feels she owes him some truth. Some knowledge. "My mother, yes." She burns only a little at the thought of her mother now. "My siblings...are gone." That truth is sufficient, she tells herself.

"Gone." His tone asks for more. For elaboration.

She nods and decides she has her own questions. Elaboration isn't required. "And yourself?"

"Myself?"

His tone is innocent, as if he doesn't know that she is asking him the same questions in return. She represses an impatient noise. "Your home. Is it near?"

"No," says, his own elaborations apparently as unnecessary as hers.

She knows the answer he'll give before she asks the question, but he provokes her stubbornness. "And your parents, and siblings, are they at your home that has no name?"

He gives her a smile. "No."

She draws in her breath and looks away into the dark corners for the patience she knows she won't find.

Chapter Five

The chill of the night has seeped into Meadbh's bones, causing her to shiver and nurse the dull ache in her backside, stiff from yesterday's ride. She rises slowly from the makeshift pallet of fir boughs that Diarmuid had constructed for them the day before. She hasn't slept much, and her sleep-encrusted eyes struggle to focus on her surroundings. Dim light filters in through the ragged gaps and chinks of the dwelling, and seems to create shapes where none should be, and emptiness where she'd hoped there would be none. The space next to her. The occupant that had emanated enough heat for her to take comfort and more from the night before, is now gone. She'd been shivering enough during the night that he'd folded his arms around her, drew her in close. She'd refused to consider the propriety of such a move and strove only to appreciate the warmth it brought. The comfort, too. Even now, she can feel his arms encasing her, a ghost shadow haunting her, a haunting she wants to keep with her.

She feels the absence of that comfort now though, as she stares at the vacant place beside her. The thought settles in her a moment before alarm kicks through her body, helping her limbs and mind to wakefulness. Has he deserted her?

Meadbh has no idea why that's the first thought she casts her mind to, she knows only that the distressing conclusion about her dependency on him certainly fuels the caution and fear she carries with her constantly. She hears the voice of Máthairab in her head, chiding her about her distress, and reminding her that she has God and St Gobnait to watch over her. She thinks again of the *beacha* and the strength of that connection that leads to her connection to St Gobnait. The *beacha* are no longer there for her, and whether they're content at Teampall Gobnatán is something that she doesn't know. Not with any certainty, though her body still feels their hum. Was it due to the honey on the oatcake? She feels she must dismiss that thought, but part of her won't. Has St Gobnait given her that blessing to feel them constantly with her? But without her regular attention to the *beacha*, would St Gobnait still watch over her? It's a question she feels might be put to the test.

She hears footsteps and turns to see Diarmuid enter the dwelling, ducking under the low lintel.

"You're awake," he says.

She nods to him stiffly. "Just now."

"I've watered the horse.

The name she gave the horse comes to her now. "Fintan."

"Fintan?"

She lifts her chin a fraction. "Fintan. I've named him Fintan."

He nods, saying nothing, but she can see the gleam of humour in his eyes. He crouches down to the bundles and begins to work the ties that fasten the bundle of food. There is enough left for the day, maybe two, if they ration it. She'd noticed that yesterday evening when they last ate.

He spreads the food out and takes a seat. Meadbh lowers herself down, careful of her stiffness which has eased to some degree, and takes a small oatcake and the pot of honey. Even though it's still the luxury it was the day before, and she knows that she should be saving all of it for medicinal use, she pushes that thought aside, as she had the day before.

They eat in silence and Meadbh tries to use the time to consider possibilities, actions and the consequences of each one for the life she'll now face. She could count them, but the moment she puts her mind to one thought, she turns stubborn and pushes it away. How can she possibly know the prospects in a time of such uncertainty? How can she know?

But she does know, and the knowing is part of the problem, part of her anger.

Meadbh sways a little, Fintan's steady amble lulling her into a doze that creates illusions of warmth, comfort and support, her body easing, releasing all its anxiety and tension to a brief moment of contentment. She feels herself fall, and before she can catch herself, strong arms pull her in more firmly against a hard chest. She opens her eyes, recalling her surroundings. Solid, muscled arms stretch out before her. Diarmuid. She's riding in front of him today again, a decision she now realises he made knowing full well he's less able to defend them should the need arise, but despite that knowledge, a knowledge that was so obvious even in the face of her own ignorance about battle, she feels safe. So safe that she had been easily lulled into a doze.

The track has widened and become muddy and rut-filled from the wheels of numerous carts lugging goods in the wet early spring. She looks around, and with sudden clarity, recognises the small group of dwellings of packed clay on either side. Further along is a stone limewashed dwelling. She's home.

A once glorious history reduced to a few clay dwellings clustered around an old *ráth* that sprawls haphazardly and the few wooden and stone outbuildings attached to it spreads out before them. Diarmuid pulls up short, studying the surroundings, his right hand moving from his reins.

At its core, the *ráth* comprises several rooms situated on an earthen bank erected at the height of the power of the Éoganacht Raithlinn, proud descendants of Mac Cass, the son of Conall Corc, the first King of Cashel. The Ui Fhlionn had returned here, to this old *ráth* after the Mac Carthaigh's had forced them out of their more recent castle at Achadh Durbchon. The words echo in Meadbh's head, her father's voice so strong and clear from the countless times he stated it to her and to so many others, whether they cared to hear it or not. It's part of her, the words and the meaning, regardless of her wishes or her fate. It's in her blood.

Diarmuid dismounts behind her and rests his hand on her thigh, stilling her progress to follow him. Blackbirds sing overhead from the trees beside the furthest hut and a lone bird takes flight, soaring over their heads. It's a large hooded crow. Taking in the visitors? She wonders for a moment if he will report back. What will he say? That the errant daughter has returned? That she's now flung from her safe abode on some fool's errand? For fool's errand is what it seems as the silence from the huts and the *ráth* greet them. On closer inspection, she can see an overturned cart, one of its wheels split in half. A door hangs ajar, half off its hinge.

"Stay here," says Diarmuid.

She makes no move to disobey and watches silently as he roots around in the sack on the far side of Fintan's flank and withdraws a long, slim cloth-wrapped bundle. It takes her only a moment to realise it's a small sword, though it's shorter than any other sword she remembers. That he's now armed both comforts and alarms her as she watches him slowly approach the hut closest to them.

Diarmuid eases open the door, calling softly. It's then that Meadbh makes out a flash of colour on the track just ahead of her. Studying it, she concludes it's a piece of cloth. She glances back over to the hut and sees that Diarmuid has disappeared inside. No sound comes from it, so she takes that as a good sign. Slowly, she eases off the horse and goes to investigate the cloth. It only takes her a moment to grab the protruding end, but it's buried deeper than she'd imagined and its size means that it takes more than a few tugs to work it loose. When she does unearth it she sees it's a child's mantle, its dun colour relieved only at the bottom edge where some red cloth has lengthened it.

It's too precious to be flung aside or discarded, even among the more prosperous of labourers. Sure, they would have passed it on, she has no doubt, to someone else who would make use of it. The reasons this half-buried garment is here, in the middle of the track, cause her to look up and search out Diarmuid once more.

It's the frown that has her stiffening, she knows, even as she stands there now, at the threshold of the third hut, staring at the small pallet with a blanket rumpled atop it, the smoored fire in the hearth, embers still glowing at the hut's centre, and the three-legged pot containing potage beside it. The frown has her move towards him, her stride determined, instead of waiting for him to come to her and recount his discovery. The frown tells her all that she needs to know about his thoughts. But still he speaks them.

"I asked you to remain on the horse," Diarmuid says quietly.

She gives him a feeble smile. "I discovered something."

He raises a brow, saying nothing, just waiting for her to explain.

She holds up the mud-caked mantle she still has clutched in her hand. "I found this half-buried just off the road. It's a child's mantle."

He looks up a moment later and fixes his arresting eyes on her. She's caught in them, searching for answers, wondering if he will give them here or later.

"The pestilence?" she asks and hears her tentative tone. She thinks of the child's garment, hastily tossed away from the dwellings. But not yet burnt. A death and hasty departure?

He casts a glance over her shoulder in the direction of the first two huts. "I think so. There are signs of some illness. Herbs for medicine scattered on the floor in the first hut and air that's stale, malodorous. All the furniture is gone, along with bedding, clothes and everything else. Burnt perhaps. But there are also signs of hasty departure." He looks down to the mantle.

Meadbh feels prompted to ask, "Perhaps it was missed in the burning?"

"Perhaps."

She looks around the hut again. "But here someone hasn't left or died."

"No."

"Will we wait for them to return?"

Diarmuid frowns again. "Come with me."

He takes the mantle from her and sets it on the earthen floor, just inside the hut. With his hand on her back he ushers away from the hut, back towards Fintan who has discovered a small patch of untrodden grass just off the track and is munching it lazily.

Diarmuid gives Fintan a pat and then takes up Meadbh's hand and heads toward the whitethorn thicket that surrounds the *ráth*.

A soft neigh sounds. Diarmuid stops and looks around, surveying the area. "Where's the *bawn*?"

She points over to the left, away from the huts they'd just visited to the two that are on that side.

A man emerges from behind the nearest hut. He stops when he sees them, his body stiff with alarm. He raises the bow at his side, removing an arrow with one swift, steady motion and notches it. "Leave here, now. We need no one to bring more pestilence!"

Meadbh pauses, scanning the features of the man who stands at a distance, his fingers poised at the bow string, arrow ready to fly. There's something familiar about him. White threads his fair hair. His *léine* is below his knee, belted, with a dagger tucked inside it. A brat drapes his shoulders, a finely braided fringe dangling from it. He wears leather boots, worn, but well made. A Gael, through and through. He studies her carefully, eyes narrowed. A man ready to defend. She casts her mind back to her family's household, the *ceithearn tigh*.

"Eoin?" she says tentatively. "It's Meadbh, daughter to Uí Fhlionn. I was summoned to come from Teampaill Gobnatán to tend him."

Eoin stares at them, still holding his bow and notched arrow in the air. Slowly, he lowers it. "You must come no further. The pestilence. Have you any symptoms?"

Slowly, Meadbh shakes her head. She has no words. Her mind is filled with terrible possibilities.

"We have no symptoms," says Diarmuid loudly behind her. A soft breeze lifts some tendrils of hair around her head and they flutter in her face, butterflies, newly released.

Chapter Six

The low stool, the pride of place Meadbh sits upon, has a slight cast to the side, but she tries to ignore it as she sips her cup of ale. It's a perfect height to tend the hearth fire, below the constant smoke that hovers like storm clouds inside every dwelling, but now it gives her a crick in her neck as she looks up to Eoin and listens as he tells his tale. Eoin is her father's distant cousin, a swordsman and smallholder who also looked after the small group of soldiers that served her father. Now, while he stands before her, she tries to find the young, laughing man she remembers from her days living here. Diarmuid sits on the small bench to her right. Eoin, his manner still cautious, nods with his words, as if to affirm every detail.

"*Tá bron orm*," Eoin says again. Those words had been first out of his mouth when he'd recognised Meadbh. And now he says them again. Meadbh just nods, still unsure exactly what sorrow weighed upon him, but it sets the tone for the words that will follow.

Eoin swallows. "Your father was away with Colm." He clears his throat and looks at Diarmuid. "When they returned he was already ill. Bebhinn and her daughter tended him. We realised almost at once it was the great pestilence, but for Bebhinn and her daughter it was already too late. They nursed him in Bebhinn's dwelling, for the safety of all." Eoin gave me a sorrowful look. "We sent for you immediately upon under-standing its seriousness, hoping you could save him. It wasn't to be. Bebhinn was already laid ill upon her bed and her daughter as well. They were both dead in a short span of time." His gaze shifts to me. "It was your mother, you know, who realised first. That it was the pestilence."

Meabdh is bemused to think that her mother would have realised this first, but she knows her mother could be quick witted when under threat. "She helped tend my father?" Meadbh knows her question doesn't come from a kind place in her heart.

Eoin shifts a little. "She did organise the household, as was her duty."

"Organise?" Meadbh asks. "No, sorry for my interruption, please continue."

Eoin gives her a tight smile, but it's his eyes that tell her he knows her implication and his response to it is resignation. His mistress provides no surprises for him.

"Once we knew what it was, it was then that people started to leave. Some at night, for their shame, taking their belongings, if they could. After Bebhinn fell ill..." He stops and looks out of the small window. "The numbers who left increased. Bold they were, leaving in the day, taking tools and animals they'd no right to. I hadn't the men to stop them." His voice is angry. "Some of them were among those leaving, the traitors." He looks over at Meadbh again and she sees the distress in his eyes.

Meadbh swallows. The words take time to sink into her mind in this tale that has seized her insides, churned them and set her mind on fire. "Too late," she whispers. "I was too late."

Eoin nods slowly. *"Tá bron orm."*

And now she knows the sorrow in its full weight as it descends upon her, too. Heavy, knocking the wind out of her.

Diarmuid leans to her, takes her hand and squeezes it. *"Tá bron orm."*

She looks over at him, studies him and gives him a puzzled look. *Tá bron orm.* "I have sorrow upon me." How can he have the weight of sorrow upon him? The thought hits her, even as she knows the words he speaks are courtesy, they are commiseration, an appreciation of what she is feeling. But still they feel wrong.

The wrongness drives her forward. "My mother?"

Would she know if her mother had died along with her father? She scoffs at the idea. She hasn't felt her father's death where some bond has once existed, even though it's fizzled with each passing year at the Tempall Gobnatán, but the bond she'd felt with her mother, and still feels now, was formed from bitter vitriol that had deepened over the years.

Eoin winces. "She didn't take your father's death well."

It's the worry in his eyes, the frown on his face, that tells her his statement "didn't take your father's death well" obscure something far more serious. And the knowledge she has of her mother tells her that it could very well mean danger. A general danger. Or a more specific danger. She feels her pulse increase its pace.

Diarmuid's quiet presence behind her helps her move forward, even as the hut comes into sight, Eoin leading them with stoic resignation. The hut where her mother has been living. Her mother. The woman that wouldn't leave the bedchamber unless she had her hair combed, braided and pinned, headcloth arranged in the most becoming manner possible. And her shoes were always of the finest, softest leather imaginable, impractical as that might be in their often mud filled surroundings. Sure, why would she step outside of the *ráth*?

Her pace slows and Diarmuid rests a hand on her shoulder. It calms her racing heart and the thought catches her. When had the need of his company replaced the resentment? The wonder and appreciation of his physical body aside, her deliberate cultivation of antagonism seems to have slunk away, a failed assault, a lost battle. She sighs, not able for this rumination. The thought of facing her mother seems a slightly better prospect.

Meadbh breaks from her thoughts, movement catching her eye. A woman strides out of the hut towards the three of them, feet bare, her gown torn and stained, her hair flying wild about her. It takes a few moments for Meadbh to recognise the woman. Her mother.

Arriving in front of Meadbh, her mother wields a mighty slap across Meadbh's face. "You're too late. He's dead. And you're to blame."

Meadbh stares at her mother, cheek still stinging with the force of the slap, her mother's tirade pouring forth. Her cheek will bruise, she knows, and she tries to remember what herb is best for bruising. Witch hazel? Her mother continues to throw insults at her, her voice rising with her ire. The screaming mess of words thrown at her becomes just noise, but Meadbh doesn't need to hear them, she knows the gist. It's everything she's heard in the past, only louder and with more elaboration. She closes her eyes, tries to distance herself from this awful woman.

"You, you, you!" shouts her mother. "It all lies at your door. If not for you, this wouldn't have happened! I told them not to summon you, but finally they persuaded me, they said I was being foolish, that you knew the ways of healing at the nunnery, but I know better. I knew that you would cast curses before you would heal, and so you have!"

Her mother's voice has become hoarse, but still she rails on, hands clenched at her sides. Meadbh opens her eyes and finds Diarmuid has pulled Meadbh's mother from her and with a sinewed arm clasped around her body, restrains her at a short distance from Meadbh. She thinks of the *beacha*. Her *beacha*. Her hives. The *beacha* loved her, she was theirs. Though she knows everyone calls the main *beach* a king, she's always felt like their *banrían*, their queen. But this isn't her hive, if anything

41

she's a renegade queen, evicted early, a threat in the making. And now that she's returned, the king dead, she's already under threat from the other queen, who's ready to rid the hive of Meadbh yet again. She shakes her head of the image and tries to focus on her mother.

Her mother quietens, though her eyes still blaze with anger. No, hatred. Her hair lies lank and tangled around her shoulders, the once burnished gold now dull and dark with neglect. Her fine gown hangs loose on her, the close weave clogged with what appears to be dried food and perhaps spittle. The bare feet, once visible, are now hidden behind the gown's hem, though the glimpse Meadbh caught of them told her nothing good about her mother's state.

Meadbh stiffens and meets her mother's gaze. It's then she sees something that stops her cold. Any sense of madness, of overwhelming distress, is missing. She can only see calculation behind the vitriol. She glances over to Eoin, his face turned towards her mother. His expression is filled with concern, worry and something else. Compassion.

Meadbh turns around and walks away. She can hear the shouting resuming as she retreats back to the *ráth*.

It takes her little time to find her father's grave. There's no mystery attached. There's nothing hurried about it, she can tell, so finding him in the place where his ancestors, the other clan heads, are buried, is a simple feat. The earth is newly turned, the marker stone already in place, and behind it the *ogham* stick, with its carefully carved symbols of strength, a concession to times past her family has long honoured.

She stands there, staring down at the damp sod, her breath still coming in pants and tries to clear the fog of rage, grief and hurt from her mind. She concedes the hurt, though berates herself for its existence, and why? Why is she still so ridiculously inept at making her heart understand the stupidity of it? It's a "why" she's carried for too many years and it's time she stopped.

She feels a presence behind her. His presence. She has no need to turn, she knows the feel of him by now. How his body takes up the space, the energy, the something that he emanates and displaces when he comes in a room, in an area. She shoves the idea away, though she'll take the calming that she currently feels from it.

"Your mother is deranged," he says.

His tone is firm, assured. She knows his words are meant as a comfort, a support, a way of telling her that her mother's accusations are baseless, but she can only snort. She hears Máthairab's chastisement in her mind, even as the sound emits from her mouth.

He sighs. "She says that she'll do anything to prevent you from having any claim to remain here. She's threatened to give it over to Desmond. Or the English king."

Meadbh whirls around, gasping. She hadn't expected this. The "why" plunges into her like a spear, ever ready to stab her once again. This time, it slices through her gut and pins her to the ground.

Chapter Seven

The damp, pungent earth is seeping through her gown to her knees, chilling them. She welcomes the chill as she kneels there in front of her father's grave, striking a devout pose of mourning, her hands only now coming up to touch each other to complete the picture. The chill reminds her that she's here, that she must gather herself and think, not remain helpless, fallen to this position out of shock and horror, as if someone had taken the legs off her. Though legless she might be, she's not without her mind, her wits, and now, of any time in the past, she must employ them to their fullest.

Diarmuid places his hand on her shoulder once again. A comfort. But it's not comfort she wants or needs, it's time. Time to find a clear path out of this unspeakable mire she's found herself in. She tries to think, but her mind is a whirl of possibilities, potential outcomes, none of them good.

Diarmuid squeezes her shoulder, bringing her back to her surroundings. She rises slowly, turns towards him.

"We must ensure that there's no one else ill anywhere in the holding," he says quietly. "I spoke briefly to Eoin about it and he says not, but it's best we check every building in the wider area." He pauses. "Just in case."

She nods, glad for a stated, clear purpose that defers her decision making. She knows the "just in case" means that there might be some who've fallen ill before they'd gone very far from here and, unable to go on, have taken refuge in the first available shelter. It's a step that she knows must be taken, and she can mull her choices while it's implemented. And it will give her time to see if there's anything to be gained by seeing her mother once more.

Meadbh watches from a short distance away as Eoin and Diarmuid, cloths covering their mouths, carry a body wrapped in coarse sacking from the small tumbledown outbuilding erected long ago for herdsmen who took the cattle to the hills for the summer. It's in the outer reaches of the clan lands, and according to Eoin, really directly part of the O'Mathghamhna holdings, taken from her father's oversight through pledges he made in return for cattle and goods to barter. The knowledge leaves her somewhat shaken, because it challenges the plan that's slowly and carefully forming in her mind. All the questions around *oireacht,* the holding and the exact terms, the rites and tributes of this lordship, as well as who was *cean fine,* because it's increasingly clear, that though she knows that her father wasn't a powerful *taoiseach,* as much as his pride would have him more, was he even now a *ceann cuibhrinn,* heading up their *sliocht,* with a small bit of land, but little else? The questions, the uncertainty, cloud how she must act. She needs to discover who the real overlord is, and the exact nature and specifics of her *sliocht's* obligations.

Eoin stumbles over a protruding stone, muttering a curse, his vision obscured by the top half of the stiff and unyielding body he's carrying. It's enough to startle Meadbh out of her thoughts and pull her back to the matter at hand. It's late afternoon, now, the time evaporated as a result of the careful yet extensive search they'd conducted for any further plague victims. She'd gone with Diarmuid, her knowledge of the land, though not recent, still better than his own. Eoin had taken the opposite direction, the two groups slowly circling back to each other. It was Eoin who'd discovered the body, but Meadbh had entered the building and confirmed the death at Eoin's request, though she'd puzzled the reason, since she had no reason to doubt his capability. And when she saw the body, that even in its bloated state she could still recognise, she understood. Colm. Her father's youngest nephew, born to Eoin's older brother, now dead. Though it has been many years since she'd seen him, the flame red hair and crooked teeth were unmistakable. As was the realisation he had fled. Her father's nominal heir since her brother died. Though she'd never liked him, and the years should make it matter less, the pain of his betrayal is still acute.

"I'll send for the priest when we arrive back at the *ráth*," she says.

Eoin stops, causing Diarmuid to jolt in surprise. The body sags between them. "The priest is gone. Besides, it's best if we bury him here. Away from the *ráth*. No point in risking the miasma."

His voice is hard and she knows he feels the same betrayal she does. She nods at his words, glad for them. She regards the body, the words "traitor", "coward", running through her mind.

The light is poor in the corner where her mother sits, rocking back and forth on the stool. It started the moment Meadbh entered the small dwelling where Eoin, his wife and son now live. She pauses briefly again to wonder at the state of the *ráth* that Eoin, who'd would have surely lived in one of the *ráth's* large chambers as the head of her father's *ceithearn tigh*, now lives here.

Eoin's rail thin wife Ita hovers over like a mother hen worried for her chick. She strokes her hair, making soothing noises, and tries to persuade her mother to eat something from the spoon Ita has poised before her mother's mouth. Meadbh resists the urge to shake her head. It will only encourage her mother. She catches her mother's eye, and even in the dim light she can still see a hint of calculation before her mother swipes the spoon away, spilling the bowl's contents over her already soiled gown. Her mother wails, throws her hands over her face and rocks with more force on the stool.

Meadbh straightens, rising to her full height and makes her way over with purpose. "Let me try," she says to Ita. "Why don't you attend to Diarmuid and your husband? They should be in any moment. They're just washing down outside."

Ita hesitates, but Meadbh doesn't give her an opportunity to refuse and kindly removes the spoon and bowl from her hands. Ita gives her an uncertain smile and a hint of relief appears in her eyes. She casts a worried glance to Meadbh's mother and then leaves. Meadbh can hear the men talking outside, their voices low, and wonders briefly at their conversation. Colm's burial had been hurried and less than dignified, an object flung into a hole, a layer of lime slung on top, and then filled in with little care to anything but securing it against any scavengers. She can only hope their discussion is limited to those kinds of practicalities.

She turns to her mother, eyeing her carefully. "Mother," she says her voice low but firm. "I have no doubt that you feel some distress at the loss of my father and that the pestilence that caused his loss only added to it, but it's time you put it behind you. Think of the household. The *sliocht*. You must be strong."

Her mother emits a loud derisory snort. She looks directly at Meadbh, her eyes filled once more with the hatred, the anger Meadbh had seen earlier. "What do you know of it?" she says, her voice pitched low and vitriolic. "You know nothing about the duties and obligations here. You're not even worthy of knowing. Go back to your nunnery, where at least God might have the patience to deal with you."

Meadbh pulls back from the force of her mother's words. She remembers coldness, she remembers even the numbing rejection of being ignored, but this anger. This, she doesn't remember. Her mother had been too busy with her brother

Felim to give Meadbh much attention or thought. At least, that's what she remembers.

"Are you angry with me?" The words were out of her mouth before Meadbh could stop them. They were the words of a small girl. One who still had hope that her mother will love her. Meadbh squashes the sentiment immediately. She stiffens, her body and emotions hardening against those stupid words. Weak words. "Why are you angry?"

Her mother gives her a sly sour smile. "That hasn't changed, has it. Still begging. I suppose it suits life in the nunnery. All that practice. Shouldn't you be begging God now? Or has he grown tired of it, like I did?"

Meadbh wills herself not to flinch. Instead, she focuses on the confirmation that her mother isn't deranged. The words she utters, though anger-filled, are evidence that her mother is fully aware of what she's doing and saying.

"Go back to the nunnery and leave us be."

Meadbh mentally bats that comment away without an effort. "What will you do?"

"It's not your concern. You've done enough."

There is something in her mother's tone that prompts her next question. "What have I done?"

Her mother's eyes narrow. "If it wasn't for you, your brother would still be alive." Spit comes with the words, flung into the air, the voice gutteral. Meadbh steps back, stunned.

"I-I had no part in my brother's death," she says, her voice wavering. "He was the one who climbed that tree."

Her mother raises her hand, points her first finger. "You are responsible. And be sure you'll gain nothing from my husband's death."

Meadbh has no words. Any rebuttal flies from her head.

What madness is this? And is it madness? The discomfort and pain since her brother's death rises up in her now. She knows it's unreasonable to take responsibility for something he chose to do. But he was younger, she reminds herself. The argument continues, until she pushes it down, back where it constantly lurks. And something in her gut tells her that this time her mother isn't pretending.

Diarmuid enters the dwelling. Her mother gives Meadbh another angry look before lowering her head and resuming her rocking.

Chapter Eight

The chamber is bare of everything Meadbh remembers. The carved chests, the bed, the woven blankets, the chair that once stood in the corner. Even the carpet of rushes is gone, the beaten earthen floor bare. An eastern wind echoes in the room, a whine that surges and withdraws suddenly as if to emphasise the loss these walls contain.

Meadbh doesn't know whether to be grateful that it's more difficult to picture her father lying on the bed, taking his last breath while her mother sits with the mending on the chair by the window. The last part is false, even as she thinks it, for her mother was never one to do what she could have others do. But what does she know of her mother now, anyway? Her recent encounter has her at a loss, though she must think, she must.

Behind her, she hears the sound of boots approaching. Turning, she finds Diarmuid at the entrance, the sadly askew door open barely wide enough for him to squeeze through. He holds a pile of blankets, and the sacks that had been slung across Fintan's back. His eyes are expressive, filled with concern. She looks away, unable to allow herself to fall into that concern, to unburden herself. She can't trust. She shouldn't trust, even though every part of her urges her on. Is it enough that he's here, still with her, even helping her this night in her unreasonable urge to put as much distance between herself and her mother, and sleep in the *ráth*, in her parent's chamber?

Darkness shrouds them both. His breath is soft, even, filled with calm. A presence that's there, beside her, providing a warmth that helps to fight the chill that's gripped her from deep inside, almost to paralysis. There's a part of her that wants to bury herself into his side. Bury her mind, her body. Dig a pit the size of the one they'd recently dug. Only instead of the cold earth surrounding her, it would be Diarmuid's warmth. The heat of his skin, the muscle strong and supportive around her. It's an image she finds unable to let go. A soft whimper escapes her mouth.

A moment later his hand rests on top of hers. She stiffens, her mind now unwilling to let him see her vulnerable, to trust that he wouldn't press the advantage for his own gain. Though what he would have to gain, she can't imagine.

"Your mother will recover," he says.

She strangles a laugh and the hysteria that seems to erupt inside her with it. "Oh, yes, she'll recover." The bitterness in her tone takes her by surprise, but it helps to smother the other emotions that had threatened to overwhelm her moments ago.

"Will you stay with her?"

The words tell her what she knows is expected, what Eoin assumes, along with the few remaining people that are left here. Here, where she would be at the mercy of the O'Mathghamhna chieftain's decision about her fate. A woman to be distributed or assigned to a person or role of their choosing. Yet Diarmuid poses it to her as if it were a question. As if there was a choice.

"Teampall Gobnatán will not have me back," she says, pleased with the evenness of her tone.

"No."

The response is simple, and a truth she knows, but still it unnerves her with its finality.

"We haven't been directly exposed to the pestilence," she says. She makes her tone reasonable, yet it's an almost childish urge to contradict him. Has she kept it as an unconscious hope? A sense of safety for herself?

He squeezes her hand. "We can't be sure of that."

Meadbh knows he's right, but still she resists. She opens her mouth to say something and then shuts it.

"They would most likely not believe us, whatever we tell them. It would be too great a risk."

He says nothing, but his silent agreement hangs in the air, eventually to sink down, weighing on her, compressing her chest.

"You won't return either, so." She makes it a statement. He knew this even as he left the nunnery, even as he offered his services to Máthairab. "Where will you go?"

She feels suddenly bereft at the thought of his departure. Though she's known him really only a few days, she feels she knows him better than anyone else. The days they shared, the journey, has somehow linked them in ways she can't even understand. He's familiar, that much she knows, and though this place is her home and these people her kin, she feels no closer to them, or this place, than a guest would. An unwelcome guest, in her mother's eyes.

She thinks of her *beacha*. Stills herself to hear their quiet hum that seems to always resonate inside her, to be heard only when she's truly unmoving. And she feels them now, a soft vibration in her chest, her gut. Communicating with each other, with her. If only she knew what they were saying.

A moment later she realises the humming sound is Diarmuid's voice and the words have passed her by. He gathers her up in his arms, pulls her in close. She sinks into it, imagines a worth to it that leaves her wanting more.

Meadbh twists her long fair hair into a plait, tying it off with a bit of leather that she keeps for that purpose. Her hair had come loose in the night, her body unable to settle after her conversation with Diarmuid, her thoughts caught up trying to piece together the fragments of phrases and words that he'd said to her while her mind became wrapped up in itself. The *beacha*. It was as though they'd distracted her enough for their own purpose, but in the end she'd heard neither them nor Diarmuid. And was that in itself a message? To listen to no one but herself? She sighs, knowing she'll get nowhere with this train of thought, nor understand why she hadn't just asked Diarmuid to repeat himself, instead of pretending to be asleep. Was it just too tempting to plead with him to stay, or to take her with him?

She makes herself stand, tidying up the makeshift beds, folding the blankets and placing them into the sack. She fixes her headcloth back over her hair, smooths her gown and tugs the sleeve of her *léine* down. Diarmuid is already up, seeing to Fintan, she thinks, and then most likely after that, off to talk to Eoin. She knows what she must do.

She smooths down her gown again, noting the travel stains, but since there's only one other gown packed away that she must keep for better occasions, she moves off, heading towards Eoin's dwelling. Regardless of whether her mother is alone or not, Meadbh must keep her wits about her and prevent her mother from besting her in any way.

She makes her way out of the *ráth*, through the hall chamber, noting once again how bare everything is. She recalls the hangings, the warm fur rugs, the large carved chests filled with precious linens, wools, furs and the ancient family torc, arm bands and a ring that her father would wear on special occasions. Were they all gone?

She exits the main hall, thinking too of the swords, beaten metal shields and other battle items she remembers vaguely from her childhood. She stands a moment, stares back into the hall, trying to conjure up her father, her brother, bright eyed and smiling, gaps showing where his teeth would later come. The room doesn't hold the image well. It's another time and even seems another place, another home.

Something catches her eye on a stone just across from the

entrance and she moves toward it, drawn like a *beach* to honey. It's an image she scoffs at, but the hum comes to her unbidden, low, barely heard. She nears the stone, close enough to touch it and reaches out, tracing her fingers over the marks etched in that stone years before. Marks she made with a small knife, taken from the table while she crouched at her father's feet, hoping she wouldn't be banished upstairs to her mother's company. The etching was a small sword, with two *ogham* symbols on them. One for "D", oak, for strength, and the other "M" her name, and also an image of a vine, which at the time she had reasoned had its own kind of strength. She'd carved that even as she heard her father talking with his men as he explained her fate, and that they must escort her to it. It was only a formality, because, as she soon realised, they'd all known. And now, as she views this etched stone, she realises that her father had allowed her presence so that she should know. Know from him and not her mother. But her mother had hissed her fate to her years before, and Meadbh had kept it quiet, hoping against hope that her father wouldn't allow it to happen.

She traces the etching once more, the "D" and the "M" and sees the message she'd tried to give herself back then. The message reads for her now, even more so. Strength.

Chapter Nine

Meadbh hears her mother before she enters Eoin's dwelling, her mother's plaintive voice rising and falling. It's a familiar sound but at the same time it isn't. It's not her mother, not that keening sound she's perfected, a woman bent with grief. Meadbh straightens, takes a deep breath and enters.

Her mother looks up from her place near the hearth at the room's centre. The chair she sits upon Meadbh recognises from the *ráth*. Her mother's chair. She gives a silent snort but feels reassured that her mother would have of course ensured her comfort as much as possible, even as she assumed the role of a desperate, grieving widow.

Meadbh greets Ita, who rises from her task stirring the thin oat potage. Meadbh notes the patch on Ita's gown, just above the belt that cinches her waist. It surprises Meadbh, that Ita would be reduced to a patched gown. Has the situation become so dire here? She glances around for Eoin, to ask for a discussion later but Eoin and his son are absent. Meadbh has no doubt the two would understandably find any chore or task away from the dwelling to attend to if possible, leaving Ita to care for Meadbh's mother. Meadbh takes the stool near her mother and draws it closer.

"Mother," says Meadbh, "You are well?"

Her mother narrows her eyes, the low mournful sound that she's switched to since Meadbh entered ceases. She begins to rock. "How can I be well?" she says. "How can I be well?"

"Is there some way I can help? Would you like me to go to the priest? Ask that mass be said for my father, your husband?"

Her mother continues to rock, the mournful tone resuming.

Meadbh takes a deep breath, tries again. "Will I ask the priest to attend you? Or perhaps we can arrange to have Eoin accompany you to the nearest nunnery and you can seek comfort among the nuns."

Her mother gives her a sharp glance. "They wouldn't allow me to find comfort there, for fear of the pestilence. The pestilence that took my own dear Cormac." Her mother heaves a sob at the end and resumes her mournful keening.

"But they are bound by God to give succour to all who seek

it," Meadbh says, although she knows this can sometimes be a lie.

Her mother shakes her head, raises the skirt of her gown to her face and resumes rocking.

Meadbh leans back a little, deep in thought. The ruse is obvious to her, but not to Ita who hovers uncertainly over Meadbh's mother, a bowl filled with potage in one hand, a spoon in the other. Is the ruse meant for Ita and Eoin, so that they will take pity on her and stay to tend her? How would that alter her mother's fate at the hands of O'Mathghamhna, or theirs? And hers, for that matter? She doesn't know the law, be it Brehon or the law of the Gaills, the law the English king has seen fit to foist upon the land they controlled. But it would be Irish law here, surely?

She pauses, the thoughts that had taken her since she arrived now taking shape. Perhaps it's assurance of the future that her mother is waiting on, that keeps her feeling and acting her grief so that she retains the protection of the few people she can win to her side?

Meadbh leans forward and takes her mother's hand. "Mother, all will be well. I'll find someone who knows the law and I'll go to O'Mathghamhna, ask that we may stay here. We're just a small number, I'm sure he'll allow it. Even if we may not have the *ráth*, we can still make ourselves comfortable in one of the dwellings."

Her mother drops her skirt, anger in her eyes. "This is Ui Fhlionn land. The *duthaidh*. The *Oireacht*. The holding of your father's *sliocht*."

Meadbh frowns. "But my father ceded it to O'Mathghamhna. The land pledges."

Her mother gives a low growl. "It is Ui Fhlionn."

Meadbh pauses. "Are there documents? Something to show that?"

Her mother lifts her chin. "It's known. All know it."

Meadbh resists lifting a doubt-filled brow. "Well, I shall go to O'Mathghamhna to confirm this."

Her mother reaches out and grabs Meadbh's arm. "You will not."

Meadbh looks down at her mother's tight grip, the fingers digging into her flesh. She lifts her gaze to her mother's face, scanning it carefully. "And why not?"

"It's not necessary," her mother says hastily, her gaze shifting away.

"But it will bring certainty, if I do."

Her mother turns to her, a flash of anger passing across her face. "Certainty that you'll have a fine marriage at O'Math-ghamhna's whim? Is that what you plan?" She gives Meadbh a severe look. "You will not go to O'Mathghamhna." She lowers her voice further but the menace is still there. "If you do, and they come here, I'll tell them that you killed your brother. It's the truth, in any case."

Meadbh draws back, too startled for words. She looks at Ita, alarm filling her face. Meadbh shakes her head, for what else is possible in the face of this statement and the rage that suddenly fills Meadbh. Rage that only her mother was ever capable of eliciting?

Meadbh stares at the tree branch where a crow has settled, its piercing caw a warning. She gives a grim smile, acknowledging that although she knows it's not meant for her, she feels it is.

Spring scents the air, earthy and grassy. A small flurry of pollen swirls in the stiff breeze. She draws her mantle tighter around her. It's still the time for storms and blustery squalls, and she hopes there isn't one in the offing. She scans the clouds above, looking for any telltale signs and is relieved to see there are none.

Another gust sweeps up the skirts of her gown and mantle. She feels a presence behind her and turns. Diarmuid. He's close enough that she can reach up and touch his face, wipe the concern from it. If she had the mind for it. But her mind is on other things. Her mother, their future. Or are their futures so intertwined she would link them? It's a question that has plagued her since she left her mother some hours ago and walked the paths of woods and fields in an effort to get some sense of her old home. Some sense of where she belonged and what she might do.

"Do you have any knowledge of the law?" she asks Diarmuid.

Diarmuid gives her a startled look and his eyes suddenly become wary. "Perhaps a little."

"A little knowledge of the law governing property?" She notices the hope in her voice and gives herself a mental shake.

He gives her a careful nod. "A little."

She nods, bites her lip. "The land here. Well some parcels of it at least, I think, were pledged to O'Mathghamhna. In return for cattle and other things, I presume."

Diarmuid nods. "When was that?"

Meadbh shakes her head. "When I was very young. Before I left. So perhaps some ten years ago?"

Diarmuid studies her carefully, his blue eyes sharp and focused. "Do you know if the land was redeemed?"

Meadbh sighs and shakes her head. "No. Is there some way I can find out?"

"Why is it you want to know?" His tone is even, containing only a mild hint of curiosity.

She considers his question, taking her time, filtering her thoughts, and the words she'll say. "I would know what my situation is. What our situation is," she says correcting herself.

"O'Mathghamhna is your overlord. Your *Ceann Fine?*"

She gives him a wry look. "I presume so. I think that's who it was before, but I can't be sure."

"What does Eoin say?"

She gives him a cool look. "It's O'Mathghamhna. I'm certain of it, now that I cast my mind back. My father spoke of it and would send his tribute and he'd go to the *Ráth* for assemblies."

Diarmuid nods. "Then there's no question."

"No question."

"Yet you want to know the current status of your father's pledges. I assume the land your father pledged had been held for the *sliocht* and was by rights the *sliocht's* and not O'Mathghamhna's?"

"Yes of course. O'Mathghamhna wouldn't have accepted the land otherwise." Her tone is sharp. Does he think her a fool, or was he the fool?

Diarmuid laughs, his eyes filling with amusement. "I'm sorry. I didn't mean to insinuate anything about your grasp of the situation, but I wanted to be certain I understood the full implications. But still, my question remains. Is there a reason you must clarify the status of the land? Will it change the outcome for you, or for your *sliocht?*"

She studies him a moment, weighing once again what she'll tell him. It takes her only a moment to realise she must tell him all. Or at least all that's necessary for her to get his insight using what knowledge he might have. She has no choice. Who else could she ask? The priest? Even if the priest did know, Meadbh wasn't certain who he was anymore, or if he was trustworthy. Priests were appointed by bishops, and they had their own purposes and reasons that weren't necessarily aligned with hers. She'd learned that much, even at the small nunnery of Teampall Gobnatán.

"If I know as much as possible, I might be able to approach O'Mathghamhna and ask if he would let someone in our *sliocht* assume the role of *Ceann Cuibhrinn*. Perhaps Eoin." She knows Eoin is the only choice, though there may be others she hasn't been able to locate. Eoin as leader of her father's men, as the leader of the *Ceithearn Tigh* surely would be a fine *Cean Cuibhrinn*.

Diarmuid nods. "And you would approach O'Math-ghamhna yourself? You wouldn't wait for O'Mathghamhna or one of his men to come here when time allows them? Surely that would be safest."

"No. It wouldn't be safest," she says firmly. "Because if I wait for them, O'Mathghamhna is just as likely to appoint a replacement, or rather "elect" them out of his own *sliocht,* wouldn't he?"

Diarmuid folds his arms and considers her statement. "Perhaps. But you risk much. He may not want to speak with you. Why not send Eoin?"

She shakes her head. "I can't leave my mother and Ita here on their own. I'll take Eoin's son with me. He's old enough." She's discounted Diarmuid. This isn't his concern. Though she finds herself reluctant to bid him go elsewhere if he has the need to, she knows she must.

He frowns, stares at his feet for a moment, then raises his head. "I'll escort you. We can go together. If you know where O'Mathghamhna is."

She stares at him, unable to say anything, or decide if this is a good offer, or one she should turn down.

Chapter Ten

She sees Eoin through the doorway of the stone shed, leaning over the hocks of a horse she doesn't know. It surprises her, and for a moment her purpose for coming here leaves her as she moves forward into the shed.

"You have a horse still," she says.

The horse is dark, nearly black and finely made, the back straight, haunches well-muscled, the legs strong. The coat is glossy, well groomed and even now, Eoin strokes its side with care. His side, for the horse is a male, she realizes that now.

He looks up and smiles, the light catching his eyes. She can see now how age has etched a path around his eyes and mouth, but his warm expression gives contradiction to the recent hardships.

"Ah, Fionn is your father's own horse. I made sure they couldn't steal him away. Though I doubt they would have succeeded. He allows few to mount him."

She grins at him. "Fionn?"

He shrugs. "A joke of your father's. He may not be fair in colour, or temperament, but he lightened your father's spirit whenever he rode him."

She gives a small laugh and then moves toward the horse carefully. She sees then that Fionn isn't the only horse here. Two others share space, but Fionn stands taller and finer than the other two. She recognises the tired sagging back of Fintan, munching slowly on a small pile of threshed oats. Beside him is another horse, a mare by the looks of it, her dappled colouring barely visible in the dim light of the shed. The brood mare, she remembers. Part of her mother's dowry.

"The others are gone. Taken." His tone is flat, but the implication is clear that they were taken by people fleeing the pestilence.

Hearing his words and watching Eoin stroking Fionn, her resolve on her course of action grows stronger. She won't be deterred.

"Eoin," she says. "It's important to secure our future. The future of our clan."

He looks at her, cocking his head. "Of course. And so we will."

She takes comfort from his reassurance. At least it's something he wants. Something he won't surrender easily.

"One of us must go to O'Mathghamhna. Convince him that we can continue as we have before. That the Uí Fhlionn will continue with the holding."

He gives her a careful look. "Continue as before? How do you propose we do that?" The scepticism is strong in his tone. "Do you have kin to call upon? I know there are a few households remaining in the outlying lands. *Scológ mhaith* who are Uí Fhlionn. And labourers perhaps. But as it stands, we cannot meet the tributes. We've barely been able to make them before the pestilence. The debt of provisioning and housing O'Mathghamhna's troops on his periodic visits were too much. It forced your mother to pledge a good portion of the land to O'Mathghamhna in return for cattle, just so that we could continue."

She stares at him, tries to absorb the terrible impact of his words, his meaning. Behind her Fionn snorts and bobs his head. A strand of straw twirls in the air, catching a soft spring breeze.

"You will not."

Meadbh stares at Eoin, her mouth set in a stubborn frown.

"It's better if I go."

They have been circling the issue in the stone shed among the horses for some time, so much so that Diarmuid now stands next to her, his whole stance a question.

"His words are reasonable," says Diarmuid.

Up to now, he's remained silent. Up to now, Meadbh had thought she might count him on her side.

"His words may be reasonable, but that doesn't mean it's the best approach to ensure the *sliocht's* survival. To ensure the *sliocht* inherits the land." Her tone is terse now, just short of anger. She's tired of arguing her point. "Someone must stay behind to protect my mother, the *sliocht* and the land. You're the best one to do that, Eoin, I'm not."

"Diarmuid can stay, then," says Eoin. He glances at Diarmuid, his eyes questioning.

Have the two discussed this beforehand, wonders Meadbh? She considers it only a moment before she sets it aside. "Diarmuid is obliged to do nothing. His task is complete."

"I'm willing," says Diarmuid with no hesitation.

Meadbh spares him a sidelong glance and frowns at Eoin once again. "Whether Diarmuid is willing or not, it's of no use. Diarmuid is not Uí Fhlionn."

"That's of no matter," says Diarmuid. "I would protect the *sliocht*, the land and the people, regardless."

She lets that thought settle in her, a glimmer of something taking hold. But can she trust him? The offer is generous, but still, there are flaws. She turns to face Diarmuid fully. "I appreciate the offer, but if someone from O'Mathghamhna...or anyone else should come and find there's no one from Uí Fhlionn here...well, they might draw the wrong conclusions and the results would be worse."

Eoin sighs. She looks over at him and he shakes his head. "There is reason there, too. But you can't undertake this journey alone."

"Diarmuid has already offered to escort me," Meadbh says.

Eoin looks over at Diarmuid, surprise on his face. "So you knew of this plan?"

Diarmuid shrugs. "I knew she was determined. I was waiting to see what your thoughts were on the matter."

"And now you know my thoughts?"

Diarmuid sighs. "She has reason and determination. It's best that she at least have someone accompany her, if you know where O'Mathghamhna is?"

"And you have no other obligations?" asks Eoin

Diarmuid's jaw tightens, his mouth thinning. "I have no other obligations at present. My time at Teampall Gobnatán has come to an end."

Eoin shakes his head. "I don't like it."

"I'm sorry, Eoin, but it's the best approach," says Meadbh, a conciliatory note in her voice, now that she's swayed him. "And O'Mathghamhna? Where is he?"

Eoin nods slowly. "The best place to start would be Caish-leán na Leachta, just south of here."

Diarmuid assists Meadbh as she mounts the mare, rather than Fintan, whose strength seems to need more time to recover. She straightens her headcloth, tucking in a stray strand of hair, spreads her skirts carefully, using her mantle to cover calves exposed as a result of sitting astride. Fionn stomps the ground impatiently next to them, a padded cushion already strapped to his back, the snaffle bit in place, awaiting Diarmuid. He wears *truibhas* tucked into his boots, an over top which is a shortened *léine*, her father's quilted leather jacket over it, straining at his chest. At his waist is a sash from which her father's sword hangs, the dagger tucked in next to it. Instead of a mantle, he wears a colourfully patterned *fallaing*, leaving his arms free to use any of the weapons. A bow is slung across one shoulder and the quiver hangs along Fionn's flanks. She wonders about her father's battle gear – the helmet, the targe – but she imagines they, too, have disappeared, either with the recently fled, or battered beyond use and then discarded.

Meadbh has waited two days for this departure. Two days where her patience nearly wore thin from her mother's anger, her mother's continued outrageous accusations against Meadbh about her brother's death, so that even now Eoin looks at her with a measure of doubt. Doubt that now fills the faces of all who are here to see her off. The group of four *scológ mhaith* that Eoin has rounded up, and who have pledged to remain here at Raithlinn, until this matter is settled and she returns. And now, in the course of two days, two precious days of time wasted, her cause, her purpose is even more urgent, because she has no idea what other mischief her mother might stir up that would hurt her cause. The last few words remind her of Diarmuid's comment the previous day. "It's best she's not coming with you. She won't help your case."

The words warm her now, because of all that now look at her with their measure of doubt, Diarmuid's own expression contains none. And for that she's glad. It gives her courage.

She watches now as he mounts Fionn, wearing bow, sword and dagger, and wonders if he has experience with battle. She looks at his hands and sees evidence that contradicts experience, but the sinewed muscles in his forearms, legs and back speak differently. She knows that the muscles of the man she saw working in the fields of Teampall Gobnatán were honed, the sweat glistening off their contours, but she recalls the economy of his movement, an economy she witnesses now, along with something else. An ease is there, an ease that tells how confident he is with his bow, this sword and dagger. And how the fit of her father's battle-scarred jack is too tight, a tightness he allows and will endure, rather than chafe against, or consider removing. It causes her to pause. She should take comfort in it, she decides.

She pulls her mantle closer around her. Diarmuid looks over and frowns slightly, his expression considering. He scans her, taking in her postulant's gown and headcloth, as well as the mantle.

"Does your mother have a chest of clothes?" he asks.

She gives him a puzzled look, then turns and scans the group of men, her eyes alighting on Eoin.

"My mother's chest?"

Eoin nods. "Safe."

She looks back at Diarmuid. "Yes. Why?"

Diarmuid looks over at Eoin. "If there is a gown or a mantle more in the style of the Gaills, would you be able to fetch them? Without causing a stir?"

"She has a mantle," Eoin says slowly. "But as for fetching them...."

"It's to help ensure Meadbh's safety. Though we are travelling on Ui Fhlionn and O'Mathghamhna lands, we could easily meet with Gaills or even Saxain. Times are uncertain. This may help. We can be more flexible with our allegiances should the need arise and anyone we encounter won't be certain either than if we are distinctly one allegiance."

"But your own dress, manner, even your lack of saddle, surely that marks you as one allegiance," says Eoin.

"You would have me change into a gown in the Saxain style?"

"A gown of a Gaill woman," says Diarmuid. "My *fallaing* is Gael, but my boots are not. It will suffice."

71

Meadbh looks down at her mantle. It was warm, functional. She'd no idea what a Gaill mantle looked like, but couldn't imagine it would be an improvement on her own.

Chapter Eleven

Though the mantle she wears is of a much finer and tightly woven wool than her own, and the colour a beautiful shade of deep blue that Meadbh is certain flatters her mother's colouring, it's still not proof against the damp chill that hangs in the air in the manner that her own mantle would have done. Its length is just that bit short, so there's a little gap between her leather shoes and the mantle, leaving the bare skin colder than she would like. The memory of

Diarmuid's approving looks and fine compliments when she'd donned the mantle do little to banish the sour thoughts in her mind now.

Up ahead, Diarmuid rides Fionn, his grace and ease with the sturdy muscled mount providing her with another little piece about him. Her stomach grumbles, the morning meal they'd had now a distant memory. They'd passed a small stone dwelling sometime back and she'd looked longingly at it. Surely, they would be at Caislean na Leachta soon. Hadn't Eoin said it was only a short distance? Although "short" to a warrior like Eoin could mean anything from one day to three, she supposes.

It's only after the sun makes a watery appearance that Diarmuid halts by an outcropping of stones. He turns and points to it. "We'll stop here for a bit."

Meadbh nods, and a moment later he's assisting her from the mare. She doesn't know the mare's name and Eoin hadn't mentioned it either in passing or deliberateness. She knows it's petty of her to refuse to know if there was a name for the brood mare belonging to her mother and tries to tell herself that she felt it would betray Fintan. Both are silly reasons and she almost laughs at herself. The mare has served her well enough, only once showing a temper when she refused to journey past some heavy thick furze after a hare had bounded out from it.

She gives her mount a reassuring pat and Diarmuid throws her a quizzical look as he removes the sack tied to the back of the mare. Meadbh smiles weakly.

It isn't long before they're perched on one of the rocks of the outcrop, each with an oatcake and a chunk of cheese in hand. Meadbh thinks of her *beacha* as she bites into the oatcake, wishing it were coated in honey. The *beacha* at Raithlinn had long since gone, it seems, even before the arrival of the pestilence, according to Eoin. It's another sad reflection on the growing impoverishment of her *slíocht*. She shoves the thought aside with the promise that she's doing what she can to rectify the situation.

Meadbh huddles into the damp cloak, wishing for the hundredth time that she had her own mantle around her, instead of this this one that provided more for her mother's vanity than her bodily comfort. A summer luxury would have been the only occasion to wear it, she's certain now, and even for that, she has no use.

She suppresses a shiver, watching Diarmuid pack away the food stores and prepare the area for them to sleep. The shelter is merely a tumbledown stone dwelling, one that's more rubble than anything, but at least there are trees and a few shrubs to block some of the wind that has begun to blow.

Diarmuid comes over to her, removes the sword and dagger that haven't left his side this day, and sets them on the ground, next to the bow he'd laid down earlier. He takes the seat next to her. She shivers. The cold is penetrating, something the heat from his body starts to drive away. She resists the urge to scuttle closer. She closes her eyes and tries to imagine that she's warm and dry and lying in her bed, back at Teampaill Gobnatán. It's a false memory, she knows, for although she'd been dry, it was seldom that she was very warm there. At least not on the small pallet in the cramped dormitory she shared with Siúr Ethne, Siúr Máire and the other nuns. Out by the hives with her *beacha* in summer, there was certainly warmth.

"You're cold," says Diarmuid. It's a statement, not a question and with it he encircles her with his arms.

She falls still, unable to move, her body stiff and uncertain in the shelter of his arms, suddenly struck again by the shift in their relationship. It had slinked up on her, this shift from a servant at the bidding of a *nuasachán*, to what now seems to be a man, a warrior, protecting a vulnerable woman. He still escorts her, but the escort and the destination are so much different now.

"Surely we'll reach Caislean na Leachta tomorrow," she says. The sound of her voice startles her, but the compulsion to speak, to break the pattern of her thoughts is overwhelming.

"We should be," says Diarmuid. He pauses before speaking. "I haven't taken the most direct route. It seemed best with the pestilence clearly about as it is."

She nods, acknowledging the truth of his words, and wonders what tomorrow's outcome will be once they arrive. Tomorrow it may be settled. Tomorrow she may know her fate. The thought gives her pause and she burrows tighter into Diarmuid's side. He rests his head on hers and she thinks she feels him kiss her head, murmur soothing sounds before she allows herself to drift off to sleep.

Meadbh startles awake. Something has disturbed her rest. She looks around in the early morning light, her eyes unfocused with sleep, and shoves the hair back from her face. Her mantle has slipped from her shoulders and she shivers with the cold, until she realises that Diarmuid is no longer at her side.

She glances around and finds him strapping on the sword and dagger. In the distance she can hear hoofbeats.

Meadbh watches Diarmuid speak to the group of men. She strains to hear them, to understand, but she realises after a short while that they're speaking a language that's foreign to her. Is it the language of the Saxain? A few moments later and she detects a few words of her own language scattered throughout, though most of them come from Diarmuid. She wonders bleakly how it is that Diarmuid has their language, and has it well enough that he's not struggling for words, but rather they issue forth almost like water pouring from a jug.

She reminds herself to be grateful that he does speak with ease, for some of the men are obviously dangerous. Their menace is conveyed in their scars and ragged faces that have spent too much time in scowls, as well as the long mailcoats, helmets and the strange axes they carry, with a handle taller than any man, providing a threat that seems impossible to battle successfully. The thought of it unsettles her, and she finds herself shifting her gaze from the tall, ginger bearded man who's speaking and seems to be their leader, and Diarmuid, as she struggles yet again to get a sense of their discussion. Facial expressions and stances seem to suggest there's no immediate threat, but her heart is still in her throat. She touches her thigh through her gown, for the small dagger strapped there that she had from Eoin, a request she made, and he granted willingly.

The words of the foreign language slide around her, their meaning still elusive, except for the smattering of Irish that leaves her no clearer about the discussion, other than what she can imagine. Glances in her direction, questioning faces, tell her only that they want to know her identity and purpose. They must be Saxain, or perhaps Gaill, but something tells her they are not. Either way, she draws her mantle around her and smothers a laugh. For once she's grateful for its obvious Gaill design.

Chapter Twelve

Wind flails Meadbh's mantle up around her knees, a symbol of her confusion, anger and worry. That she's been taken so close to home, so close to her destination, by men who are clearly not where they're permitted. But is permission required now? Is there no one to challenge them on their journey north? For north is clearly where they're heading, now the sun has made an appearance through the clouds. Her mind is a whirl, trying to find her way through to answers that will keep her safe.

She glances ahead, studying the back of the red bearded man in front of her and the large roan coloured horse he rides. The saddle is of a fine leather and the stirrups, though well used, are finely made too. The other four who are armed ride behind her, and have similar saddles and other accoutrements, but not as finely made or well kept. The remaining three men are younger and unarmed, and dressed in clothes that are more foreign than she's seen before, though all of a muted dun colour.

Diarmuid rides behind her and she can feel his eyes on her. He'd spoken words of reassurance to her as he prepared first Fionn and then the mare for her to ride, the sword and dagger no longer at his side, the bow missing from his back, all now in the possession of the warriors. The words he spoke were nothing of note, nothing that explained the ones he'd exchanged so easily with the red bearded man. A bland expression was all she'd given him in return. Now she wonders what his thoughts are, and how he hopes to make all well, as he told her he would.

His words mean nothing to her now, she'll rely only on herself to make all well, though how she might achieve this, she doesn't know. They're obviously taking her and Diarmuid to someone of greater note, otherwise they would have killed her and Diarmuid on the spot, she has no doubt about that. They believe she and Diarmuid have possible value and she knows she must determine if it's a value she can meet, or at least appear to do so. She's a failed *nuasachán*, with her father recently dead from the pestilence, a mother who appears to all to have lost her wits, and her *sliocht* is teetering into complete landlessness, under obligation to a more powerful *sliocht*. She's nothing really, a woman without significance, a woman who once cared only to tend her *beacha*. *Beacha* that are no longer hers to tend.

It's then she realises that though her *beacha* are no longer within easy reach, they continue to give. Their hum is still there in her heart, telling her what she already knows in her mind. She can heal. In times like these that is no small thing. It has some value, though it's a value that has risk.

Meadbh stares at the damp stone, feigning sleep as Diarmuid takes a place by her side and slips an arm around her. It's the third night he has done this, and though she welcomes his warmth against the damp, chill nights they have passed in hollows and stone ruins, she doesn't want to trust it. His easy discourse with red beard, and the gangly slim warrior that tries to befriend her, still unsettles her, though he's assured her that he'd only picked up the language when he was working on a farm further north, on Mac Carthaigh lands which bordered with the Gaill lord, Desmond. But land and borders are changeable, she knows, even when the old laws wouldn't have it so. These Gaill and the Saxain who claim to rule. They have shoved all the old ways aside like so much rubbish.

But Diarmuid seems neither one thing or the other, and his claim to be a free farm labourer she now doubts, along with his claim that he has no idea where these men are taking them. There's no fear, anxiety or even wariness in his manner, nothing that indicates worry about what's to come.

She hears the other men talking lazily a short distance away behind her. "Have you learned anything more about where they're taking us?" she asks him in a soft voice.

"No," he says, his low voice right against her ear.

She feels the heat of his breath, and for a moment, his response is awash in how it warms more than her ear. "All will be well," he adds, the tone soothing. She allows it to lull her and her anxieties to slip away, lost in this moment. She relaxes back against him.

Meadbh has lost all sense of feeling below her waist. She wonders how she manages to be mounted still, following these men endlessly, stopping only on occasion when she's nearly fainting from the strain of it all. Diarmuid at least seems to have noticed and requested more than once that the men stop, but they rarely listen to him. At least that's what she imagines as she hears him speak to them, the scattering of familiar words that seem to refer to her, like *"bean"* and *"tuirseach"* because she's a woman and she's tired.

By the time they stop, she can hardly stand when Diarmuid assists her from her horse. In the end he lifts her up in his arms and carries her over to a small rock and places her on it. He spreads a mantle she hasn't seen before on the ground and lifts her down upon it. She leans back against the rock, glad for the support.

"Rest here," he says. "I'll bring you something to drink and eat in a moment."

She closes her eyes, sinking into the feeling of rest, of stillness, and tries to ignore her aching limbs. Her thighs are throbbing and her back is stiff. Resting seems to find a new way to enable these pains to fill her mind and body. She's not sure how many more days of this gruelling riding she can take.

A hand calls her back to the present and she opens her eyes. Diarmuid squats before her, placing an oatcake in her palm and a cup of clear water from the stream nearby.

"Can you ask them how much longer we'll need to ride?" she says, her voice a rasp.

Diarmuid squeezes her hand, his expression full of sympathy. "It won't be much longer, now, I think. Tomorrow is only a short ride and we'll be there."

She stares at him, stunned and gratified, but also alarmed. "How is it you know? Where are we going?"

"I'm not certain," he says. "I'm merely guessing. But it's to someone with authority, someone with power, because these men are clearly galloglass. And only powerful men employ galloglass."

"Galloglass?" she asks, confused. The word is vaguely familiar. "What are they? Who are they?"

"*Galloglach*," he says with no elaboration.

"*Galloglach*," she repeats softly. Memories assail her of tales in her father's hall. Tales of brutal warriors, who fight for payment and without mercy. They have long served some powerful men in the west. Are they Mac Carthaigh's men? The fact that Diarmuid understands who they are only adds to her growing anxiety. "And what's your guess at who the powerful person is?" she whispers, afraid to hear the answer.

He pauses. "Maurice Fitz Thomas Fitzgerald, Earl of Desmond."

The name means nothing to her, except for Desmond. But Mac Carthaigh is the only connection she knows to Desmond. And he is the *Ceann Fine* of Desmond. What they once called King. "Earl" is a term for which she has no understanding. Chills rise up her back.

Chapter Thirteen

The chamber is small, but at this moment Meadbh allows herself to note its dry comfort after so many days spent damp and chilled to her bones. She assures herself that's what accounts for the shivers that don't seem to leave her. And the way she cannot seem to focus her mind on the problems at hand. The decisions and strategies that must be made and devised. She must find dry clothes.

That thought directs her to see the sack containing her clothes that has been placed on the floor between a pallet and a plain chest set against the stone wall. A small narrow slat window is above it, a waxed linen cloth covers it, blocking out some of the light but also the wind. There's a stain on the cloth, as if someone has flung a cup of dark liquid at it in a temper. She wonders who this room belonged to, or perhaps still belongs, and she here, only having its use for the time it takes to change her clothes? She wonders over this, even as she knows her mind must wonder about bigger things.

An older girl enters. She's short, fair haired, her bones delicate as a young bird's. She wears a plain *léine* of sorts, but over that a simple dun coloured wool gown whose sleeves go only to the elbow. A simple headcloth covers half of her head and a long plait dangles down her back. Sturdy ill-fitting shoes encase her feet. A servant? Perhaps, though she's dressed in a manner that Meadbh thinks might be Saxain or Gaill. The girl gives Meadbh a small nod and offers her services. Her Irish is fair enough, though heavily accented.

"I'm fine," says Meadbh.

The girl shakes her head. "No, I'm told I must make you presentable."

Meadbh is startled by those words. How is she to be made presentable?

The answer it appears is in the sack that the girl sorts through, withdrawing a gown that Meadbh is surprised to see and knows belongs to her mother. Diarmuid must have put it in there.

"Are you kin to Desmond?" asks Meadbh, curious. "I mean the earl?" The word 'earl' is strange on her tongue, another foreign word to join the others that have come since the arrival of the Saxain, she supposes. What it signifies specifically she can only guess, except that it gives him authority.

The girl gives her a funny look and laughs. "No, I'm only a servant. I'm Derbhla. My mother was a Gael that worked in this castle for the Poers before the earl defeated them." She shrugs. "So I work here as my mother did."

Meadbh nods slowly, considering Derbhla's tale, and submits more kindly to her ministrations. Derbhla helps Meadbh out of her gown and headcovering and into her mother's gown, or kirtle, as Derbhla informs her of its name. Derbhla fingers it with admiration, calling the fabric silk, something that astounds Meadbh. How has her mother come by such an extravagant gown? It's round necked, and the sleeves are tight fitting, something Meadbh isn't used to, even though her slender frame finds some room to manoeuvre. Around her waist Derbhla ties a woven silk sash. Derbhla searches around in the sack again and withdraws another garment, gives it a shake and whips it over Meadbh's head. A surcoat, Derbhla explains. It's sleeveless, with deep armholes.

Once dressed, Derbhla sits her down on the chest and begins to fix Meadbh's hair. After meticulous combing, she weaves Meadbh's hair into two plaits and coils them in a strange manner on each side of her head, securing them with finely carved wooden hair pins. Meadbh can't begin to imagine what she must look like. The strangeness she feels tells her enough. From the sack, Derbhla produces a finely woven veil that she fixes to Meadbh's head. All of it feels strange. Her head, her body in these clothes. Clothes, beyond the gown, she can hardly imagine that Diarmuid would know to bring. The thought of it brings a flush to her. Until she considers what it might reveal about his past.

The solar is rectangular and a good size, at least to Meadbh's eyes, and a vibrant fire burns in a brazier in the centre of it. Several wooden benches line the walls on each side, men draped across them, talking and cleaning weapons. Even without the fine woven wool hangings that are displayed on most of the walls, the sweet-smelling rushes strewn on the floor or the chests, armour and pewter plate that decorate the spaces between the hangings, the journey into the castle told her of the wealth and importance of the figure she sees seated on a carved high backed wooden chair where men gather around him. Next to him, seated in a lower chair, is another man.

The castle itself, she'd noticed, had two storeys, a turret, a stone courtyard bawn filled with wooden buildings of wattle and daub, and huts clustered on their outskirts. More indications of wealth and power. A man of authority indeed. She scans the room for signs of illness, but everyone within here and elsewhere that she's observed seems well. Perhaps the pestilence hasn't reached here yet. Still, her urge to be vigilant holds her back, and she wonders if she should pull off her headcovering and cover her nose and mouth with it, but its loose filmy weave would have little proof against pestilence, she decides. Her kirtle is longer than she's used to and she clutches a portion of the skirt in one hand so that she won't trip.

Meadbh has entered the hall at the back, descending a narrow, winding stone staircase, escorted by a different servant girl who had enough Irish to summon and direct her to her destination. Small and wiry, this girl wouldn't give her name, as if the giving of it was somehow admitting, or perhaps betraying, something.

She spies the back of Diarmuid's head, just to the side, talking to the red bearded man. He turns as if sensing her presence, and she stiffens. He smiles. She can only stare, her eyes wide as she struggles to assemble her thoughts.

Meadbh learns from a strange man that she must call this burly, fair haired man of middle age, "my lord Desmond", but then Diarmuid has already told her how to address him, as if that meant anything to her. Or if it would help her in any way to deal with the conversation that has flowed between the two men since she and Diarmuid were formally presented, the earl taking only cursory note of Meadbh's presence. The earl speaks her tongue, and for that she's both grateful and not grateful, for part of her would stay in ignorance of this tale that's spinning out before her, and she a figure in it. It's all she can do not to gape at Diarmuid, that such words could spill out of him, as it were a jug pouring forth frothy ale. Froth. The tale is froth and nothing more.

She has no idea who Desmond is, except for his title and embroidered wide-sleeved tunic of thick velvet cloth and the tight fitting wool *truibhas* underneath it. A thick sash gathers in the tunic and a sword hangs from it, resting on the chair. The scabbard is exquisite, the work of a true craftsman, the designs ancient and familiar. Had a Gael made that? It causes her confusion even as he issues orders to someone in the tongue of a Saxain. Yet he calls himself lord over an area that she knows already has a Gael *ceann fine*. She knows that because all who live here know that. Even at Teampall Gobnatán, all knew that.

"Though these times are difficult, it does pain me to see any *fili*, let alone an *ollamh* without a home," says Desmond, tapping the arm of the chair in which he sits. He has a restless energy, as if he would spring out at her at any moment. "No man can be without poetry, for without it he's but an animal."

"I thank you for your concern for me and my wife, my lord Desmond," says Diarmuid, his tone sober. "But with the clergy against us, banning the purchase of the services of any *filí*, let alone a formally trained *ollamh*, my patron, cousin to Mac Carthaigh was reluctant to support me."

The shock of Diarmuid's words distract her for a moment, but she pushes it away for a moment, intent on the exchange.

Desmond expression darkens. "That wasn't a good business at any level. But I hope that turmoil is behind us now," he adds, his expression neutral. "Though some won't honour such art, I'm not one of them. My son, Gerald, has an interest in poetry too, and composes a little himself, and though I am only a little acquainted with the art, I find his verse very fine." He gives Diarmuid an assessing look. "And where did you learn your art?"

"At the feet of the great Seán Mór O Dubagáain," says Diarmuid calmly.

Again Meadbh stares in wonder at his answers, so ready and spoken with nonchalance. This man beside her talking, not a bother in the world, is not the man she thought him. A labourer. Sweat drenched, work roughened hands. Perhaps it's just that he has an imagination worthy of a bard.

"Impressive," says Desmond, nodding slowly. "I've heard tell of him. He's from the north, is he not?"

Diarmuid nods. "Though I'm not, but being a son of lesser count in a *slíocht* of poets, and having every inclination to learn this art form, I travelled to his home and asked to be one of his many students and fortunately, he consented."

Desmond continues to nod, but Meadbh struggles to take in

all his words. All this time she's travelled with him and he spoke of none of this. Not once. Is it pure imagination?

"Well, I'm fortunate to have you here," says Desmond. "Given these uncertain times, and with pestilence abroad, it is, without a doubt, a blessing. We thank God every day that we have been spared." Desmond crosses himself and everyone else follows, Meadbh as a hasty afterthought, for she can no more think of God's blessings than she can think of the prayers that accompany it.

"Have you encountered any pestilence, yourself?" asks the man who sits near Desmond. He's a stocky, dark haired, ruddy faced man. His long tunic is of fine woven wool and meets his boots, and the style of his hair, beard and even his manner mark him as Gael.

"Do you know mac Diarmada?" Desmond asks Diarmuid.

Even as the earl asks this, he studies Diarmuid carefully. The name has no real meaning for Meadbh, she knows only what it tells her in and of itself. He's the son of Diarmaid. But which Diarmaid?

Diarmuid gives mac Diarmada a small bow and shakes his head. "I don't believe we're acquainted. And no, we haven't encountered any pestilence and since leaving Chiarraí, we have seen no sign of it."

"And where were you heading?" asks mac Diarmada. His tone is careful, his eyes narrowed.

Diarmuid flashes a grin. "We'd heard that O'Mathghamhna had a liking for fili and bards, but it seems fortune brought us here."

"You say O'Mathghamhna were in Chiarraí? In Mac Carthaigh territory?" asks Desmond. "And here is your overlord, mac Diarmada, right before you." He gives an impish grin. "It wasn't mac Diarmada you were escaping, was it?" He gives a hearty laugh, shaking his head. "But how could it be when mac Diarmada has been here with me, all this time, winning lands for us, while that usurper, Cormac deigns to call himself the Mac Carthaigh." Desmond slaps mac Diarmada on the back. "Our poet is doubly welcome here now, is he not, mac Diarmada?"

Mac Diarmada gives Desmond a sour smile and manages a nod.

The words should reassure Meadbh, along with the knowledge that Diarmuid's lies are skirting the truth, but given the whole conversation she can only feel deep alarm Diarmuid is claiming a skill that she doubts he possesses, and a skill for her that she knows she doesn't possess. His claim about his origins she has cause to doubt, or that he trained with a famous *ollamh*. But the statement that claimed her as his wife has her the most astounded. The outrageousness of it still leaves her breathless. And he makes this claim to this man who calls himself the Lord of Desmond. A man, in his own eyes, who would have the power to determine the future of her *sliocht* and their inheritance. And Diarmuid has delivered her and his false story about her to this very man. Her eyes sting with the anger of the one word raging through her that explains what has occurred. Betrayal.

Chapter Fourteen

"Mac Diarmada?" Meadbh says to Diarmuid. "Lord Desmond? These people, these men of authority, have power to do us harm, no matter that mac Diarmada is a Gael."

"All will be well," he says, his tone soothing.

His tone, she thinks, is what loosens the slim thread that holds her temper in check and causes the concerns and the outrage to spill out, filled with all the venom, the scorn, the putrid evil elements she can infuse in her rage, because her anger knows no bounds. "Your bard?" she says, her tone strong, piercing. "I'm not your wife, let alone your bard. How dare you take such liberties? You, who are no more than a labourer for a religious house."

An amused expression flashes across Diarmuid's face as he leans against the wall of the stone chamber to which they were led following their meeting with Desmond. That brief glimpse of humour only incenses Meadbh more.

"You claim that I am something, when you have no knowledge if I possess the skill," she says. "A skill that is uncommon among women. A skill that when practised by a woman in a household such as this is seen to equate her to someone who likes to bed every man in sight!"

Meadbh knows that her last words contained exaggeration, but she did it to emphasise her point, and give focus to her rage. "And for that matter, you're claiming to be something that you aren't. What will happen when he asks you to recite a poem?"

"Then I will say that my *reacaire* isn't with me." He shrugs, unconcerned, reaches out a calming hand, but she shakes it off.

She gives a frustrated sigh. "But if he should ask you to compose?"

He pauses a moment. "Then I shall compose."

She narrows her eyes, studying him. "You know the method of composing, to the level of *ollamh,* with its intricate metre, its clever phrasing?" She notices now his finely made *ionar* of burgundy wool over his *léine* that barely covers the knee of his *truibhas,* and the embroidery stitching picked out at its neck. It has the Gaill look, without a doubt. Where has he obtained such a tunic?

"You seem to be knowledgeable about the elements of poetry," says Diarmuid, giving her an assessing look. "I'm gratified and impressed. I knew you had music, but that the little nunnery should also teach you poetry is more than I could hope for."

His words take her aback for a moment, they're so out of the course of her knowledge, ideas and imaginings about him. "I-I had Father Aban, the bishop, teach me some of it. At least what I could persuade him to share. He came once a month to meet with Máthairab and to take confession."

She pauses, shakes her head, clearing her mind of the memories from those times and earlier. When the music gave her joy. When she first heard the hum of the bees and it reminded her of the plucking of máthairab's harp. The thrum of it. Deep inside her. Even now she can recall it.

She looks up at him, tilts her head. "You are an *ollamh*. And now you've arrived at the household of someone who believes himself to be the king of Desmond. And there would be no better addition to the household of a king than an *ollamh*."

Her words are not questions. She has no need of his confirmation. She sees it all now. It's been his plan. His response, though, isn't what she expects.

"It's the best protection for us I can fashion, Meadbh. At least for the moment. I assure you, I didn't plan for us to come here. I promise, I'll find a way to get you to O'Mathghamhna and secure you and your *sliocht's* future."

The words leave her speechless. Part of her wants to believe him, but she knows she can't. Every instinct in her tells her it's best to trust no one, least of all Diarmuid.

94

Torches mounted on the walls of the castle chamber flicker, casting uneven shadows over the solar. Voices echo, no one conversation distinguishable, creating only a blend of noise, a dull roar that gives Meadbh a feeling of claustrophobia. She has no desire to be here, seated at this oak trestle table that nearly groans under the weight of the platters of food, in a place that should be reserved for someone else. The haunches of pork, beef and venison and the carcasses of wildfowl of various sizes that crowd the fine carved trenchers tell her that. Even the rare sight of plates of limpets, eels and mussels are tucked in among the other platters. She feels out of place not only because of the food's plentifulness, but the manner of its cooking, the bread that accompanies it. It's an abundance and in some cases, a type of food she's not used to. It confuses her. Confuses her stomach, which growls at the deep rich scents of these dishes and wars with the bile that rises to her throat. A bile that is in part anger, she knows, while the cheese and oatcakes that sit on the trencher she shares with Diarmuid, the only bits of food she allowed to be placed there for her, are untouched. She's not sure what she'll eat, or if she can eat. All the deprivation that she's known, from war, from famine, from the imposed aestheticism of the nuns, compel her to reject the abundance these people enjoy. She refuses to be a part of it while her own *sliocht* at home have only the meagre rations they can barely eke from the land and the few cattle that graze it.

She casts a glance over at Diarmuid. She admits to his handsome appearance, dressed now in finery she's never seen. Have those clothes come from his own sack? And when? She'd remained in the chamber until Derbhla brought her down for this meal. She's drawn to his eyes, which are twinkling at some joke the earl makes as Diarmuid plies himself with the fare from the trencher they share. He certainly has no scruples over the food. Hefty portions of venison, beef and some small fowl are piled there, with a single onion and some kale at the side. She looks fondly at the onion. She hasn't seen, let alone eaten one, since last year. The spring onions hadn't yet come up before she left Teampall Gobnatán.

Thinking of Teampall Gobnatán brings the *beacha* to her mind, and with them, the thought of honey. Honey is what she could eat. Honey would soothe her mind as well as her stomach. She hears a tune in her head. She closes her eyes and hums it softly, hoping that its sound vibrating through her body will go at least some way towards what the honey would do if she ate it now.

"Ah now," Diarmuid says softly into her ear. "That's a tune right from a harp I've no doubt."

She halts her humming, her eyes flying open, the moment passes and all the calm she's achieved vanishes with it into the air. She flushes and scans the room, hoping no one else has heard her hum amidst the general din of voices.

He places a hand over hers, leaning down once more. "Worry not. I only heard you because I'm close and I'm attuned to such particular arts." He casts a look towards Desmond. "My lord is too engaged with his men at the moment."

She follows his glance, sliding her hand from underneath his, but Desmond, perhaps because the movement catches his attention, looks over to them.

"Ta tú an bantiarna bhean chéile na Diarmuid, nach bhuil?" asks Desmond.

She understands that he's asking her if she's Diarmuid's wife, but the word before wife, "lady", is unfamiliar. It's a term in a context for which she has no understanding and she can only hope it's no insult. Diarmuid finds her hand once again and gives it a squeeze.

She pauses a moment, Diarmuid's hand still covering hers. The words come to her, though she wonders if she should utter them. "Yes," she says, finally, and clears her throat of nerves. "Yes, I am Diarmuid's *bean chéile*."

"You must excuse me that I haven't given you a formal welcome before now. My own lady wife, Elinor, wouldn't have permitted such an omission. But sadly, she's not here. You must therefore endure a less refined audience."

Meadbh nods, struggling to keep up with his words, to understand his pronunciation, his phrasing, which is unlike anything she's accustomed to. Diarmuid's own phrasings and words hold only a hint that he wasn't of her area, but a man at least from her region. A Gael. At least she thinks so. But a *fili* can mimic, she thinks a moment later.

Desmond nods to her plate of food, still untouched. "I hope you can find something to savour and enjoy among the fare here. We would all have you well fed so that when you and your *fear chéile* perform later you won't be distracted by an unsatisfied belly."

Her mind refuses to catch up and fully understand the words that Lord Desmond has just spoken. She can't fathom how it came about. Has she misunderstood? Or has Diarmuid once again spoken for her as well for himself, claiming ability that neither of them possess? She gives a slight shake to her head, as if to clear the fog, to find new meaning, better meaning in the phrases that have been spoken. She looks over to Diarmuid, hoping for assistance. He squeezes her hand once again and she wants to laugh at the futility and meaninglessness of such a gesture.

Diarmuid strikes a pose, arms out, palms up as if he is opening himself up for inspiration from God above. Or perhaps it should be gods, Meadbh thinks, for they'll need all the gods of old to enable them to perform at a level that Diarmuid has claimed for them. Though this man, this Lord Desmond, is only a Gaill, and it hardly seems likely that he has the experience or the knowledge of the intricacies and quality of an *ollamh's* work. Or a bard's, her role tonight. And she has no harp.

She moves to stand in front of Diarmuid, as they hastily agreed earlier, closes her eyes and seeks to find a connection with her own special link. Perhaps through the song of the *beacha*, she can find a course that will help her make it through these next moments safely.

She draws a hum from deep inside her, a vibration and tone that has the command of a hive, working in harmony. And she their house where they work. The hum is strong and she follows its path. Diarmuid begins to intone his poem, finding her rhythm, a rhythm that she recalls from the past. Her father's hall. Father Aban's descriptions, relayed at her insistence after he told her of the great woman *ollamh*, Gormfhlaith. The metre, the rhyme and the emphasis carefully created. Twenty-four syllables making up four lines of three, seven, seven, and seven syllables. Rhyming, alliteration are all intricately woven, required. All this she hears, and her humming rises and falls with it, as if the *beacha* are speaking the words, sharing their thoughts through this poem.

Tánic sam slán sóer, Dia mbi clóen caill chiar
langid ag seng snéid, Dia mbí réid rón rían

. . .

Summer has come in the land, in thy time, o ruddy face of
brown eyebrows,
As thou has brought down every moistening shower, thou has
given milk to our milch cows.

Diarmuid continues on, his voice rising and falling. Deep, rich
toned words spill forth. She continues to hum as he intones the
ancient poem. Its metre and language are old, composed before
the rules she learned, the words barely understandable. But the
joy, the magic of the tones are more than enough.

Diarmuid speaks of 'each hazel is rich from the hero',
alluding to old rites of ancient times when gods were invoked
and the king merged with the land, drawing his power. His
might. Meadbh is mesmerised by his words and the deep, rich
tones of his delivery. She intones the hum on instinct, as if her
hum and his words are entwined. His words end just as her hum
fades away, and Meadbh opens her eyes, aware only now where
she is and who is in front of her.

Desmond is attentive, his expression intent. Mac Diarmada,
seated to his left, looks mildly interested, and Meadbh sees the
irony that the Gael, whose life blood should be steeped in this
art form, hasn't the real wit to appreciate the verses that Diarmuid has recited in a manner worthy of any *reacaire*. And
beside him the Gaill, who wouldn't have such a heritage to call
upon, should find so much appreciation for it clearly evident in
his gleaming eyes, the mouth slightly agape.

Chapter Fifteen

Back in the small chamber, Derbhla attends Meadbh. She offers to uncoil her hair, help her undress and settle her into the pallet on the floor. A small ewer of water is on the chest and Meadbh wonders at it.

Derbhla sees her glance. "To wash your hands and your face, if you should wish."

Meadbh nods and sighs. If only she could wash away this day, this night, this last month. She remains silent as the girl helps her out of the surcoat and kirtle, leaving Meadbh only in her *léine*. On the pallet stuffed with straw and perhaps moss to soften it, is a woven wool coverlet that might also serve for a brat. She's uncertain about the night and what it will bring. Will Diarmuid be here? She left him in the solar, drinking ale and other beverages of the sort she's never tasted. She only drank sparingly of some watered ale and left soon after the performance, excusing herself with the plea of tiredness. But Diarmuid stayed, engaging mac Diarmada and Desmond in lively conversation about the fine points of his performance and the wider issues of the times. She too should have followed suit, if only to discover what she can about Diarmuid and the others, so she can make plans, to formulate a course of action that will serve her best, for she can't count on Diarmuid to do it. This past day and more have proven that. But she'll use these moments now to decide what she'll do as she considers all that she's learned and what she's observed.

She turns to Derbhla. "I must thank you for all you've done today. You've been most kind."

Derbhla flushes and waves her hand. "It's no bother. It's what I'm here for."

Meadbh pats her hand. "I'm Meadbh. I'm sorry I didn't say so earlier, but I was so preoccupied."

Derbhla shrugs. "It's understandable. But really, you've no need to worry that you didn't tell me. It's hardly my place to request it in any case."

Derbhla's words are modest, but she beams with pleasure at Meadbh's comments.

Meadbh gives her a ready smile in return, the fragments of a plan already forming in her mind.

Meadbh lies still on the pallet under the wool coverlet, her hair in a single plait hanging along her chest, her *léine* tucked around her like a caterpillar's cocoon awaiting its transformation to a butterfly. Waiting still. She wonders briefly if it will in truth be a transformation. Will she become his wife fully this night? She knows the statement they both made earlier to Desmond carries some weight under Brehon law, but what of his law? Or the law Desmond follows? She continues to wait, her mind drifting to Teampaill Gobnatán and to her *beacha*. She thinks of tonight, the hum that rose from her and Diarmuid's words that something tells her the *beacha* would understand. Was it always like this with a *reacaire* and a *clarseoir*? The thought carries her to sleep.

A hand touches her shoulder, waking her from a deep sleep. She feels a figure ease down beside her, hot breath at her ear. "All will be well, Meadbh. All will be well."

The warmth is welcoming, the support at her back. She continues to feel the press and heat of his hand on her shoulder. It gives her the most comfort and she knows it will send her back to her sleep. A troubling thought, though, a soft disquieting one that lingers low, beneath the surface of her mind, tells her she shouldn't trust this warmth, this comfort, or the hand that gives it.

He's gone the next morning when Meadbh awakes, and she tells herself that she's glad. There are so many reasons to be glad, and she won't enumerate them all, just assures herself there are countless. She hums to herself and stretches, acknowledging the quality of her sleep the night before. The cause is assuredly the pallet, the warm dry chamber. She slowly rises, giving only a cursory thought to Diarmuid's whereabouts. He'll be attending Desmond, or perhaps checking on the horses. That thought reminds her of her task at hand.

She makes her way to the ewer, still half filled with water. She pours some of the water from it into the small bowl and splashes the water on her face. The slight sting its temperature gives is refreshing, even in the chill of the morning, dressed only in her *léine*. She pats her face with the linen cloth tucked beside the bowl. No wet marks from Diarmuid's possible use.

A knock sounds on the door, and at Meadbh's bidding Derbhla enters, droopy eyed, her dun-coloured gown hanging slightly awry, as if she dressed in haste. Meadbh's gown from the night before is brushed clean and draped across her arm. She nods to Meadbh, yawning, covering her mouth.

"Ah, sorry now," says Derbhla. "They were all at it until the small hours. It was very late before I could have my bed." She takes the gown from her arm, folds it and places it on the chest.

"No worries at all, Derbhla," says Meadbh. She rubs her shoulders absentmindedly against the cool air that has wafted in.

"Oh, let's get the gown on you, now, so," says Derbhla. "Before you catch a chill."

Derbhla picks up the gown from the night before but Meadbh shakes her head. "I want to ask your help."

Derbhla gives her a doubtful look, shrugs. Meadbh quietly explains her needs and any doubt about the story that she's created evaporates after a few moments.

103

Meadbh picks her way through the muddy path, a sack filled with provisions clutched in her hand. Her short leather boots are already mud clagged, the damp seeping through. It can't be helped and she shoves thoughts of it away. Around her, she can hear the song birds in full voice. The sound of a sparrow hawk cuts the air shrilly, calling to a mate perhaps, or sounding an alarm. Something rustles the scrubby bush that has sprouted up at the back of the stables she's skirting, beside the stone wall, playing host to plant and animal life. It seems to emphasise that Desmond counts this only as a temporary resting place and puts no effort or time into maintaining it to a high standard.

She hears voices, and pauses. She can make out the sounds, but the words are foreign. The *galloglach*? Listening carefully, she waits until she hears them stomp away and then moves forward again. She rounds the corner of the outbuilding and slips inside. The light from the doorway helps her make her way along the horses that are tethered there, looking for the familiar form of the mare. She's considered for only a moment taking Fionn, but decided the mare was best, since she was used to her and fixing the cushioned padding would be easier.

Meadbh hears a soft neigh and recognises the mare, tethered in a small enclosure away from the others. She goes inside, finds the snaffle bit and slips it on just as she hears the sound of footsteps in the distance. She waits again, hoping they'll pass. A moment later they're gone, until she hears some shouting. Without any further hesitation she leads the mare out of the shed, circles around the rear of the building and the other buildings, to go across to the track road that leads from the castle.

Her lack of size, as well as dressing as a young lad in an

ionar and *truibhas*, with her Gaill mantle on top, she hopes supports her role as a servant intent on delivering a message for the earl to the blacksmith in the small town nearby. That's her plan to get her along the road, safely away from the castle. She has every reason to trust that Derbhla felt true sympathy for her need to return to an ailing father in the south, without the knowledge of her husband who has forced her to travel with him in this foolish and dangerous endeavour to seek patronage. She has no choice but to trust Derbhla, and the directions Derbhla gave her to her kin's dwelling, where there's someone who would willingly accompany Meadbh south for a small recompense. The fact that the only item she has that might approach recompense are the wooden hairpins she took from the chamber, now tucked in her sack, she chooses not to think about.

Chapter Sixteen

A clammy fog, perhaps drifting from the nearby sea, or due to the overly warm weather, clings to Meadbh as her horse picks her way through the boggy hills. The weather has been so cold in early spring, and so it makes her feel the heat all the more now. Her tunic clings to her back, which is too warm under the weight of the mantle, tunic and *truibhas*. Droplets gather on her lashes and at the edge of her hairline, where short tendrils are gathering in tiny curls. The long plait is tucked under her tunic, so that only the top of her head is exposed to the fog's dampness.

She scans the land for the signs Derbhla told her to look for. She has yet to see any. After a while, a windblown ash, its branches reaching in front of it like so many arms begging for mercy, looms ahead and she breathes a relieved sigh. The first marker, at last. She can push aside the doubts that have gripped her since first stepping outside the chamber this morning. Thoughts of Diarmuid rise up and she wonders over his reaction when he finds her gone, suppressing the pang of concern and guilt that accompany these thoughts. She tells herself that it was unwise to trust him. So many of his actions and words proved that, and the "all will be well" statements were just words to lull her into cooperation.

She examines the possible reasons for his duplicity. In the forefront is the desire to somehow make Raithlinn his. It's no great prize, but for a man who might now have nothing, it would have appeal. The fact that she knows very little about his background, and what she does know is probably a lie, gives no support to either guilt or innocence. He's clearly a man of learning, a man who has studied with an *ollamh,* and might just be one himself, though probably not an *ollamh* of the highest rank. He seems too young for that. She recalls his performance the previous night. Its quality. She presumes it was accurate, though the metre sounded very old. Another thought creeps into her mind that she quickly shoves out, appalled at herself. Diarmuid at Raithlinn. But no, it must be Eoin. Eoin is of the Fhlionn *sliocht.* She thinks of her father. A sharp pang cuts across her. Her father would want Eoin.

The dwelling, Meadbh notes when she arrives at her destination, is small enough and the thatched roof is in need of repair, Meadbh notes. In the fog she took a wrong path and had to double back, so that it's past midday when she arrives, and the sight of the rectangular clay packed home gladdens her.

She slows the mare, suddenly cautious. She's been so intent on finding the way and arriving safely, thoughts of pestilence had fled her mind. Now, she lifts her the neck of her *léine* and covers her nose and mouth.

Light from the weak sun that has now broken through the skies sparkles off the fog-damp grass that hugs closely to the long hut. An odd holly and a few willow trees hover nearby. A scrubby clearing is to the east side of the hut, where a small pen houses a few cows. They low in unison at the sight of her.

She halts the mare a respectable distance from the doorway which sits at one end of the long side of the dwelling, near the clearing. The weathered door is shut and she wonders if she should hail the inhabitants.

Just as she opens her mouth, the door swings wide and a figure appears. A woman. She leans against the door frame, clad only in a blood splattered *léine*. Sweat plasters her hair to her head.

"Help," she says, her voice barely above a whisper.

Meadbh stares at her, unable to move. The mare moves restlessly under her, uneasy at the sight of the woman.

The mare has turned before Meadbh realises it. She makes no protest but allows it to retrace her steps, eventually breaking out into a swift trot. Meadbh blinks, her mind trying to catch up with what she's just seen. Pestilence? She can't be sure, but the shocking sight of that woman is something she's never seen before. She halts the mare as her reason and training rises up, telling her she must return. What would Máthairab think of her? She's a healer. She repeats those words. Thinks of all the prayers everyone at Teampall Gobnatán has offered up over the years, protecting Borneach and their nunnery. The nuns were convinced of its effectiveness. Should she now offer up those prayers for herself, when even in the past, as she knelt on that cold hard floor of packed earth, she doubted?

She takes a deep breath, turns the mare around and heads back to the woman, her pace slow and deliberate.

And still, as the hut comes into sight, she halts once more, staring at the dwelling. The woman is collapsed at the door's threshold. The mare, once more unsettled, begins to shift about. Meadbh tightens the reins and remains in place. Her mind whirls, thoughts at battle.

"*Dia duit.*"

Meadbh turns and sees a gaunt, lanky youth making slow progress towards her. He pulls a young calf behind him with a rope that has been tied around the cow's neck. The calf gives a high pitched bellow of protest as the youth increases his speed to meet up with Meadbh.

Instinctively, Meadbh raises the cloth that had slipped during her trot over her nose and mouth once again.

"*Dia is Mhúire duit,*" she answers.

She scans the youth and judges him to be a few years younger than herself. Still, he's tall enough despite his gauntness. His spare frame is clad in a worn but tidily mended *léine* and a serviceable frieze mantle with sections of wool tufts missing across the shoulders. His legs and feet are bare and chafed.

"Is it shelter you seek?" asks the youth, politely. "My home is just up along, I'm sure my mother would give space to rest and take some food."

He spares a glance for the dwelling. Meadbh stiffens, prepared for what he sees. He drops the rope and starts to run. She can only sit on her mare and watch as he scrapes up his mother and takes her inside.

Meadbh hovers in the doorway, her nose assaulted by sour smells, and waits for her eyes to adjust to the light. That's what she tells herself, but she can't find the will to move forward. To discover the state of things. "The state of her" is what echoes in her mind, the tone derisive. "The state of her own self".

She knows she's ashamed. But the shame isn't enough to overcome her hesitation, her absolute fear of what she'll encounter, and all its possible consequences, some that she's personally experienced, if she steps forward. Shame, shame, shame. She'll confess it to any religious who would care to hear it and absolve her, but the fear she tries to stifle, because the fear has nothing noble about it. It makes a mockery of any belief she might have possessed in the power of prayer.

She closes her eyes, takes one step forward. The neck of her *léine* is up so high her eyes are almost covered, and for a moment she wonders if perhaps she should cover them and try her best to see through it. The thought is ridiculous, but still she feels compelled. Would the pestilence enter through her eyes?

"Will you stay with her while I fetch some sour milk for her to drink?" says the youth.

Meadbh nods slowly and locates the youth standing by a straw stuffed pallet at the far end of the room. She can see now that he's bent over the woman and is holding a bowl. Dark bile fills it. The woman retches and spews more bile into it. Slowly, Meadbh makes her way towards the youth and the woman, uttering prayers under her breath. The prayers she only moments ago rejected surprise her, as do all the other instincts of protection she's learned in her life. The scrap of cloth she was given, soaked in the ancient well by Teampall Gobnatán and then wrapped around the saint's sacred statue on her feast day, comes to mind. Where is that? She feels a desperate need for it, even though she knows it's probably still back at Teampall Gobnatán.

When she arrives at the youth's side, he shoves the bowl into her hands and she finds herself holding it under this woman's mouth as the youth disappears outside. It's then she notices the swelling on the woman's neck. Meadbh suppresses the retch that arises suddenly from her gut. She can hear her mare neigh outside, as though she too can taste and smell the death that hangs in the air.

Chapter Seventeen

Meadbh is still holding the earthenware bowl when the youth returns. Her head is turned to one side, away from the horror of this woman, the bulge on her neck, the retching in the bowl. The foul odours that assault Meadbh are nearly more than she can handle, and they prevent her from imagining she's somewhere else. It's the thoughts of her father and what he might have experienced that brings her from her turmoil to take note of the youth. He's holding a mug full of milk and is talking to his mother.

"Come Mother, try some of this sour milk. It's cold, just as you like it."

The woman groans in reply and falls back on the pallet, turning her head away. The youth turns to Meadbh, his eyes red rimmed and clouded with tears.

"She's very ill," says Meadbh. "I doubt she'll be able to swallow much. Maybe some water."

The youth nods. "I'll get some fresh from the well."

Meadbh forces an encouraging smile, knowing that the youth just wants a purpose, to do something that will help his mother. She, on the other hand, would rather her purpose be far away, but she's here now and feels trapped at this woman's side.

The woman rests on her back, her eyes closed. Meadbh rises from her crouched position, bowl still in hand and pauses, contemplating what she should do with the bowl's contents. She goes outside, and spying a squat furze bush, heads there and tosses the contents on it. She watches it splash across the thorny branches, the prickly needles and budding yellow flowers. Dark splotches spread across branch, needles and petals, dripping. She turns, hurries away from the sight, and slips inside the dwelling, taking time to dig out her headcloth from the small sack that's still tied to the mare's cushion strap. She ties it firmly in place over her nose and mouth.

Back inside, the woman lies still on the pallet, her breathing now tortuous. As Meadbh draws closer, she sees the woman's mouth is bruised blue and the swelling on her neck is dark and suppurating. Meadbh's first instinct is to utter a prayer and it runs through her head even as she tries to recall what she must do for this woman. Her healing skills are at a loss. She realises she knows nothing about how she must treat someone with the pestilence, despite everything she learned at Raithlinn. She stares at the woman, still hovering a distance away from her as the woman's breathing becomes even more laboured.

A few moments later Meadbh hears the youth's footsteps, his panting breath. "I've tied up your horse." He looks over at the bed. "How is she?"

Meadbh turns to the woman and sees that her chest no longer rises and falls, her breath is no longer tortuous. She's dead. Meadbh crosses herself and turns to the youth.

"*Ta bron orm*," she says.

The boy looks at her, stunned.

Meadbh knows what must be done to prepare a body after death. That much she can do. She's assisted Siúr Eithne enough times, and even completed the rituals on her own, when the need arose. But now, she can hardly think. She remembers Diarmuid and Eoin's caution with Colm, though his treachery most certainly contributed to his perfunctory handling, she knows the pestilence paid a part. Diarmuid was careful to keep her at a distance, and both he and Eoin wore cloths over their mouths and made it a quick task. There was no careful washing of the body. No priest in attendance to give him any rites, even though he lay dead. And what of her father? She'd not asked the details of her father's death and burial. No priest to shrive him, that she knows, but surely prayers were said.

She looks at the woman, unmoving on her pallet, her mouth slightly open in death. An opening for her spirit to escape, thinks Meadbh. She inhales deeply and starts to intone the Lord 's Prayer. The youth falls to his knees and joins her, his voice halting, stuttering with tears.

When they conclude it, Meadbh finds herself launching into *Faeth Fiada*, St Patrick's *lorica*. It's a prayer for protection, its meaning an ancient invocation that penetrates the mists of all times and beings, covered though it is in the words of the god of Christ, she feels the need for it now. The words of binding, the words of protection against all things harmful.

Crist domimdegail [indiu]
ar cech neim ar loscud,
ar bádudh, ar guin
conimraib ilar fochraici
Crist domimdegail [indiu]
ar cech neim ar loscud,
ar bádudh, ar guin
conimraib ilar fochraici

Christ, protect me today
Against poison, against burning,
Against drowning, against wound,
That I may receive abundant reward.
Christ with me, Christ before me
Christ behind me, Christ within me,
Christ beneath me, Christ above me,
Christ at my right, Christ at my left,
(Christ in the fort,
Christ in the chariot-seat,
Christ in the mighty stern.)

When Meadbh finishes, she opens her eyes and feels a sense of calm. The youth stares at her, wide eyed.

"Do you have any *sliocht*?" Meadbh asks him.

They are walking to the well together, she and the youth, so that they may draw enough water to wash the woman. It's a task that Meadbh could name to remove her from the dwelling, give her time to gather her thoughts and create a course of action. Though once the water is drawn and they return to the dwelling with it, the woman must be washed. But all in good time, she tells herself, even as she fingers the cloth that is now fallen around her neck. Its use seems long past. But still.

"We are *betagh*, owing allegiance to the Poer family, I guess," says the youth in answer to her question, shrugging. "I have an uncle and his family. He lives in the next field over."

Meadbh nods. "And your name?"

"Cathal, and my mother was Finoula."

"I'm Meadbh."

They arrive at the well, draw the water and make their way back to the dwelling as Meadbh tries to form a plan.

Meadbh holds the damp cloth in her hand next to the straw filled pallet. The woman lies where they'd left her, in the bed, arms at her side, hands clenched and mouth slightly open. A bucket stands beside Meadbh. She feels Cathal's presence beside her, waiting, wondering at her hesitation.

On impulse she turns to him. "I think it might be best if you go to your uncle, tell him what's happened and ask him to come so that he may help and bear witness to her burial. And his family too."

Cathal looks at her, nodding slowly. "I will, of course," he says. "They'll want to be here. My aunt and my mother enjoyed each other's company on fair day."

The last statement appears mindless and disconnected, Meadbh thinks, but she imagines the grief directs his tongue to some extent.

Cathal gives his mother a last look, turns and leaves the dwelling. A moment later she can hear his running footsteps. Meadbh stares down at the woman, contemplating her next move, the cloth still in her hand. The body is already growing stiff and she knows she should begin the washing of it, but she can't bring herself to lay the cloth upon the woman's face, let along remove her blood and sweat-stained *léine*. And what then will she replace it with?

She looks at the meagre wool blanket that's covering the body. Felim. It's difficult for her to think of this body, so putrid in its last moments and even now, as a woman, a mother. For Meadbh it's a vessel of pestilence. She pulls the cloth up over her mouth and thinks again of the *lorica*. Prays to Padraig, prays to Gobnait. With one swift motion she takes up the blanket and pulls it over the woman. Rolls her on her stomach and draws up the sides of the blanket. She casts around for a needle, or anything that will serve to close shut this blanket. She knows she's a coward. The shame that's upon her now is almost as unbearable as this task. But she will do it.

117

When Meadbh hears the footsteps and voices, she's standing by a smoored fire, the embers only a tiny glimmer in the hearth. She stirs it with the iron poker in an effort to bring it to life. The fire will be needed in the days to come. No one lets a fire go out, if it can be helped.

Behind her, the newly shrouded body lies on the pallet, the badly sewn end of the blanket under it, and the large rust-pitted needle is safely tucked away where she found it, wrapped back up in its oiled cloth, next to the tallow candle in the small cubby hole in the stone wall by the pallet.

Cathal, a short stocky fair haired man and a sturdy brown haired woman clatter into the dwelling. The woman is weeping openly, and when she catches sight of the body on the pallet, she throws her hands up to her face and starts to keen. Cathal gives the woman an awkward glance and nods to Meadbh.

The man approaches Meadbh, his expression hesitant. *"Dia duit,"* he says. "My nephew tells me you've been a great help in this time of trouble." He eyes her carefully, suspiciously.

"Dia is Mhúire duit," says Meadbh. *"Tá bron orm.* Ah, no. I have done nothing."

The words are more than courtesy, because she knows she hasn't done enough. She has done less than nothing. This woman deserved more than what Meadbh gave her. Meadbh didn't even treat her with contempt. She treated her as if she weren't human. An object. Meadbh turns her head away so they won't see her shame. She pokes at the embers that refuse to spark into life.

Cathal's aunt lowers her hands, tears still tracking down her face. "No," she says. "You have done so much. And you a stranger." She sweeps her hand to the bench at the small table on the other side of the room. "Sit," she says. "We must show you some hospitality, if only for a moment. And then we'll try to find a priest. Though how we'll manage that, with our own just dead from the pestilence, I don't know." The tears well forth again and she looks up to her husband, takes a breath and says, "We'll find a way, though. We can't bury Finoula without at least the benefit of a priest."

The conversation disturbs Meadbh, not only because it seems private, something that should be done without her presence, but because of the growing sense of dread inside her.

"Is there much pestilence around here?" she asks, refraining from looking over at the bed where Finoula now lays shrouded.

The aunt wrings her hands, glances up to the uncle. The uncle speaks. "There is some, in the town. The last time I was there, selling my wool to a sea merchant, a few were dead of the pestilence, the priest included." He looks at the bed. "I told Finoula when I brought the sack of grain from town, to keep Cathal close and to avoid the town if possible." He frowns. "She was fine when I left her and Cathal only a week ago." He studies Finoula carefully, but remains at a distance and stops his wife when she attempts to go to Finoula's side.

Meadbh nods, watching the silent scene. "The pestilence seems to be fierce and determined no matter what people do to avoid it." She feels the cloth, now at her throat, useless once again.

Chapter Eighteen

Meadbh watches with a sense of hopelessness as Cathal and his uncle lower Finoula's body into the ground. The poorly sewn blanket that she made a shroud, thin and precarious in its weave, still envelops her. Once she is placed in the ground, the uncle and aunt, who she now knows are called Seán and Máire, stand next to Cathal.

The tears that come to Meadbh's eyes are born from frustration, self-pity and self-loathing. She should be well on her way to her destination. To Caishleán na Leachta, to the O'Mathghamhna, to make her request. Instead she stands here, watching this woman that she never knew be buried.

Máire turns to her. "Cathal said that you know all the prayers. Will you say them now?"

Meadbh reddens, because what she said was more of an invocation, though some would call it a prayer. Meadbh knows the thought that was deep in her heart at the time. But she needs the prayers now, and these people do as well, she tells herself. She opens her mouth and begins, but this time her former sense of desperation is replaced by something akin to resignation, futility.

Meadbh stands awkwardly at the door, searching for the words she knows she must find. She hears the mare neigh in the pen by the cows. She's grateful that Cathal has seen to the mare since her arrival. Though it's been a day, a night and not yet a full day, she feels she's been here for a fortnight and more. Her body is limp with exhaustion. Hopelessness. And it's that hopelessness that paralyses her mind. Numb, she's forced herself through the motions of these last hours. And now, she must take her leave.

Does it matter if she has an escort now? And the only escort possible, Seán, seems a choice that's both wise and unwise. Wise for any stranger who might have been asked, but unwise for her. And they still think she's a youth. She utters another prayer under her breath. A brief one to St Gobnait – the closest she can come to her *beacha*. The hum is gone. Her *beacha* seem so far away now. Maybe St Gobnait can reach them. She knows, though, her punishment is to come. A punishment filled with ironies, because though her cowardice tried to keep her safe, in the end it failed to protect her. She sighs, knowing she must accept it now. Accept her fate.

She steps forward opens her mouth and makes the request. To ask if it's possible for Seán to escort her to Caishleán na Leachta. To show her the way, at least, as far as he may.

The mare walks steadily along the track road, Meadbh swaying slightly with the mare's motion. She notes the budding oaks, the birch. A sparrow hawk flies overhead, searching for prey. She swipes the hair that has blown across her face and looks down at Seán, his hand grasping the reins, leading the mare as he trudges forward. Seán refused to ride the mare and Meadbh wasn't certain if it was more that his pride wouldn't allow him to ride a mare like any other Irishman, or that he had no experience on a horse and didn't want to take the risk of embarrassment. Whatever the case, she didn't press him on it. The consequence is that their progress is slow.

His acceptance of his role as escort had been slow. Only the urging of his wife and nephew had made him decide to take on this responsibility. He had reasoned that there was too much to be done at both homes, but his wife had said their sons and Cathal would manage. The suspicious, watchful looks he's cast her way since he first saw her have become regular. She stiffens now as another such look is cast her way.

The mare's motion has done nothing to lull her today, her careful plodding only emphasising the turmoil in Meadbh's mind, where she spends most of her time. Seán speaks only when necessary. In the two days since the journey began, Meadbh has never felt so aware of everything inside her. The bruise on her cheek her mother gave her is gone, no longer tender to the touch. Her stomach has been only able to manage the smallest of drinks of ale, or fresh water from streams that they pass. Milk, sour or otherwise, is beyond contemplation, even if they were to find someone to give it to them. Only the few bits of oatcake, cheese and salted beef have been consumed. Nerves, she tells herself. Anxiety over what lies ahead. But still, she monitors her body, now clammy as they stop for the night. Will it happen this night? Will it be fever, or chills? She tries to recall what Cathal had told her about his mother's experience, but finds she can't. Her general knowledge is only vague, but she does know of the swellings. She can't forget them. Each night she's run her fingers along her skin, waiting to feel their tell-tale presence. Will tonight be the night?

Meadbh huddles in her mantle in the small shelter of a clearing. The night is warm, but she's chilled. Dread seeps through her. Is it beginning? It's been three days, no, four, since she entered Finoula's dwelling. She has no idea, except that Finoula had been fine about seven days previously.

A short distance away Seán lies on the ground. His worn mantle has become pushed aside, revealing the long, belted *léine* he wears underneath, a large neatly mended section near his shoulder clearly visible. Meadbh thinks of Máire, needle and thread in hand, working the hole carefully. It makes her sad and she has no idea if it's because someone should show such care for another, or that Seán may not receive that care in the future. Because if she should fall sick, it's inevitable that he will. Or so she imagines. The thought strikes her and a fear grips her. A fear that compels her to utter the *lorica* yet again. She speaks aloud, her voice a whisper. Seán turns over and mutters in his sleep.

The mare halts a moment, then proceeds forward at Seán's urging, resuming her steady pace. Meadbh catches herself, the sudden halt causing her to sway a little. She realises she's lost sense of time and place. The trees around her have become a green blur, the sounds muffled. She's fallen into a kind of trance, she thinks, brought on by hours of Seán's silence, the steady pace of the mare, and the relentless trees that comprise her scenery. She no longer listens to the birds whose spring song rings out, a music that used to keep her attention for long swathes of time. She's failed to notice the animals, or any other signs of wildlife that she would find amusing or fascinating in times past. And she no longer has the bees to hum her to awareness, to keep her filled with a vibrant sense of life. The steady rhythm of the mare is her world, until they stop for a meal, or for the night. The world is only in this rhythm. She closes her eyes, pushes her mantle back, suddenly feeling warm. The spring heat is in full force. Soon it will be Bealtaine, she thinks. Summer. She licks her lips, conscious of the beads of sweat that have gathered there. A moment later she feels herself falling from the mare. Seán's curse rings out as she hits the ground.

Chapter Nineteen

Meadbh is lying on the ground, eyes closed, the breath knocked from her. She struggles to find the energy to open her eyes, but it seems impossible. All that she knows is that she's incredibly thirsty. She forms the request in her mind to ask for a drink, but the words don't come. She can only lie here, on this piece of ground, glad that her mantle has fallen from her sides, so that she can feel the cool of the air upon her skin. But it isn't enough.

Meadbh opens her eyes. They feel scratchy, her lids scraping across her pupils as she makes a huge effort to open them fully. Her hair is damp with sweat, clinging to her scalp. Her gown feels clammy. She can see through half raised lids that the day is nearly gone. A bird calls in the distance. A crow, she thinks. Trees rustle overhead in the breeze. The soft chomping of grass sounds near her. She thinks of the mare. She can hear nothing else and wonders where Seán is.

A cooling hand rests on her forehead. She sighs with relief and the words to ask for a drink form in her head so strongly, she thinks she utters them. She must have, she realises, for a moment later her head is lifted and the neck of a waterskin appears at her mouth. She tries to drink from it. The cool liquid spills in her mouth, but a large portion dribbles out, down her chin and onto her neck. The liquid chills her and she starts to shiver, her teeth chattering. A voice utters soothing sounds and words, their tone and pitch high and raspy with age, unlike Seán's deep tones. Meadbh opens her eyes and sees a woman. A worn, wrinkled face amid a halo of grey hair escaping from her headcloth. She wears a dark mantle, and sturdy calves and bare feet peek from under it.

The woman attempts to lift Meadbh from the ground and Meadbh moans with the pain of it. Her teeth are still chattering, and it's all she can do to stop her whole body from shivering. Meadbh tries to assist, knowing her efforts are meant for good. The woman struggles under Meadbh's weight, but eventually, between the two of them, they manage to get her upright. She scans the area for signs of Seán. The mare stands idly, the sack still tied to her back. There's no sign of Seán, nor his small sack.

The woman urges her towards the mare and Meadbh tries to comply. After a lot of stumbling, the woman supporting her, Meadbh makes it to the mare's side. She stares at the mare's flanks, willing herself to raise her arms and hoist herself on the mare's back, but the effort just seems too much.

"I'll help you up," says the woman. She places her large, sturdy hands on each side of Meadbh and counts. On the third count, Meadbh feels the lift and she grabs the mare's back, trying to rise with the momentum of the woman's efforts. She collapses half way and finds herself draped across the mare's back. She has no more energy. Her eyes close.

Meadbh sees her brother, his body lifeless on the bed, her mother at his side, in turns wailing and shouting at Meadbh. Meadbh holds herself tightly, tears streaming down her face as she keens, softly berating herself for daring him to climb that tree. Even now she sees the tree, it looms large, its branches treacherous, suddenly coming to life, transforming into serpents. The serpents hiss, their tongues flailing, their jaws open, teeth sharp, ready to strike. She draws away. One has the eyes of her mother and she retreats, stumbling, and falls on her back. The serpent looms above her, ready to strike. She feels the bite of it on her neck. She startles awake.

Meadbh shivers and searches for warmth, her eyes still closed. Another wool covering, a fur skin. Anything to make her warmer. The cold has awakened her from her dreams. Her neck is stiff and she tries to raise her arm to check it, but the weight of it is too much. She forces her eyes open. The woman hovers over her, her face filled with concern. Meadbh notes the woman's eyes are hazel, with gold flecks. Eyes that had once been pretty. The woman places another threadbare cover over Meadbh, who tries to express her thanks.

The woman shakes her head. "Don't try to speak, *a chara*. You're very ill and you must save your energy."

Meadbh thinks of nodding but even that effort nearly exhausts her. All she knows is that her head is aching and she's in need of a drink. "A drink" she rasps.

The woman nods and takes a small earthenware cup from beside the small pallet Meadbh lays on. The woman leans over, lifts Meadbh's head and puts the cup to Meadbh's lips. Meadbh takes a sip. She can feel the moisture pass her lips, fill her mouth. She gags, spitting out the watered ale. The woman tries again and Meadbh manages to swallow a little liquid. A moment later, her bile rises and she lifts her head higher, turns to the side and vomits. Meadbh goes to wipe her mouth with the back of her hand and discovers the small swelling at the side of her neck. She draws her hand back in horror. She hasn't imagined it.

Meadbh feels a cool cloth on her forehead. She struggles to open her eyes. They're crusty with lack of use. Lids raised, she waits for her eyes to adjust to the light, to focus, to understand what's happening to her and where she is. A thatched roof is directly above her, its supporting beams worm riddled and burlap sacking torn in places. Her eyes drop to the area just in front and she sees the woman bending over the small hearth, muttering to herself. Her grey hair is wispy, poking out from her headcloth, and the heavily mended belted *léine* she wears hangs down to her calves. She's tending oatcakes that are cooking on the iron griddle that hangs on a crane over the fire. The griddle is old, bits of it are missing, rusted off, but still usable.

Meadbh raises her hand to the cloth on her forehead. It's warm now. How long had it taken her to open her eyes since it had been placed there, she wonders. The woman, hearing Meadbh stir, looks up, swings the griddle away from the fire. She unbends, placing a hand to her back to ease the strain, before making her way over to Meadbh.

Once by Meadbh's side, she smiles. "You're awake again. Good. Do you think you can manage a drink of something?"

Meadbh nods her head, not wanting to use up her strength just yet. The woman returns a moment later with a cup and, lifting Meadbh's head, helps her to drink. This time Meadbh manages on the first try. This time she keeps it down. She pauses before trying again, though, just to be sure. But another sip is managed, and another.

"I'll make you some thin potage in a short while," says the woman. "This is enough for now. This is good."

Meadbh gathers up her strength, her courage. The questions are crowding her mind, and she sees that as a good thing. A need to know. A need to feel that information will help her. Will give her an immediate future. She moistens her lips, takes a breath. "Where am I?" She manages eventually, her voice a whisper.

"You're in my home," says the woman. "At Gort na Tubrid."

"How long?" Her voice is half whisper half rasp.

"I found you on the track road about ten days ago. I'm Síle. But hold your questions for now. You need to rest. You've been very sick."

Meadbh lays back on the pallet and contemplates what the woman has just said. Ten days. But she has no idea how long she'd lain there on the ground. She thinks not long, but the number of days still confounds her. She thinks of the castle, and Diarmuid. That seems so long ago and yet it still causes pain. The betrayal, the danger. All of it. And to lead her here, to this moment. Sick, perhaps dying, on a stranger's pallet, in a stranger's home. Her own home is so far away. At least she thinks so. But the homeplace Síle the woman gave her, Gort na Tubrid seems impossible, because this townland bears the same name as the one for Teampall Gobnatán. But sure, there must be more than one of named after a well in a field. Its name would label many a place. A holy place though. A holy well.

"The well?" she asks. "Is it holy?"

The woman smiles. "Ancient and holy, so surely blessed it has now led to your recovery. We must thank the saints and all the gods for that power."

Chapter Twenty

Meadbh sits with her face turned upwards, taking the full benefit of the weak sun that shines down. She's counted the days, no, endured them, fighting to regain her strength enough so that she can sit here enjoying this moment. The pure joy of it. To feel the light on her face, the warmth of the sun, the music of the birds. To inhale air that isn't poisoned by the foul smells of her illness, or clouded by the smoke of the peat fire.

She hears Síle's footsteps behind her. Carefully, Meadbh

turns from her position on the wobbly stool and sees Síle just outside the dwelling's doorway.

"Ah, you're looking better, now," she says. "You've a bit of colour in your cheeks."

Meadbh smiles and nods. "Thank you. I feel better than I have in a long while." She gives a weak laugh.

Síle returns the smile, nodding. "You're doing so well. I never thought you would be up and about so quickly."

Meadbh takes comfort from that. "Hopefully, I shall be able to ride soon."

"You're doing grand," says Síle. "But it's best not to rush. The pestilence is rarely survived. You've much to be grateful for."

"I know. And I'm deeply grateful, don't mistake that. It's just that I have spent too much time being ill. I need to be on my way as soon as I'm able." Meadbh notes that Síle hasn't mentioned anything about Meadbh's choice of clothes when she found her collapsed and she doesn't mention it now. Discreet? Incurious?

"Ah, you're more than welcome to stay here as long as you like. I've no one left, now, so you've been grand company for me."

The words resonate in Meadbh. "You've no one?"

Síle shakes her head. "All dead from pestilence."

Meadbh takes time to consider Síle's words. "All of them?" The thought fills her with immense sadness. She isn't certain of the specific cause, though it might be because at that moment she feels bereft of all her own family, her sliocht. "*Tá brón orm*," she says.

Síle nods. "It was a great sorrow for me and there's sorrow still. I nursed them all, and yet, I, who should have been taken, was spared." She gives Meadbh a bewildered shake. "But the actions of God and the saints aren't for us to question." Síle crosses herself. "My sins are certainly not any fewer. But perhaps it was for you that I was spared."

Meadbh takes a sharp inhale of breath and belatedly crosses herself. "And I'm eternally grateful, whatever the reason or cause, as much as I'm grateful to you."

Síle waves her hand. "It's nothing to thank me for. It's what anyone would do." She pauses. "Or should do. If they were a good Christian soul."

Meadbh thinks of Seán. She thinks of herself, begrudging the care to Finoula. How can she blame Seán, though? "You have more than Christian goodness."

Síle. "Ah, there was enough selfishness, too. As I said, I enjoy the company. I have no reason to be worried about nursing you. If my time has come, it has come. I'll join my family. Otherwise..." She gives a shrug.

It's a pure impulse, one Meadbh can't help. "Come with me when I leave. If you'll consider it."

The air is damp from a misty rain that has hampered their progress in the morning, but now the rain has stopped, and there's promise in the scudding clouds. The mare ambles along the path, taking her time. Meadbh does little to urge her on, because the mare is now carrying two, and Meadbh isn't certain of the way. Síle has done her best, directing Meadbh on this path, assuring her of its southerly direction, but she knows little more than that, having ventured no further than the surrounding dwellings, the fair at the crossroads, and a few other places whose names Meadbh doesn't recognise.

The sun's presence a little while later tells Meadbh that Síle's directions were accurate and she now urges the mare on with some confidence. The direction is correct, at least, she thinks, but there's little else that's known. Their location, and how it relates to their destination is still in doubt. They are questions she tries to avoid so they don't press in on her. She'll enjoy the journey. She's alive. And surely that's what she must have in the foremost of her mind.

Seated behind her, Síle taps her shoulder. "We must rest," she says. "You shouldn't exert yourself too much. You aren't fully recovered."

Meadbh nods, though she doesn't feel tired. She wonders if Síle feels the need to stop, both from physical discomfort and the discomfort of riding the mare. Meadbh had noticed her uneasy look when Meadbh had first urged her to ride. And the manner in which she tightly clutches Meadbh's waist hadn't gone unnoticed, either. Regardless, for both their sakes, it's a wise move to stop.

The rock barely holds the two of them, but the sun is out and the now clear skies give Meadbh a new feeling of energy. She takes a deep breath. In the distance she hears the cry of a gull. She smiles and looks down at the large chunk of cheese in her hand and breaks off a good portion and hands it to Síle. Síle has given her the biggest portions of all the food they're now sharing, saying that Meadbh still needed to build her strength, but

Meadbh doesn't want the woman to cheat herself of what is due her.

Sile hands the cheese back. "No, no. I'm grand. I can eat no more."

"Ah, no. That's nonsense. You must eat as well. I need your sturdy strength."

After a moment Sile relents and takes the cheese, breaking it up into smaller pieces, before popping them one by one in her mouth. Meadbh looks on, amused, while she eats her last oatcake, a thin layer of honey spread across it. She savours its flavour, wanting to treasure this small luxury and remember her own *beacha*, her own honey. Sile only had the one small pot, obtained from a neighbour and distant kin, because the *beacha* had feasted on the flowers and tree blossoms from her family's field. An ancient practice, part of the old Brehon law, but one Meadbh can feel great appreciation for at this moment. She resolves that once her own future at Raithlinn is settled, she'll somehow establish new hives. The thought settles inside her, a small idea that generates the smallest piece of joy. She closes her eyes, all her senses alert, hoping for the hum, but all she can hear is that same gull crying overhead.

Meadbh stretches, easing herself out of the sleeping position she'd assumed the night before. She hasn't slept much, too aware of the noises of the night and possibilities they contained. Too many possibilities and none of them good. More than she can imagine, but those that she managed to conjure up in her mind were enough to have her turning restlessly under her mantle.

Beside her, Síle sleeps on, her night seemingly as restful as Meadbh's was disturbed. The restfulness of a person who has long ago come to terms with death. It's a calm that Meadbh can't adopt, as much as she might want to. Her recent experience tells her that now she wants life. To live well. She looks up at the sky, notes the darkening clouds, and frowns.

They're on a wider track now, the path well-worn. The trees have receded to a fair distance, furze and wildflowers replacing them on either side of their track. A chill fills the air and birds are swirling above, circling and swooping in the bracing wind. The weather is changing. Ominous clouds have been gathering since Meadbh and Síle left their place of rest by the stone outcropping.

Behind her, arms still encircling Meadbh's waist, Síle snorts. "Not long now before the rain."

"I know," says Meadbh.

"Will we look for shelter?"

Meadbh is still debating as the first drops of rain come. She opens her mouth to speak, scanning the area around her. It's then she hears the thundering hoofbeats of horses in the distance.

Chapter Twenty One

The rain is heavy and Meadbh's hair is plastered to her head when the horsemen arrive. Síle remains behind her, clutching her waist. Meadbh has kept the mare standing, moving neither forward nor turning and retreating. There's no use, and not enough time to take cover, even if they hadn't been visible to the mounted men the moment she heard the hoofbeats. To hide could suggest something more than they mean. To remain where they are hopefully means they have purpose here, and the remote protection of someone powerful. Meadbh can only hope.

The riders draw up, a brawny dark haired man with a matching beard at their head. His nose is gnarled purple. The years haven't been kind to him, but his blue eyes glitter brightly. Everything about him and his men – the saddles, the bits, the mantles, boots and swords at their sides – tell her they're Gael. She can only hope that counts on her side. She can only hope.

The man surveys her, his beard dripping in the rain. "What brings you to this land?" he asks. His tone is curt, but there is some politeness behind it. A rusty, forced kind.

"We're only travelling through," says Meadbh. "Though we would gladly take refuge from this foul weather at some nunnery or monastery if you could kindly direct us."

She tries to keep her tone strong and firm. She is a woman of standing, undertaking an important journey. Her bedraggled appearance, female mount and lack of attendants negate the words. She sniffs, trying to dispel those thoughts.

The man stares at her, considering her remark. His horse stirs restlessly under him. The other mounts copy his horse. The mare gives a challenging whicker and his horse snorts in return. He eyes the mare and frowns.

"How is it you're mounted on a mare?" His voice is filled with disdain.

She straightens. "The mare was the only horse available."

He shakes his head in disgust. "Mares aren't for riding."

"There was no choice. And haste was needed, so walking was out of the question."

She owes him no explanation, and she might point out that his welcome was hardly hospitable. She scans the men behind him, some faces filled with amusement, some with boredom. One or two show the disgust that this man wears.

He studies her carefully. "And where is it you and your servant have to go in such haste?" He asks.

She refrains from lifting her chin and from correcting him. Síle isn't a servant, she's a friend, but Síle's poor manner of dress says differently. Her own gown, the stained, travel worn habit from Teampall Gobnatán under her mantle with which she'd replaced the youth's clothes isn't much better. Her headcloth has slipped to her neck, further proof that she's hardly someone of consequence. But for now, Meadbh thinks it will protect them both from deeper questioning if Síle were to act the servant. At least for now. Síle's silence coveys her agreement. Meadbh straightens, holding herself erect. A display of fierceness she doesn't really feel. The rain is still pelting and they have to raise their voices to conduct this conversation. She's wet and the mantle has little protection against such heavy rain.

She sighs inwardly, resigned. "We go to Caisleán na Leachta."

The man narrows his eyes, surveying her closely. "And what business have you at Caisleán na Leachta?"

She ponders her response only a moment. "I would speak with O'Mathghamhna."

"O'Mathghamhna? And what would you say to him?"

She looks at him, taken aback by his forward manner. "That's between myself and O'Mathghamhna."

"Ah, but you see, I am O'Mathghamhna's eyes and ears. I am Feardorcha O'Mathghamhna, close kin to O'Mathghamhna."

Síle tightens her arms around Meadbh's waist, communicating her alarm.

The rain is soft now, a misty bloom around the riders as they make their progress on the track. Meadbh takes no notice of her wet garments, or the hair that drips like tears across her face, manifesting what she now fights inside her. There's no time for tears, no time for worry. She must put her mind to her situation and see her way clear. This man, this Feardorcha O'Mathghamhna, as he belatedly told her, hardly seems trustworthy, but she can see no reason why he wouldn't take her to O'Mathghamhna.

She shifts uncomfortably on the back of his horse. He's made her mount behind him, swinging her up there with one swift motion that left her breathless. The wool from his mantle smells of wet lanolin from the woven tufts. The arms she has around his waist bring her closer to the smell and the tufts tickle her nose.

Instead of trying to look over his shoulder, she turns her head to the side and glances over to Síle, who peers over at her from behind a short, stout man where she rides as instructed. The mare is at the back, out of scent and sight of the other horses, pulled by the last rider. Síle gives her an encouraging smile, but Meadbh can tell it's forced. She appreciates the effort. They'll face what's to come together.

They stop for a break. It's well past midday. The rain has finished, but Meadbh's mantle still clings to her, and the weight of it when she dismounts makes her want to fling it off. She pushes her wet hair from her face, even as she feels the end of her plait drip on her back from under her mantle. The dismount is an awkward effort altogether, and she owes thanks to this man Feardorcha for it. For his lack of assistance, and that he dismounted with no care for her, walking to his men and giving orders for the pause in their journey. Were these men kin to O'Mathghamhna as well?

Sile comes alongside of Meadbh, her own dismount effected with the help of the sturdy man. At least she had help, thinks Meadbh. Sile would need it more. Meadbh can see the strain and fatigue on Sile's face. This is more than enough to deal with. Sturdy Sile may be, but she's no longer young and she's endured much.

Meadbh scans the clearing for a place to sit that's had some semblance of drying. Although with the state of her mantle, it hardly matters. Eventually, she finds a small rock. It has space enough for the two of them, and she motions for Sile to join her there. Meadbh looks over to the mare, their sacks still tied to her back, and wonders if she should retrieve some food. It's been a long while since they've eaten.

A handful of oatcakes are shoved towards her. Feardorcha. He lifts his chin, pointing at her. "Eat. We won't be long. I want to arrive before dark."

She takes the oatcakes. There's nothing to coat them. She thinks of the small pot of honey in the sack and decides that it's better kept there. Sharing out the oatcakes with Sile, she sits on the rock, and watches the men take their own places in the clearing, munching on their fare. Some remain standing, opting to avoid any additional wetness, but others sit in clusters, talking amongst themselves. Meadbh sees the man that Síle rode with, chatting to one of the others. His hair is nearly dry, the fair curls she sees he possesses cling tightly to his head. He's younger than Feardorcha and his eyes are friendly, not hardened like Feardorcha's. Seeing her look, he nods to her pleasantly. The man beside him, brown haired and wiry, sees his nod and turns to look at her. His eyes slide over to Feardorcha and frown. Meadbh follows his glance and finds Feardorcha's eyes studying her carefully. He's leaning against his horse, a short distance from her.

"You've yet to tell me anything more than it's a family matter that you wish to discuss with O'Mathghamhna. Who is your family?"

Meadbh considers what to say and decides the truth would suit fine. She draws herself up. "I'm Meadbh, inghean Cormac Ui Fhlionn mac Dugall."

A surprised look crosses Feardorcha's face. A moment later he breaks out into a roar of laughter. It echoes in the clearing, as some of the men take it up, sharing the joke, while others shift uncomfortably, looking down at their food, or the ground.

Chapter Twenty-Two

It's when Meadbh begins to recognise the surrounding countryside in the gathering dusk that an uneasy feeling forms inside her. The outcropping of gnarled trees, ivy embracing them in its stranglehold now. A booleying hut in the distance, towards the uplands. Has he decided to take her home after learning who she is, she wonders? The thought starts to worry at her, like a stone in her shoe, a constant growing irritation. Sitting on the back of his horse, this stone is growing larger and many more gather with it. She would rather they go directly to Caisleán na Leachta. To go to Raithlinn would reveal far too much about the dire straits of the holding and their *sliocht*. And what would O'Mathghamhna do when he heard that, for she can't imagine that Feardorcha would keep it from him? But whatever he says, she knows it won't benefit her *sliocht*. Eoin would be seen as too weak to be Ui Fhlionn, to be *ceann fine*, or even *ceann cuibhrinn*, if that was what the Ui Fhlionn was now. There's no time to even warn him, to give him a chance to at least create the illusion that things are no different now her father is dead. Even a diversion will suffice. A kernel of an idea forms in her mind.

Meadbh's mind is telling her over and over that it's an opportunity. A small one, but one that's worth the risk, for there's all to lose, otherwise. She hasn't long before this opportunity will slide away and she'll be at his mercy. She inhales, withdraws a hand from around his waist and taps his shoulder.

He ignores the gesture and they continue on, his horse setting a brisk pace for the others to follow.

"Feardorcha," she says after a moment. "Are we making for Raithlinn, instead?"

His answering grunt tells Meadbh little, but she takes it as a yes and plunges on. "If so, then I think you must be careful. There's pestilence in the area."

"There's pestilence everywhere," says Feardorcha, his tone dismissive.

"But that's one reason I need to speak to O'Mathghamhna. It's now at Raithlinn. You wouldn't want to endanger yourself or your men by going there, so I thought it best to warn you. If indeed that's where we're headed now."

Feardorcha chuckles, shaking his head. "I'm grateful for your warning, but it doesn't change my mind. We go to Raithlinn."

His answer stuns Meadbh to silence. She bites her lip, trying to conjure another reason to avoid Raithlinn, or at least give Eoin some notice. But what can he do anyway in such a short amount of time? She knows now, by the shape and number of the looming stand of ash trees, that they're not far from the Raithlinn stronghold.

The track is just as muddy as before, but the cart tracks have disappeared, dissolved in recent rains, she imagines. The dwellings are there, just ahead, quiet and undisturbed. A moment later a figure emerges from a doorway out into the clearing, followed by another. She has a small surge of hope that some of the *sliocht* that had left are now returned, and that her worries aren't as large as she imagined, but then she realises these men are strangers. She reasons with herself that she's been a long time from Raithlinn and there would be many she wouldn't recognise. But she spies their clothes, the swords at their side, and knows that it's not a case of time passing and people changing in appearance, these men aren't Ui Fhlionn.

She looks to the *bawn* by the *ráth* where the stone buildings for the horses and animals are kept, and the pen for the animals next to it, hoping to see Eoin, or his son, Aedh. She sees only more men milling about. Strangers. One man leans against the stone wall, his arms crossed, watching another who sits on a rock, working a strip of leather, oiling and cleaning it, she imagines. A few scraggly dogs fight over scraps near them, while a cat emerges from the shed that houses the animals. These small details help Meadbh's thoughts from flying into panic, but these details also tell her that any deception or delay is fruitless. Others have already taken up residence in Raithlinn. She has no idea what *sliocht* or what authority they represent, she just knows they aren't Ui Fhlionn.

The sound of the horses draws all these strangers' attention. Those sitting or leaning stand and the rest halt in their tracks. The one that had been leaning against a wall, watching the other man, makes his way forward and Meadbh can begin to distinguish his fair hair, his rounded, beardless face, the greyness of his eyes and the smile that's forming on his mouth.

"*A Feardorcha, Dia duit,*" he says, continuing towards them.

Feardorcha greets him back and realisation starts to dawn on Meadbh. She waits to hear more. Perhaps she's wrong.

Feardorcha brings the horse alongside of the young man, who catches hold of the reins, steadying the animal. Feardorcha dismounts, leaving Meadbh. She's consumed with tension. Carefully, she begins to manage her own dismount, until she feels a strong pair of hands ease her down to the ground. Once there, she turns and sees the young man beside her, surveying her with an appreciative look. His brown hair is tangled, his beard barely there, but still he licks his lips. She flushes at the notice he gives her, uncomfortable.

Meadbh scans the area again anxiously, looking for any familiar face. Even her mother's.

Feardorcha hands off the horse to one of the men and walks inside, ignoring her.

Meadbh sits on the chest opposite the door in the hall of the ráth, quietly watching the activity around her, hoping that she won't be noticed. Síle sits tucked at her side. Meadbh's mantle still sits cold, damp and heavy on her shoulders. She needs time to regroup, to fully understand the situation, and find Eoin, if possible. What he might say fills her with dread. She knows she must hear it, though.

The hall floor is scattered with food scraps, as well as over-turned and upright tankards and cups. The trestle table leans against the wall, forgotten. Benches are aimlessly arranged around the hall, some of them occupied. An Irish wolfhound lounges in the middle, chewing on a discarded bone. Men amble in and out. A lone woman Meadbh doesn't recognise, wearing only a belted *léine*, rests against a tall dark-haired man, his arm around her as they sit on the settle against the wall to the right of Meadbh. She thinks of the last time she was here, with Diarmuid. It's an unsettling thought. A path she won't follow, but painful still. Meadbh pushes the thought away and looks again at the men around her. They hardly seem a threat, at first glance. Second glance shows more. Hardened muscles. Battle scars. Swords and javelins in close proximity. Sharpened. Ready. She bites her lip, hoping that Eoin hasn't succumbed to the end of any of these blades or javelins.

Feardorcha enters the hall, his boots scattering the mangled rushes that cover the beaten earthen floor. He scans the room while he combs his beard with his fingers, and spies Meadbh over on the stool. He snorts and beckons to her with two fingers. Meadbh rises, bracing herself, and makes her way over to him. Is he going to banish her to one of the huts? She thinks she can bear that, as long as she's left alone. Though she knows the more likely scenario is that he'll drag her to the large chamber. The one that used to belong to her parents.

When he arrives at her side she can see a trace of speculative humour in his eyes. "Now that you're here, see if you can organise the food store and get the cook to produce something edible."

Meadbh does her best to conceal her surprise. Since she has no idea what stores they have brought with them, or if they've hunted or fished, she can only nod and tell him she'll do her best. This is a good turn of events, she tells herself. It gives her an excuse to leave the hall. It allows her time to find Eoin and discover the exact nature of the events that have taken place. Though she knows what's happened. She does know, deep in her heart.

Chapter Twenty-Three

Meadbh heads to the stone building that contains the food stores, keeping well out of the way of the men who are still outside. After careful consideration she'd left Síle back in the hall. It seemed safer, in the end. For Meadbh, for Síle. That's what she tells herself, and hopes that the men and Feardorcha won't take advantage of her absence and prey upon Síle in any manner.

Some of the men milling around still as Meadbh weaves her way through to the store, giving her curious looks, while others hardly spare her a glance. Though her mantle is still damp, she's glad for its protection. A brief breeze stirs the bottom and she hopes that might begin the drying of it. Still, the evening light is nearly gone. It's only as an excuse to leave Feardorcha's presence that she has ventured to the store, weighing the odds of meeting any ill out here over trying to discover if Eoin, or any other of her kin, are still here.

She arrives at the small shed containing the food store and slips inside. It's dark, and she can only make out shapes on shelves, but it's enough to see that there are at least a few sacks here, presumably containing milled oats, and hopefully some onions for flavour. Meat haunches and whole fowl hang from hooks embedded in the cross beams. At the far end is the hearth, perfect for smoking and some food preparation. Tomorrow is soon enough to discover the exact kinds of meat and fowl, but at a guess she would say a haunch of beef and mutton and some ducks. She spares a thought to wonder if it might be her family's mutton and beef, but doesn't linger on it. Again, she knows the answer. And that answer is a path that leads only to wretchedness.

She slips outside, careful to close the door quietly, and checks to see if anyone notices her. Once the way is clear, she heads in the opposite direction, towards Eoin and Ita's dwelling. She prays that he's there, for otherwise, she'll have to search further afield, and she knows she doesn't have much time.

Once outside Eoin's home, she places her ear up against the door. She hears voices inside and thinks she recognises one, though her heart sinks a little. Her mother's.

It takes Meadbh a moment to understand the scene in front of her. A fire in the hearth provides a backdrop. Flames hop and crackle, red hot. A pot hangs over it, issuing deep, rich aromas of meat and onions. Ita stands at the hearth, a spoon in her hand, midair. Her face is flushed. Tendrils of her fair hair float around her head. Her gaze is fixed to the right of her, on the bench where Meadbh's mother is. Her mother, who sits with her head tilted, face flushed, eyes shining, mouth pouting. Her mother whose gown isn't stained, or coarsely woven. Her mother, whose hair shines and is woven into a long plait that hangs along her shoulder, with the merest of transparent veils covering her head. Her gaze is fixed on the dark haired man above her, who stands, arms lazily crossed, stance casual, expression amused. Feardorcha.

Eoin is absent.

The bench feels hard underneath Meadbh. She grips it tightly, holding in this grip all her anger, fear and disgust at the same time. She's said nothing since she entered. Feardorcha has ignored her, Ita has fussed, taking her mantle and seating her on the small stool next to her mother.

Ita presses a bowl towards Meadbh. She looks down, contemplating it. She takes the bowl, feels its heat. Steam rises and assails her nose with its succulent odours. A rare feast of tender meat. Famine, war and now pestilence have made such feasts infrequent. She slides a glance over to her mother. The end of her plait, gold bright, is circling slowly around the fingers of her right hand. Suggestive.

"Ah Feardorcha," says her mother. "There's much to

commend how you oversee my husband's holding. It would bring him much joy to witness it."

Feardorcha gives her a considering nod, his face impassive. "I've done my best to assure your wellbeing. But it's for O'Mathghamhna that I do this. And for myself, with his authority."

Meadbh hears in those words the answer that she wants to deny, but has known all along. The answer that she's dreaded. But still, now she has it. She has more, though. More than she wants, or could have imagined. Her mother's plan. She shakes her head softly. There's no surprise, but yet there is of course. Deep down.

Meadbh's potage has grown cool in her hands. The aroma has lessened with the steam. The exchange between her mother and Feardorcha keeps all her attention, though her eyes are focused on her lap. Ita stands off to the side, uncertain. Meadbh spares a moment to wonder where Eoin is, and Aedh. Are they on some errand for Feardorcha? Hunting? Nothing in her surroundings gives her a clue. She must ask Ita. Yet she hesitates.

"Will you have a bowl of potage with us?" asks Meadbh's mother.

The tone makes Meadbh stiffen, even as Feardorcha turns her down, amusement in his eyes. The tone brings back memories, none pleasant. Memories of other guests. Her father. The carefully calibrated words that Meadbh hears deepens those memories. The preening. A different woman than Meadbh knows. Not her mother. Not *her* mother.

"Meadbh," says Feardorcha.

His voice startles her out of her reverie. She tries to clear her expression. Everything is written on her face. She knows this. She's been told this countless times by Máthairab. She looks at Feardorcha and clears her throat. "Yes?"

"You're not eating," says Feardorcha. "Isn't it to your liking?"

Meadbh blinks. Nods her head. "Yes, yes. It's grand." She makes a show of taking a mouthful, the wooden spoon clutched tightly in her hand. A fisted hold. Steady, unshakeable.

Her mother stirs beside her. "You must excuse my daughter, Feardorcha. I tried to instil manners in her, but she was ever a stubborn child. Spoiled by her father." She frowns at Meadbh. "She hasn't even greeted her own mother."

The tone is pleasant, but pouting. Meadbh sighs inwardly, reining in impatience and anger. They're to be buried, as ever. She turns to her mother. Forces a smile. This smile she retrieves from the past. A past clouded with recriminations, condemnations and occasional slaps. Slaps that still echo in her jawbone.

"Mother, it's good to see you looking well. You had me worried sorely when last I saw you."

Her mother waves a hand. "I'm well enough now. Of course I wasn't myself before. I was a newly made widow. It's natural for a widow to grieve. Since you're a nun that would, of course, be something with which you'd have no familiarity."

Meadbh tightens her lips. "Not yet a nun," she says. The tone is pinched. Filled with the history that hangs like a heavy shroud between them. Opaque.

"For all intents and purposes a nun fully pledged. You're over the age." Her mother nods, sealing the statement in her own truth. A knot that can't be untied.

Feardorcha gives a hearty laugh, his head falling back. A

joke, heavy with amusement. When he finishes, he grins. "A nun?" He shakes his head. "Not you. No, we can't have that."

She regards Feardorcha cautiously. She finds his words both welcome, yet not. "It's not possible now. Not since leaving Teampall Gobnatán. Not with the pestilence."

He nods his head slowly. "The pestilence."

"My father died of the pestilence." *Here*, she has a mind to add, but doesn't. It's something he most likely already knows. Something, given the state of Raithlinn, that must have been obvious, at the very least. She glances over at her mother. The expression she finds there is coy. A hint of caution creeps in. Perhaps Feardorcha hasn't been aware of the cause of death. Her mother is more than capable of creating alternative versions of the truth.

Feardorcha shifts his gaze to her mother, studying her. "Yes," he says slowly.

"Did O'Mathghamhna discover it before you arrived?" Meadbh ventures to ask.

Feardorcha nods slowly, looking at her. "He did indeed. He sent me here to confirm it. To assess the state of the holding. Ui Fhlionn, after all, is indebted to O'Mhaithmghamna. Heavily."

Meadbh stiffens at his words. The implication. "Yes. We're aware of that. But a fresh start will help shift the situation. Eoin is more than capable...." Her voice trails off at Feardorcha's raised hand.

Feardorcha shakes his head. "Enough of your plans. I have my own plans."

Meadbh hears his words and again feels that dread. She knows. Again. She knows what's in his mind. She glances over at her mother. Her mother gives a smile that Meadbh recognises. Seductive.

Chapter Twenty-Four

Meadbh opens her eyes slowly. Stiff, cramped muscles greet her. She stretches slowly, like a cat, conscious of Síle's sleeping form next to her. The straw pallet underneath rustles at her movement. Fatigue still claims her body, the few hours of sleep she did manage haven't satisfied the need borne of so much travelling and sleeping outdoors. And her illness. It seems so long ago now, yet her body tells her it isn't. At this moment she's weak in body, mind and spirit, if she were truthful. Yet she pushes herself slowly from the pallet. Things must be done, regardless of her lack of strength.

She slips her gown on over her *léine*, seeing the small stain from last night. She hadn't noticed it before, but she hasn't any doubt that the spill of her potage happened after Feardorcha's statement about having plans. Plans that he felt no need to tell her mother. Her only clue is that he instructed the men before bedding down for the night that he would be going to Caisleán na Leachta in the morning. Her mind had been on his choice of bed at the time, rather than any details or questions the men asked, but she remembers nothing of any consequence. She'd stood uncertainly in the hall, watching him make his way to the inside door, until he halted, turned and lifted his chin towards her.

"You and your servant can sleep in the small chamber, if you wish. I'll have one of my men put a pallet there. Unless you'd prefer to stay with your mother."

The comment she'd suppressed still stays with her as she silently makes her way down to the hall. Men are there, scattered around, finding sleep on the benches, the floor. Wherever there's space. Snores emit from a few. Shifting positions from others. She picks her way through them. Quietly, carefully. A rat scampers across the floor, under and over the rushes, until it disappears altogether. Startled, Meadbh halts. Catches her breath. A moment later she resumes her journey, her muscles still stiff from the night before.

Once outside, she blinks at the sun just peeking through the clouds at the horizon. It's early yet. Dew drips from the trees and grass around her. Birds greet the spring morning with enthusiasm. She spares only a moment for the freshness of it all. Lets it cloak her. Then, she heads towards Eoin's dwelling.

Meadbh tries to peer in the small window of Eoin's dwelling, pulling aside the cloth that hangs down against the night air. The angle is wrong and she gives a frustrated sigh. She can only see the wall opposite and the bench that lines it, along with the space next to it. It's too dim to see beyond on the left. If she angles her head, she can just about make out the hearth. A quick glance tells her Ita isn't there, stirring up the fire for the day's use.

A figure crosses her vision. Ita. Meadbh calls her name softly. Ita turns and locates Meadbh at the window. Puzzled, Ita makes her way over.

"Meadbh," she says in a low voice. It's a question, more than anything.

Meadbh gestures to her and Ita, understanding, disappears from sight. Several moments later she's outside at Meadbh's side. Meadbh draws her to the back of the dwelling. "I've come to ask about Eoin. About what happened while I was gone."

Pain crosses Ita's face. Meadbh fears the worst.

Her mother. Meadbh should have known. She did know. It couldn't have been otherwise. Ita continues to talk, but Meadbh's thoughts drown out Ita's words. Her mother was the one who told O'Mathghamhna of her father's death. She sent Aedh with the message.

Questions halt her swirling thoughts, and she focuses on Ita's words. "Wait," says Meadbh, holding up a hand. "Sorry, but can you go back a little in your account? My mother sent Aedh. Did he return? And where's Eoin?"

The pain crosses Ita's face again. She shakes her head. "Aedh was sent, but only Feardorcha O'Mathghamhna and his men came. Aedh is still at Caisleán na Leachta." Tears fill Ita's eyes.

Hostage. The first thought she has at Ita's words is Aedh has been made a hostage. "And Eoin?"

Ita shakes her head. "Your mother sent him after Aedh."

"My mother sent Eoin after Aedh?" Meadbh knows she's repeating Ita, but it's a repetition that is needed. The words say so much and she struggles to allow the full implication of her mother's actions.

She nods. "She said she hadn't thought Aedh would remain behind. So Eoin is there to plead for his return."

Meadbh nods now. The plan is evident. She knows her mother. She knows she would appear to be concerned. Unaware that such instruction would put Aedh in danger. And now Eoin. Two hostages. Two Ui Fhlionn men no longer visible heirs.

"How long ago?" she asks.

"As soon as the men arrived. When we saw that Aedh wasn't with them. Seven days ago."

Her mother didn't wait long after her departure before sending Aedh with the message. She sighs, squeezes Ita's shoulder. "I'm sure they'll be grand. Feardorcha seems fair, and so we can infer that O'Mathghamhna is as well."

Ita nods hopefully, a small smile breaking out on her face. "The men haven't been bad. A little sloppy, a little dirty. But nothing bad."

The 'bad' Meadbh knows is another word for what woman face in situations such as these. What she herself fears, despite her position as *inghean* Ui Fhlionn. "Even more reason to trust that Eoin and Aedh will be fine."

Meadbh says the words as comfort. She knows there are so many other possibilities that would make those words a lie. Ita knows it too. For now, they'll both keep the lie afloat. It's all they have to keep themselves and all their hopes afloat as well.

Back in the hall, Meadbh finds activity. The snores have ceased, along with any restless stirrings. The men are up, grumbling and murmuring to themselves and each other. Hair and beards are raked clean of crumbs and tangles. Clothes are straightened and *truibhas*, stiffened leather jacks and leather boots donned.

She looks for any sign of Feardorcha and spots him over at one of the benches, talking to the stout man who'd carried Síle on his mount the day before. He looks up, and seeing Meadbh, motions her over. Hesitantly, she complies, weaving her way through the men. Some only glance at her, but others take her in from head to toe. She resists the self-consciousness that arises as much as she can, but her hand sneaks up to smooth the plait under her grubby headcloth that she'd only loosely re-woven that morning after a night's tangled sleep. Already it's falling apart, strands dangling along her shoulder.

She brushes a strand from her face when she arrives at Feardorcha's side. He regards her silently for a moment, his gnarled features speculative. Lines trace a map around his keen eyes. She sees that once he might have been considered well enough looking. The eyes trouble her, though. The eyes show things she doesn't want to see. Darkness. Judgement. A hint of anger. She attempts to find more, to change her initial assessment, but a trace of amusement enters his expression and she understands he knows what she's doing. He snorts, shakes his head, denying everything and nothing, except his own amusement at her. Her naiveté? Her blatant study of him? Again, the uncertainty sets her off kilter.

He sniffs. "We go to Caisleán na Leachta today."

The "we" of his statement puzzles her. She waits to hear if she's to be part of that "we". In her mind there is no "we". She has never been part of a "we". And in this case in particular, because she would of course prefer that he go with his men and she remain behind. That's the kind of "we" she can approve.

"Get your servant to pack some fine gowns," he says, ignoring her silence. "Your finest. You will want to look your best for O'Mathghamhna."

She looks at him. Readjusts her thoughts and the foolish meanderings on "we". But still, she finds the link with him disturbing. And portentous. But she can tell herself it's an opportunity to ensure Eoin and Aedh's safe return. It's an opportunity to plead her case for her *sliocht*. Convince O'Mathghamhna that Eoin would be a good choice for Ui Fhlionn and to inherit the holding of Raithlinn. The opportunity is there and that's no lie, but opportunity and success are so far apart, to convince herself otherwise is to lie. Still, she'll do her best. There's no lie in that either.

Chapter Twenty Five

This time Meadbh is allowed her own horse. Not the mare, of course. The mare has resumed her duties, ready to be serviced by the male horses, since she'll be in heat at any point forward until the end of autumn. Now Meadbh sits astride an unfamiliar horse, swaying with it as it navigates the muddy track. The horse is one that Feardorcha brought with him, she presumes, since it wasn't at Raithlinn before. Síle rides behind her, her arms around Meadbh's waist. Síle wears a borrowed gown over her *léine*. Meadbh has claimed her as no servant but distant kin. There was no one in the hall to provide a countering story, so Feardorcha had just accepted it.

Meadbh feels the warmth of Síle's arms encircling her waist, now. It's a comfort. The comfort of kin. The uncertainty of what lies ahead can be fought with such comfort.

Up ahead, Feardorcha rides his own horse, easy in his seat, experienced. A man who spends most of his life astride. Riding to battle for O'Mathghamhna, checking the various holdings. Would a man like that even take part in booleying cows for grazing? She decides that he's nothing like Eoin, who did such work. Eoin who was more than head of her father's household warriors, such as they were. He did these tasks more out of willingness, rather than kin obligation. He was a true *tanaiste*, unlike her spoiled young brother, or her cousin. She realises her words put Eoin and what occurred in Raithlinn in the past. A musing that takes her into darker realms.

She turns her head to the right, as if to move away from such a path. She blinks to clear her mind. An extra assurance. The alder tree that she sees is still bare, though she thinks she can detect a few buds for leaves to come. The thought lifts her up.

Feardorcha glances back at her and she gives him a puzzled faint smile. Does he think she might make an escape? The desire is there, but practicality, and her hope of achieving something for her *sliocht,* keep her on the horse and following him. The soldier behind her is more than enough to ensure that she doesn't wander by design or accident. The track should be familiar, though, since she and Diarmuid ventured out from Raithlinn to Caisleán na Leachta not that long ago. But as she passes each field, each clutch of trees, rock outcropping, she realises that nothing is familiar. Initially, she thought she might be mistaken. That she'd forgotten or hadn't noticed some of the landmarks she sees on this journey. But the pain in her heart tells her differently. She feels anger at Diarmuid, too, but the pain far exceeds it.

They pass an old *ráth* in the distance. Sturdy enough, it seems small compared to others Meadbh has seen, but still a couple of people pour out of it and watch them pass. Two men, she thinks. No doubt O'Mathghamhna kin. A small group of dwellings stand near it. Other kin? They must be an outlying manor grouping, sharing the farmland and bounty. It's just enough beyond what she knows to be the boundary of her father's holding, and at one time might have been part of Ui Fhlionn. She isn't sure. It's when they clear the next group of trees, swinging southeast, and a good-sized stone tower looms into the distant view, that Meadbh realises they are already at Caisleán na Leachta. There has been no break in the journey. There's no need. The distance isn't vast. The horses aren't tired or in need of water.

She thinks of Diarmuid once again. Their journey. The pain in her heart is still sharp. Sharper. But she must put this pain aside and think of what she must do. That's another thought she would rather push aside as well.

Meadbh focuses on the wooden bench where she sits. Its finely carved arms, the slope to the back that disappears behind her. Its generous size. The fine polish on the wood. Oak, she thinks. A good sturdy wood. It will hold many people for any length of time necessary. Right now it holds her. And Síle. Síle sits beside her, face a semblance of calm, the grey wisps of hair escaping the headcovering she donned before they left Raithlinn, but her hands tell a different story. They fidget, fingers playing with fingers. Nails are studied, the fingers splayed on one hand, while the other picks out the dirt from under first one finger, and then the next. Meadbh's nails are bitten enough that there's no dirt to pick out. So Meadbh studies the bench, following the details and any thoughts those details prompt. Because around her the din is loud with men and women coming through the doorway to the solar, talking, some stomping the mud from their boots, while Irish wolf hounds swirl at their feet, the unofficial greeters.

Meadbh knows they stare at her, survey the mantle she clutches around her. It's her old one, thankfully retrieved from Ita, and the warmth and familiarity help her to remain seated in relative calm on this bench, situated at the far end of the main chamber, near the carved wooden chair that's against the wall. A large iron brazier stands on the other side of the chair, the glow of the turf shedding an extra circle of weak light to add to the illumination provided by the two narrow windows and the open doorway. Meadbh really has little need of the light, though, or at least only as much as it allows her to study the bench while she waits.

Waiting. She has done much of that since their arrival some hours ago. She waited, as instructed, for someone to assist her and Síle in their dismount, while Feardorcha and his men disappeared into a stone building within the bawn that might have been a cow shed, a place for the horses, the food store, or something else entirely. While she'd waited, the tower rose up in front of her. The once fine bawn looking a bit worse for wear, but still functional. The cattle presumably were out grazing on the newly rejuvenated grass.

The someone who finally came to help her dismount was a young lad, pale faced and beardless. Once both she and Síle were firmly on the ground, she waited again, uncertain where to go. The lad had moved on, tending the horses. Men passed them. Dogs sniffed them, tongues wagging. Not the greeting she expected. After several moments had passed, she took Síle's hand and led her inside. Climbed the ladder to the second level, above the hall where the cattle would be gathered in, along with any other stores, during times of trouble. Finding the small staircase, she led Síle up to the large solar. It was there she found the bench she now sat on with Síle. To wait. Hoping to see Eoin and Aedh at the very least.

Her wait eventually brings her eyes to view the solar. It's larger than her father's hall. Meadbh knew that, of course. The exterior had told her at a glance. Imposing. Though perhaps not like Desmond's castle. The thought causes her to frown. The castle Desmond has taken. But from whom? One of those minor Gaill lords, no doubt. The Poer family they mentioned? These Gaill fought their own people as much as the Gael did. She thinks of Diarmuid. Or the betrayals that came with such fighting. She shakes her head slightly. Shakes out that thought.

She notices a woman directing a few of the men to carry the carved oak chair forward. It wasn't a chair to be shoved across a floor. It was a chair that required care. Its prominence demanded more than one person to move it from one place to the next. A chair of authority.

Meadbh scans the room for any sign of Eoin and Aedh. There's nothing. No sign of them and she decides it's best not to ask. Perhaps from fear of what the response will be, or fear that it would just endanger them more for everyone to see how much she values them.

She scans the room again, this time looking for Feardorcha. There'd been no sign of him when she'd first entered the solar and there was none now. Was he in one of the rooms above? She casts her eyes upwards, as if she could see through the wooden planks. Her eyes drop, focus on the carved chair now commanding the attention of the room.

Figures emerge from the arched opening at her right where the stairs upwards are presumably located. Feardorcha and three others file in, one at a time. They all share Feardorcha's dark colouring. His brawny build, the chin. The last man, though, seems brawnier, taller, his energy barely contained in his body. The beard is fuller, the nose ungnarled. His eyes are keen and they scan the room, fixing on her. His expression is unreadable and it stirs unease in Meadbh. She has no doubt who he is. O'Mhaithmhaghmna.

Chapter Twenty-Six

Meadbh is still on the bench, but the table is set up before it. Síle is no longer next to her. Her seat is further along, with O'Mathghamhna's lesser kin. At least Síle is at the table, and not helping to serve the food, or outside, tending sheep. Or any other duty of this household, now that Meadbh has claimed Síle as kin. Of Eoin and Aedh there's still no sign. She pushes away the disquiet that gathers inside her. Perhaps they will appear later. She stores that thought up, along with all the other "perhaps" that she's conjured since her arrival.

Feardorcha is beside Meadbh now, his shoulders, arms, elbows taking up space, overlapping her own, a presence that can't be missed. His voice, loud and clear, contributes to that understanding. The knowing that this man has authority. Second only to O'Mathghamhna. There's no mistaking that, or their close kinship that isn't just the physical resemblance. It's the fact that O'Mathghamhna has Feardorcha seated next to him. It's the hearty clap he gives Feardorcha's shoulder during a shared joke. The words exchanged in low voices as Meadbh strains to hear. She understands in full now that any hope she has of changing the situation in Raithlinn is useless.

A stir of activity at the corner by the stairs catches Meadbh's attention. She glances over and sees a woman enter, fair haired, slender. A girl follows her. She's no longer a child, but not quite an adult. They are both dressed in fine gowns, their feet shod in well-made soft leather shoes, the girl's with a slight curve upward on the toes. Except for the shoes, the fashion is still in the Gael manner, but expensive. Perhaps even silk. Cloth carefully selected from a merchant's special wares, shoes as well. From the French? The Burgundians? Meadbh tries to recall the names of places she heard bandied about when she was young.

The woman makes her way to the table with the young girl behind her, studies Meadbh for a moment and frowns at her husband. "Finghín, you didn't mention there are guests. And the poor *cratur* hasn't even had her mantle taken."

O'Mathghamhna looks up at her and grunts. "Ah, now, Gormlaigh, I told you Feardorcha had returned."

She gives him a little shove on his arm. "You're being deliberately thick." Gormlaigh moves to Meadbh. "You must forgive my husband. He isn't the best at welcoming women." She spares O'Mathghamhna a severe look. "There are so few women guests who visit lately."

Meadbh nods, understanding that Gormlaith refers to the pestilence. That they are welcome here, without hesitation, she knows is down to kinship and trust. Another affirmation of the close relationship between Feardorcha and O'Mathghamhna. Meadbh can't bring herself to think of this man as "Finghín".

Gormlaigh introduces herself and her daughter, Slane, and instructs someone to take Meadbh's mantle, despite her protests.

"No, no," says Gormlaith. "You've no need of your mantle. We'll put more turf on the brazier."

Gormlaith's wide smile is hard to resist, and despite herself, Meadbh surrenders her mantle. And also despite herself, she relaxes and returns the smile. Gormlaith seats herself next to her husband, her daughter taking the other side. Meadbh feels Feardorcha's gaze on her, but she won't meet it. Her food suddenly takes her attention.

Feardorcha's selection takes up most of the trencher they share, and suddenly, Gormlaith is requesting one for Meadbh's sole use. Meadbh would almost rather the gesture hadn't been made, since her appetite is sparse and she knows that hospitality will require Gormlaith to ensure that the trencher is filled. Meadbh finds herself suddenly aware of what other things hospitality will compel Gormlaith to do.

Meadbh knows it's been some time since she's seen so much food. Famine, war and now pestilence had made every table bare that she'd been to since she could remember. Even in the nunnery it seemed their sparing meals were more than religious abstention. But this table is laden with fowl, beef, venison and more than just oatcakes, cheeses, butter and honey as additions. Ale and soured milk are plentiful to wash it down. Her own stomach is more than full on the small amount of beef and oatcake smeared with honey than she can manage. It's nothing compared to what is being consumed around her. She sneaks covert glances at different people gathered around the table. An older auburn haired woman across from Meadbh, who'd smiled earlier and introduced herself as Cobhlaigh ighnean Domnall Cabaicc mac Dermod O'Donoghue, digs into a filled trencher heartily. Meadbh smiles at the addition of 'talkative' to Cobhlaigh's father and thinks that there's no doubt as to the daughter's parentage. Cobhlaigh chatters to Meadbh amiably and it doesn't seem to matter that Meadbh hardly answers. Nodding on occasion seems to be enough.

Cobhlaigh's husband, Maol, is cousin to O'Mathghamhna, Cobhlaigh tells Meadbh, and Maol, hearing his name, nods to Meadbh and greets her before turning back to his discussion with Feardorcha, who sits across from him. It's a discussion that includes O'Mathghamhna and appears to concern a specification of ploughlands and their condition. Something about its nature sits uneasily with Meadbh, but Cobhlaigh distracts her with a question about Meadbh.

"You're a nun at Teampall Gobnatán?"

Meadbh is taken aback at first that this woman knows so much about her, then reminds herself that Aedh and Eoin are here, and no doubt have been thoroughly questioned, officially and unofficially. She's yet to see the two, though, and she finds it disquieting. Hostages of Eoin and Aedh's standing should be here, eating at this table. All the stored "perhaps" now vanish when she delves into her thoughts for them. The thoughts that remain are darker, and she decides to push those down deep, out of reach.

She catches herself and realises that Cobhlaigh is waiting for her answer. Meadbh shakes her head. "I wasn't yet pledged as a nun."

Surprise crosses Cobhlaigh's face. "You aren't pledged?" She glances at Feardorcha, a speculative expression on her face. She gives a slight nod. "You put that in the past tense. Does that mean you don't intend to return?"

Meadbh is about to answer but Feardorcha forestalls her with his own. "She doesn't intend to return."

Meadbh blinks. "I'm not permitted," she clarifies. "The pestilence. It was considered unwise for me to return once I left to tend my father."

Gormlaith leans across her husband and Feardorcha to catch Meadbh in her sight. "*Tá brón orm.* It's a great loss for you and your *sliocht.*" She crosses herself. "I'll say a prayer for him."

Meadbh nods her thanks, suddenly unable to speak. There's so much here in these words from Gormlaith, Feardorcha and Cobhlaigh.

"A loss indeed," says O'Mhaithghmhna. "We'll drink to him later, celebrate his life and put things right."

Feardorcha nods. Gormlaith gives Meadbh an encouraging smile. Cobhlaigh laughs. "Ah now, it's the 'putting right' we'll all enjoy."

There's a little fanfare before the *ollamh* is introduced, followed by the *clairseoir* and *reacaire.* Meadbh finds she's pleased, antic-

171

ipating some formal honouring of her father's life, his *sliocht*. Once again, she searches the room fruitlessly for Eoin and Aedh, wanting them to share in this. They knew her father well. Better than she did. It's a thought that causes her a moment's sadness. Sadness isn't called for now. She knows that. She assembles a smile and looks to the centre of the room, a short distance from the table where the *reacaire* moves to the fore, commanding all eyes. He pauses dramatically, looking to the *clairseoir* who takes the stool provided, settles the *clairsach* on his lap, and lifts his hands in readiness.

A commotion stirs and three figures enter the hall. Meadbh's eyes widen when she sees it's Eoin and Aedh. They move forward at the urging of another man. A brawny, dark haired young man who shares the features of the two men at her table. A clear kinship to O'Mathghamhna and Feardorcha. But younger. A youthful swagger infuses his stride and the smile he sends O'Mathghamhna's way. They pause halfway through the hall.

"Ah," says O'Mathghamhna shaking his head. "Aren't you're always the one for the big entrance, Conor."

"Sorry, Father," Conor says. "We were busy with the... uh...cows."

Meadbh has hardly hears the exchange, too concerned with studying Eoin, and then Aedh, for signs of harm. Eoin's body seems whole, as does Aedh's, nothing visibly amiss. But harm can come in other forms, something Meadbh knows well. Eoin's expression is impassive, almost stoic. It's Aedh's face that tells the story. Stormy eyes, flushed face. His youth and inexperience are showing now. His father rests a hand on his shoulder.

"You must excuse my son," says O'Mathghamhna to the three performers. "His manners seem to be missing." His tone is sardonic, a hint of reprimand present. His eyes, though, are indulgent.

Conor turns to the men and nods to them. "Fergal, Tomás and Turlough, I'm sorry to interrupt. I will settle with great haste so that you may regale us with what I know will be a wonderful treat."

Gormlaith coughs. Her eyes narrow. She gestures to Conor and indicates a seat down beyond the daughter. Conor gives her a grin and makes his way there, leaving Eoin and Aedh to stand uncertainly near the three men about to perform. Concerned, Meadbh glances at O'Mathghamhna, wondering if she should say something.

O'Mathghamhna nods to someone and a young, slim youth with red spotted cheeks, approaches Eoin and Aedh and, after touching Eoin's arm, nods to a bench over against the wall. Eoin leads Aedh to the bench and takes a seat. Meadbh fights the urge to go to them, bringing her food and questions. She has so many questions.

It's the daughter who rises, her face flushed. Gormlaith puts her hand at her daughter's lower back, giving her the slightest of pushes. Just enough. The daughter straightens, picks up her trencher, now laden with food that Meadbh realises Gormlaith must have placed there, and she makes her way to the bench. The hall is silent. Rather than focusing on the three men about to entertain them, everyone's attention is caught by the current entertainment provided by Aedh and Eoin. A drama unfolding. Only there's no *reacaire* conjuring the images with the *ollamh's* words, telling the tale.

And Meadbh feels as though she's come in the middle of this tale. She's missed half the story.

Chapter Twenty-Seven

Q uestions. That's all that crowd Meadbh's mind as she sits on the bench at the table, conversations surrounding her. The question about the performance she's just witnessed hardly bears marking, except for its dubious quality. The question over whether the *ollamh* or *reacaire* are the most at fault regarding its quality is hardly worth consideration. She has little experience by which to judge it, since her father could never afford to patronise any entertainer except on an occasional and temporary basis. A bard who would sing and play for a night, his skill level passingly good. Nothing at the level of this *clairseoir*, whose skill she can't fault. She wants to sit by him, try the *clairsach*, something she used to do whenever she had the chance.

She thinks of her performance with Diarmuid. It hardly seems possible how much its quality was so far above what she's just witnessed. The rawness she feels at the memory takes her by surprise again. But there's no question there, not really. She moves on. Next question. Was that poem recited with so little intonation, drama or emphasis, something that had been created centuries earlier for someone else? A rote memory retrieved, learned in who knows what bardic school and her father's name inserted? How could a poem retracing the history of a *sliocht* and a prominent man be replaced with another's? An additional question. A question to shake a head to. Meadbh finds her own head shaking as she ponders it. Was it an insult, or just a poor performance by a man with no talent? Two men. Because the *reacaire* mustn't be forgotten.

Meadbh finds her gaze turning to Eoin and Aedh, to study their reactions, but more questions line up behind these that have held her attention. They push and shove, so that again, Meadbh has to resist the urge to make her way to her kin. But why not? Why does she have to sit here, instead of going to greet them? Another question. She answers it with her body. She rises and untangles her limbs from the bench and makes her way over there, oblivious to expressions or murmurings that may or may not be occurring. All she sees is Eoin's frown and the anger flashing in Aedh's eyes. She wasn't the only one to find the poem insulting. Another question answered. And who better to help her answer the other questions she has but her own kin. Her clansmen.

Eoin lights up when he sees Meadbh coming towards him. Aedh is too busy studying his clenched hands that are all too ready for a fight. The trencher lays half eaten next to him.

"You're safe," Eoin says when Meadbh reaches his side.

She nods and takes the seat next to him, studying him carefully. His eyes are tired, the fine lines radiating outward are now deeply grooved with worry. She feels a stab of guilt and sorrow that such cares have taken some of his years from him. She sees the same mouth as her father's, full lipped, under the beard, now pulled down into a frown.

"How is it you've come here?" asks Eoin. "Is there more trouble?"

Aedh looks up at those words, throws angry glances in Feardorcha's direction. Eoin puts a calming hand on his arm. Aedh scowls.

Watching this, Meadbh finds herself shaking her head. "No, there's no more trouble."

Eoin studies her carefully. "Where's Diarmuid? Is he with you as well?" He looks over to the table, searching for him.

"No," says Meadbh. Her throat is suddenly tight and she can't go on. She clears it, starts again. "No. It's a long tale. One best kept for later. He's with Desmond. The earl." She adds the last descriptor so he won't think she means Mac Carthaigh. To be clear that he's with the Gaills. And they're allied and beholden to the English. She wants it to be clear what kind of man Diarmuid really is.

Eoin's stunned expression provides some balm to her sore heart. She wasn't so much the fool after all. She holds on to that thought, will keep it against the pain she despises that still awakens whenever she thinks of Diarmuid. Meadbh hates that she still carries that pain around with her like a heavy bag at her back that hurts if she steps differently. The weight of it. Its presence born reluctantly. She stops her thoughts. She won't allow herself to go further. It doesn't help. Despite Eoin's words, she was a fool to trust him, to allow herself to more than trust.

Eoin has been speaking and Meadbh turns her attention back to him, asking him to repeat his words.

"How did you manage to return to Raithlinn, then?"

A brief smile escapes her. "That's part of the long tale." She glances over at Síle and captures her gaze. There are questions in her eyes. Concern. Meadbh gives her a reassuring smile and turns back to Eoin. "I had help from many quarters. One of them is over at the table. The older woman, grey haired, looking at us now." After Eoin gives a slight nod, Meadbh continues. "I have claimed her as kin, rather than servant. I thought it would protect her. Her name is Síle."

Eoin nods again, turns to his son. "Did you hear that Aedh?"

Aedh has been staring ahead, seemingly inattentive, but he nods briefly and shrugs.

Meadbh turns to the matter at hand. "Are you both well? Are they treating you as they should?"

Eoin gives her a wry look. "You mean as a hostage should be treated? Yes, well enough. Though Conor could do with a few lessons in hospitality. He had both of us retrieving some lost cows and shoveling shite today. Under his supervision, of course. And his two cousins, some bandy legged lads a few years younger than him."

Aedh's expression has become angry again. "The *bastún*," he mutters. The calming hand is back on Aedh's arm. He flares his nostrils, takes a deep breath.

"Have you heard anything about O'Mathghamhna's plans?" Meadbh asks.

Eoin gives her a considering look. "You of course know that Feardorcha has been given the Raithlinn holdings and is more or less *Ceann Cuibhrinn*?"

Meadbh's heart sinks. She does know of course, but hearing the words come from Eoin makes it seem fixed. Permanent.

"Has it been formally declared?" she asks. She thinks of the times that the region's main *Taoiseach* officially decides and confirms situations of this nature. Bealtaine is one, and it's only twelve, or perhaps fourteen days away. Hope, a small kernel is there. She feels it, deep inside her. Is that what O'Mathghamhna waiting for? And who would he declare it to?

Meadbh yawns. The fatigue slows her actions, her tired limbs aching from the riding, the tension. She knows it's tension. Tension that grips her still, but her yawn, so instinctive, overcomes it. She covers her mouth with her hand, hoping that no one notices it. The hope is in vain. Although she sits here on the bench beside Eoin still, Gormlaith and Feardorcha haven't taken their eyes from her since she sat down. There were no comments or looks of any kind, unless careful consideration is counted. She has tried to keep her own expression determinedly neutral during the conversation, but she knows that Aedh has given them an idea of the topics that have been discussed. No resolution, no plan has been made, though. There's nothing to plan. Escape isn't an option. What would that mean if it were considered? There's no shape it could take that would have any meaning. Returning to Raithlinn wouldn't change the circumstances. Heading elsewhere is too foolish to consider. There is no elsewhere. Or no elsewhere that wouldn't mean danger in too many shapes and forms that would almost certainly end in one result.

Eoin had mentioned Mac Carthaigh. O'Mhaithghamnha is more or less at Mac Carthaigh's behest, his overlord, he'd explained. It was Cormac who was Mac Carthaigh now, great grandson to Domnall Got, his brother Domnall now dead. Meadbh had nodded her head as though she was fully aware of these intricate situations. The hope she had before is still there and though Eoin dismissed the idea as fruitless, she wonders now if it might be possible. If Mac Carthaigh would support Eoin, well certainly, O'Mhaithghamna had to listen.

Her thoughts turn her gaze to Feardorcha. His eyes narrow and she fights the urge to yawn again. Her jaw tenses and muscles tighten around her mouth to keep it closed. She suddenly thinks of a chicken, the stretched ropey neck. Still trapped in Feardorcha's gaze, she tries to ease her body, release the tension. Any release she might find is lost in the hand Feardorcha lifts and the motioning finger he aims in her direction. She turns to Eoin to find that he's also watching Feardorcha. Eoin looks over at her, concern filling his eyes.

She covers his hand with hers. "All will be well." The words halt her movement. They echo in her head, only it isn't her own voice she hears, but another's. Diarmuid's. She stiffens. "I'll be fine," she amends and rises.

She arrives at Feardorcha's side and he takes her hand, standing. O'Mathghamhna follows suit. He holds his palm up and calls for silence. Gradually, the din recedes and a few moments later, silence. Meadbh's hand is sweating inside Feardorcha's meaty grasp. She attempts to assemble a calm, neutral expression on her face, but the effort is a strain.

"I would have you raise your cup," says O'Mathghamhna.

He takes his own cup in hand. It's silver, beautifully etched. Meadbh thinks of her own father's dull tin one. Ancient, he'd told her once. Belonging to ancestors they could recite back to a past so misty only bards and *ollamhs* could dare to conjure it all. They probably have, at one time or another, back when the Ui Fhlionn were a *sliocht* of prominence and covered in glory.

"The cup should be full, of course," says O'Mathghamhna, grinning. "It's the only way to drink."

Laughter breaks out. There are smiles and good will all around. Generosity, camaraderie. A family atmosphere. A *sliocht* close knit, and filled with a shared knowledge of who they are and how they're connected. Meadbh envies that. Even though she understands there are minor rivalries, jealousies and a smattering of discontent that riddle every *sliocht*, now is the moment they let that dissolve and share in the *craic* of it all. So still, the envy is there. She finds Eoin, searching for her own connection. He sends her a reassuring smile and she tucks that deep down. It will suffice. She's used to having few connections. Or none. Her *beacha*. They were her *sliocht*, she thinks. She frowns at the use of past tense. They will return, she resolves. Others might not, but they will. She refuses to name "others".

O'Mathghamhna is speaking and Meadbh tries not to let her mind wander. The urge to do so, she knows, is self-protection against what's to come. The hand grasping hers gives her more than a clear idea.

"I promised you entertainment," says O'Mathghamhna. He pauses for the shouted affirming comments. "And I kept that promise, did I not?" He waggles his brows and Meadbh marvels at his unexpected stupidly comic turn. But his audience loves it. They're his people after all, and good humour is in the air.

"But now," he continues, "it's time for the second promise." He glances in Meadbh and Feardorcha's direction. "To make everything right." He claps Feardorcha on his back. "So, my friends and relations, on the sad death of Ui Fhlionn, I'm making all right for Feardorcha, my dear young brother, and Raithlinn at one time by giving Meadbh inghean Ui Fhlionn to Feardorcha in marriage."

Meadbh hears the words. She knew they were coming. But still, she's speechless. Despite the urge to refuse, something she thinks is possible, she has no words, no voice.

Chapter Twenty-Eight

Meadbh is waiting again. Síle beside her, she sits in the dark, on the bed, gripping Síle's hand, dressed only in her *léine*. Shivering. The bed is wooden framed, box like, simple carvings adorning its head and a pallet of fresh straw covered in linen with a fine wool coverlet sit on top. It's just about big enough for two. Meadbh noted that upon entering this chamber, situated above the solar. O'Math-ghamhna and Gormlaith's chamber when it didn't serve as the guest chamber. There seems no doubt over that. The carved press, the chair, the small table, the rushes, the fur rug. She saw all that in the rush light, three tapers set on the table and the press. She tried not to think of it as a bridal chamber, just as she tries not to think of it as such, now. As she waits with Síle. In the dark, rush light extinguished.

Below her, in the solar, she can still hear voices. They're muffled, but still identifiable as male. Feardorcha is among them, she has no doubt about that, and certainly O'Math-ghamhna. Gormlaith retired to a different chamber with her daughter at the same time as Meadbh, showing Meadbh the way, and bestowing a kind smile on her at this chamber door. Eoin and Aedh had left the solar earlier, O'Mathghamhna's arrogant son leading them away for their own night's rest else-where. That it would be under lock, she hadn't had the energy to ask, her mind too consumed with her own change in circum-stances.

The lack of any "yay" or "nay" from her mouth was more from initial shock, followed by a whirling mind, than anything. Consideration, deliberation. She tried to force her mind in those frames, but still, as she sits here, in the relative silence and dark, she can't find it in her to formulate her best path.

A roar of laughter sounds below. A shout follows.

"Ah, Meadbh, *mo chara*, you can't do it," says Síle. "Unless there's no other way. No other kin."

Meadbh squeezes Síle's hand. "Eoin is my kin. And his son. He's distant cousin to me. Cousin to my father."

Síle sighs. "But he would be the one to choose for you. It's his consent they need."

Meadbh gives a wry smile. It's dark and Síle can't see it but it gives Meadbh a sense of her own self. The humour, so dark. As dark as this room, she thinks. Yes, Eoin is the person who would have her wardship. Who would choose for her? And, given different circumstances, she knows he would let her choose for herself, if possible. She has no claim on Ui Fhlionn holdings, except the dowry for her marriage. And that, she's fairly certain, went to Teampall Gobnatán, never to be reclaimed.

"He's a hostage, Síle. His consent is a given."

"I know," said Síle. "But still, perhaps he can find a way to say no." She pauses. "I assume 'no' is what's in your mind. I don't think you like him overmuch. Or at all. Though, to be fair, he is a man of consequence among the O'Mathghamhna. He's been given the holdings of Raithlinn." She sighs. "And he isn't all that awful to look at. In the dark you wouldn't see him at all."

Meadbh smiles faintly. She appreciates her friend's efforts. And it has helped to some degree. Her chilled bones have warmed a fraction.

"No," she says. "In the dark I wouldn't see him at all."

But she would feel him. She would smell him, his breath all over her. She would hear him. She starts to shiver again, until Síle persuades her to lie down and cover herself fully.

The weather has turned cold. A damp wind blows from the north, chilling everything it touches here in the solar. Meadbh is cold enough without the wind. A cold that no brazier or hearth fire can cure. It's deep in her bones. It's a solid core, impenetrable. Beside her, Síle rubs her back. It's a soothing gesture, it speaks of hope, comfort and an attempt to warm. She's done it to Meadbh repeatedly since the evening before. And not just her back. The shoulders and arms have all had their turn. Determination is behind every vigorous rub that slows eventually to a soothing stroke. The intent is there, but the hoped-for result refuses to appear. Meadbh's periodic shivers won't stop.

Around Meadbh, a few women are clearing up from the night before, still collecting trenchers, gathering up bits of food and tossing it to the dogs who mill around, waiting to be fed. Meadbh marvels that the dogs are in the hall, without the men, but perhaps the men are off on business and they'd rather not have the dogs, and securing them elsewhere isn't an option. Meadbh find herself wondering where they are. Feardorcha came last night, a long time after Síle departed to find a bed elsewhere, but he did nothing more than collapse into a drunken snore next to her on the bed. Any hope of sleep, though there was little enough of that, vanished after his arrival. But there were blessings in his drunkenness, and for that she's grateful. At the first signs of light, not all that long after Feardorcha's arrival, she rose, donned her gown and went down to the hall in search of Síle.

Already a few women were there and Meadbh asked after Síle. After a few shrugs and shakes of the head, Meadbh decided to take a seat on the bench. A short while later Síle entered and took a seat beside her. Perhaps it was due to Meadbh's intermittent shivering, or Síle's attempts to warm her, that made them take pity on her, because they turned down Síle and Meadbh's offer to assist. One woman even brought forth some watered ale and a few oatcakes for Meadbh and Síle to stave off any hunger. Food is the last thing on Meadbh's mind, though. Síle has eaten the portions for both of them, for politeness' sake, as much as any hunger on Síle's part. The woman, breaking from her task collecting cups, is about to press more oatcakes and ale on them when Gormlaith enters, her fair hair woven into a single plait that hangs along her shoulder from under her headcloth. Her eyes are tired, but a warm smile fills her face.

She greets both Síle and Meadbh, and a moment later Cobhlaigh enters. Her hair is hastily assembled into its own plait under a headcloth, slightly askew, her gown somewhat mussed and pulled a little to the side, but her eyes are alight with mischief. She sweeps a hand across her face to remove a strand of hair that's strayed from its fellows.

"Ah, the bride. There she is," says Cobhlaigh. "Did you have a good night?" She gives a hearty laugh.

Gormlaith shakes her head and smiles. It's a smile of knowledge, of experience. It says "this is Cobhlaigh's way. She means well".

Meadbh forces a smile. All wit and banter have left her. She starts to shiver again. Síle rubs her arm, more for the assurance than anything. She knows by now there's no changing Meadbh's level of warmth. Her chill has reached her soul.

"You're feeling that chill, aren't you, you *cratur*," says Cobhlaigh. She looks at Gormlaigh. "Will we give her a warm drink?"

But Gormlaith is already arranging for it with one of the women. She's one step ahead. Meadbh looks at her, sees the keen eyes that keep her one step ahead. That help her understand a situation, assess it to its full, and allow her to live a life that has advantages because of such ability.

A few moments later Meadbh is handed the cup of warm ale. Later, after the cup is empty, Meadbh isn't sure whether it's the ale or Meadbh's full view of Gormlaith that stop the shivering. Síle is beside her still, the rubbing and comforting no longer given or required.

Meadbh lies awake that night, waiting again. Síle is not beside her this time, and Meadbh is lying flat, tucked beneath the wool coverlet. Spent, after a day in which her whole life has changed course, or perhaps not changed so much as shifted slightly, for what else is she to do if she's no longer to be a nun? Securing Raithlinn for Eoin and her *sliocht* still would have left her with this course, for if not Feardorcha, it would be someone else she would marry. And who would Eoin have chosen? Who was there to choose? She knows that it would be O'Mathghamhna who would choose, ultimately, though there would be a show of consulting Eoin. And she would be right where she is at this moment. Awaiting the morning. Stating the words, accepting this man as her husband.

Would Feardorcha join her tonight? Test the marital bed before the official ceremony? She has no idea if he has any interest, despite any show of slobbered kisses he might have given her at the meal earlier. Or the raucous humour that played out between him, O'Mathghamhna and the other men during and after. She'd given her acceptance of the marriage proposal that afternoon, in the solar in the presence of O'Mathghamhna and Feardorcha and anyone else who happened to be gathered there. A formality at best, she understands, even before that. Her pride, her desire to conduct this process as befits the long and important heritage of the Uí Fhlionns, compelled her to request for a formal ceremony, utter the words again, before all who would gather. She knew Gormlaith had already been making preparations for another feast. And now they would wait until after a formal pledging and acceptance, with due ceremony.

The women had fluttered over her after O'Mathghamhna had agreed. Gowns were discussed. Hair arrangements and ornament potential arrangements assessed. Síle had hovered nearby, concern plain to see, while Meadbh fixed a smile on her face. So tomorrow it will happen. Now, she waits to see if Feardorcha will sample his bride beforehand.

The door opens, as it had the night before. Feardorcha stands there. Meadbh strains to read his expression, but the dim illumination provided by the rush light on the table is unequal to the task. He walks forward. He's steady on his feet. The rush light is extinguished and Meadbh is grateful for the darkness. She feels him sit on the bed. She hears him fumble with his boots. One by one they're tossed aside. She imagines him removing his *triubhas*, his *léine*. The pallet shifts beside her as he lifts the covers and draws the rest of his body under them. She can smell the faint odour of ale. He shifts beside her. Meadbh lays there, listening, feeling. An arm snakes around her waist, drawing her next to him. She feels his beard at her neck, then his lips. He pulls her closer. Her married life is here, now. She sighs, pushing away any other potential outcomes that might ever have been in her head.

Chapter Twenty-Nine

"Taste this," Cobhlaigh says to Meadbh. "It's a wheatcake." She holds out a piece of the object that looks very similar to the oatcakes Meadbh knows.

"Wheatcake," she repeats and takes a bite. The difference is there, subtle yet not.

Meadbh has heard of these types of cake, made with wheat rather than oats. The wheat, grown so little here, is favoured by the Gaills, and the Saxain before them, who brought the fashion of growing it with them. Few areas seem to be suitable for it, though, so most access to this grain is from merchants and the ports, where ships bring in sacks of it. She examines it carefully and takes another bite. With honey, or butter, she admits, she can like them well enough.

"It's the first time they've been made here," says Gormlaith. "One of the men bought sacks of the grain last month when he was in Corcaigh. We have a real occasion to use it, now."

"Before the rats eat it all," says Cobhlaigh.

One of the women laughs, but Gormlaith gives only a tight smile. They're all in the stone cookhouse. Sides of beef are outside on spits, turning slowly over the fire, with the help of some small boys and a few serving women. The women gathered here, on this rough table, are fashioning the cakes, baking them on the flat iron griddle on the small hearth and in the centre of the room. Nearby, whole birds plucked the day before are spitted and cooked over a separate fire.

They've been up since the first light, stirring fires, mixing, chopping and any other action that can serve to create the feast to celebrate a marriage.

Meadbh joined them as soon as she saw the light creep in the window, her body sore. Sore between her legs and sore in other, quieter, deeper places that drove her to put on her *léine* and then her gown. She's thankful for the gown and all that it covers. Later, though, when the women help her dress for the ceremony, Meadbh realises they will know. But they know already, she tells herself, even now, standing among them, sweating in the heat of all these fires.

Síle bustles to move Meadbh away from the spit of fowls where she crouches, turning the iron rod occasionally. Meadbh finds the slowly searing flesh fascinating. The pale flesh, speckled with fragments of feathers, scalded pink in places from the hot water used to assist plucking, now slowly browns, fat dripping, changing into something different. A duck become meat. And if she leaves the bird too long on one side, the way it bubbles in places, eventually turning black. Charred.

Meadbh gives the spit one last look before she lets Síle draw her forward. It's time to get ready.

Gormlaith surveys Meadbh and the women who attend her as they slowly remove her gown. Meadbh turns her head away. She knows once they remove the gown they'll see the stains. The tear. Síle moves in front of the women with an apologetic smile to them.

"Ah my dear, dear cousin," Síle says, patting Meadbh's cheek. "To see you married. You don't know what this does for my heart."

The words mean as much as the action. An action followed by another as she bunches the plain linen *léine* up from its end and pulls it over Meadbh's head in one swift motion. Meadbh blinks at the speed, and the smile she gives Síle is a grateful one. Síle knows what Meadbh is thinking, but then the other women probably do too. It's no secret, but yet, Meadbh would rather that the evidence of the night before not be there for everyone to see.

It wasn't that Feardorcha was overly rough with her. At least that's her judgement. It was just the awkward position of her *léine* and the need to push it away from his intention that caused the tear. And his greater need that caused the stains. Or some of them. She's been wearing this *léine* far too long.

She will need a new *léine*. She knows that, and only hopes that the women whose knowledge of her experience the night before understand that a fresh *léine* is required.

Gormlaith sees the issue, almost before Meadbh's old *léine* is over her head and is issuing orders to one of the women. But the words are not in time to prevent Meadbh standing there, bare skinned, for several moments before someone throws a blanket around her. She clutches it to herself, glances at Síle.

"Ah, now, *mo croí*, it'll be grand," says Síle, softly.

Meadbh gives her a weak smile. Grand. She can't remember the last time she felt anything approaching grand. With her *beacha*? She won't examine any other moment after she left them. Not even that moment when she felt them inside of her and she gave their song to a crowd of enemies. Because she thinks of them as enemies. All of them.

The woman who Gormlaith had sent for a fresh *léine* appears, but there's no garment in her hands. Her hands clutch her own belted *léine* instead. Her eyes wild with alarm. "Oh *bantiarna*, oh *bantiarna*."

The woman opens her mouth to speak again, but no words come out.

"What is it, Mairgreg?" Gormlaith says, her voice firm. She moves towards Mairgreg, places a hand on her shoulder.

Mairgreg takes a deep breath. "It's your daughter. It's Slane. She— she's ill. She's in her bed with chills. When I went to your chamber, *bantiarna*, she was there, rooting around in your chest, muttering to herself. She had a blanket around her...." Mairgreg stops. Takes another breath and turns frightened eyes up to

Gormlaith. "I went over to her. Asked if I could help. She wouldn't let me. She kept shivering. So I just directed her to her bed. Took the blanket from her. She was so pale...and...then I saw it. The swelling. Under her arm. Here." Mairgreg puts her finger to her armpit and stares down at her hands. "It took me by surprise, *bantiarna*. How is it that came there, I ask myself? But she do be poking in places all the time. More curious than her brother. Did she get a thorn from a furze bush and now it's become inflamed? Or maybe a blackthorn bush. They're the very devil." Mairgreg shakes her head, as if personal experience with a blackthorn is now being recalled. The words wander in and out, around and about, as the story ambles, dragging its heels to come to the end. To the point. Meadbh wants to wander with it, enjoy the view, the tale, and admire the skill of the teller who really should be a bard. A *seanchas*.

"Ah but no," says Mairgreg, after a short breath. "When I looked at the swelling again I see it's angry, but not in the way a thorn would make it, no, something else. And to make her shiver like there was no amount of blankets in the world that would make her warm? No, something else." Mairgreg stares up at Gormlaith now. "Something else, *bantiarna*. Something else." She bites her lip, her eyes wide, beseeching. The words "tell me it's not true" are there, plainly written in her face, spoken through her eyes.

Everyone has heard descriptions of it. Everyone has spoken of people they have heard tell who have died from it. But can this be denied? Meadbh and Síle exchange glances. They know it can't. They know with utmost certainty what it is. The pestilence.

193

Pestilence. The word is whispered in the chambers above the hall. Along the stairwell as it descends down and it echoes throughout the hall until it makes it way to the cook house. The store. The stone buildings housing the horses, and outwards, to the very edges of the *bawn* and beyond.

A momentary paralysis seizes everyone as the word grips Caisleán na Leachta and its holdings firmly. Until another woman falls to the ground in a faint of chills. The swelling this time is in her groin. A place no thorn of any kind has ever touched.

Chapter Thirty

Meadbh knows many things about tending the sick now. She knows about healing herbs and nourishing broths. The power of honey. The power of hope. Prayer. She knows that it can be gruelling, filled with anxiety, sorrow, pain and sometimes joy at the end of it. But it's that moment of decision, when the illness is recognised and a path must be taken to tend the sick that's key. What path is it for Meadbh, now? She wonders this deep inside her, as everyone in the bedchamber stands there, mind and body paralysed as the understanding of it filters in.

Meadbh remembers this moment of decision and the paralysis that came with it in previous times. The foreboding she felt. The way her body couldn't move. The horror that rushed through her. The bowl she held filling with vomit. All these things she remembers as she stares at Síle, sharing the understanding, the knowledge of what's occurred. And what's to come. Síle's look turns questioning and Meadbh finds herself glancing away. The question is clear. Her answer is not. She bites her lip. Thinks of the time to come and sighs. What will she do? What will they do? She turns back to Síle and gives her a faint smile and a nod.

"Gormlaith," says Meadbh. "Let me tend her. And Síle. We know what to do."

Gormlaith looks at Meadbh, her face and lips pale. Her eyes a well of despair. "You know what to do?" she says, her voice barely a whisper.

"I was... I am a healer of sorts. I used to tend the sick in and by Teampall Gobnatán." Meadbh nods, as if that would give added confirmation of her skills. "The honey. I had *beacha*. Well, I tended the *beacha* there at Teampall Gobnatán." She knows she's rambling, but she just isn't sure she should say anything more. Anything that will hint at her deeper experience of the pestilence. Her specific personal experience.

Meadbh looks at Síle. "Síle has nursed people through the pestilence."

"And they lived?" asks Gormlaith.

The hope, a small light in her eyes, her expression and her voice is almost painful to hear and see. Meadbh nods.

"Only one," says Síle. "I don't want to mislead you,

bantiarna." Her voice is respectful but firm. She casts an apologetic look towards Meadbh. "It's best you know what might come. Understand that I have lost all my children and their children. And my husband."

Gormlaith looks at her. "And yet you lived."

Síle nods, but her face shows more than age at this moment. Grief, struggle, and more are etched into the lines, the hang of the skin at the chin and jowls. A weathered look that has more to do with experience than the burn of the wind, sun and cold.

"So, there are two who have survived the pestilence," says Gormlaith.

Meadbh is about to protest, but Síle's subtle shake of her head leaves her silent. They mustn't think she's carried it here. It's enough that Síle has risked it.

"What must we do, then?" asks Gormlaith. Her voice, her face, her eyes, all express determination.

This time, when Meadbh stands on the threshold of a dwelling containing pestilence, her body moves forward and her mind is taken up with the tasks at hand. She has no idea if surviving the pestilence means she won't get it again, and this time, experience and outcome that will be a lot less joyful. Or if, by some small chance she's carrying new life inside her, she has no idea if it will be affected by pestilence and in turn, her too. The uncertainty of her life in these past months is something she hasn't necessarily enjoyed, but she's at least come to realise it will now be a part of her life. The dangers, the fears, the hopes, the anger and all the other range of emotions, some that she can't name, or won't name, that have travelled through her, sometimes repeatedly, since leaving Teampall Gobnatán, are more than the eight years she was there. So much more. A lifetime, she thinks, packed into a season. The season of Imbolc. The season of spring. Nearly done. Bealtaine is in a few days. The beginning of summer. The day of gatherings. Of celebration. Of decisions. But there'll be no gathering this year. At least not for the O'Mathghamhna *sliocht*.

There are four people ill with pestilence now. One of the men, Domnall, and two servant women. And Slane. Meadbh had wanted all of the ill kept together. In one room. They agreed to make the cook house the place to tend them. It has a hearth. There's also easy access to water. Means for warmth, for food, all of that important for Meadbh and Síle to tend the sick. But Gormlaith refuses to have Slane stay anywhere but in her bedchamber. Gormlaith wanted to tend her daughter as well, in fact insisted it be so, but O'Mathghamhna refused permission. Put his foot down, though only metaphorically, but the fist he slammed on the table to make his point held just as much force.

O'Mathghamhna is a man filled with rage. Rage that has targets wherever he can locate them. The sacks of milled wheat are removed, set alight and burned. He's certain it's the grain Gaills use so readily that's the cause. Grain that had no business in Ireland, let alone in his household. He scours the area for other enemies and finds that the blankets, the gowns and any other kind of garment that Feardorcha, Meadbh and everyone else who came from Raithlinn possess have the pestilence embedded in it and orders it all burned. There is no reasoning with his anger. An anger that on its underside is fear. Fear that transmits to some of his men and some of the women who slink away, either to their homes, or somewhere else.

Meadbh wipes her brow with the back of her arm as she fills the jug with water. The gesture, at face value, is to brush her hair out of her face. So much of it has escaped her headcloth and the plait beneath it. The hair, once brushed aside, falls back where it had been before, tickling her nose and the corner of her eyes. The offending hair, just like her fatigue, will not be brushed aside.

She wipes her hand across the front of her gown, showing little care for the sweat stain it adds. It will hardly be noticed among all the other stains that the garment contains. Stains that show the days she's spent helping Síle with the sick in the cook house, and then Slane, still in the castle bedchamber. She climbs those castle stairs several times a day. She and Síle take turns for the nights, especially now, when Slane is so weak. Meadbh grabs the sleep she can manage in any time, regardless of when it is, usually sitting up against the wall as she waits for the broth to heat up, or for Síle to make a special drink. The rest isn't long, not nearly long enough to even be called sleep. Her mind, on the other hand, finds no rest.

She takes the water jug, now full, and climbs the castle stairs to the bed chamber where Slane lies, frail and pinched. Meadbh's hope is that she will be able to wash some of the signs of illness away, so that at least from the doorway where Gormlaith intends to view her, she'll look something like the daughter she knew.

Gormlaith is determined to have at least that much of her

daughter, bedamned to her husband. She's said this to Meadbh, her voice so low it was almost a whisper, when Meadbh passed through the solar to go to the cook house. Most people avoided Meadbh now, even Feardorcha. It's not something Meadbh minds or has given much thought to. Except perhaps Eoin. She's seen little sign of him, or Aedh. She can only imagine Conor is staying well away and using those two as an excuse. But with no one talking to her besides Síle and Gormlaith, she hasn't heard anything to confirm her speculation. And when Gormlaith approaches, it's always about her daughter, and Meadbh under-stands and won't trouble her with anything that, in Gormlaith's view, is less important.

Meadbh enters the chamber and finds Slane lying in the bed, her breath shallow and faint. The flesh has fallen away even in the few days since she's taken ill. She'd had little enough flesh to lose. Her once slender frame is all bones, the skin stretched across it. There's an exception, though. Meadbh knows that if she pulls back the blanket, it will show the swelling at her armpit.

Slane tosses restlessly in the bed and mutters incoherently as Meadbh approaches, jug in one hand. Meadbh places the jug on the floor beside the small stool she put there when she first started to tend Slane. A bowl is already beside it. She's glad to see that Síle has already emptied its contents and washed it. It can now be used to hold the water to wash Slane.

Meadbh begins her task, her movements tender, careful, wiping brow, cheeks, chin. Neck, hands and arms. She's cautious of the swelling, knowing now that it's painful if she touches it, even by accident. Meadbh also avoids pressing Slane's back or her neck, which brings moans of pain.

When Meadbh has completed the ablutions, such as they

are, she tries to bring some semblance of order to Slane's fair hair. It's a light nut brown, or at least Meadbh recalls that it was. Before illness, sweat and restlessness cast it into a dull flat dun colour that lies dark on the pillow. Still, she's determined to try.

When she's nearly done, a plait reconstructed, ends tidied inside it, there's a low knock. The door opens and Gormlaith is there, worry lining her face, darkening her eyes. Her mouth is pulled into a tight smile.

"Slane, *mo crioí, mo leanbh. Is do mháthair mé.*"

Her voice is pain-filled as she addresses her daughter with endearments, assures her that her mother is here for her. Meadbh's heart wants to break, but she won't let it. Gormlaith knows she must speak her words to her daughter now. Meadbh has known for a while the end would come, or at least suspected it. But last night, the "when" became apparent. The "when" will be before the morning is done.

Chapter Thirty-One

Meadbh follows the path, glad for a purpose that brings no chore, no duty, if only for a short space of time. She found this path only moments ago when she walked past the cook house instead of entering it. The path called to her. It hailed her as if she were an errant sheep and it an insistent herder. She had no choice. Her body just followed its will – and its will at the moment decided that she couldn't face one more moment tending the sick. It had made the decision when she left Gormlaith crying at the door while her daughter took her last breaths. It was a grief that Meadbh felt she had no right to witness. A grief that was so large, and yet so private, it only had space for the mother and her child. With only a brief hand to Gormlaith's shoulder to acknowledge her grief, her right to be here alone with her child, Meadbh left, descended the stairs, leaving jug and bowl behind her on the bed chamber floor where she'd placed them. She descended the stairs until she found herself outside, passing people who kept their distance, and in their embarrassment, or in some cases not, looked away, for fear she'd catch their gaze. Their fear is palpable.

She ignores them, making her way to the cookhouse, the path beginning to woo her, and she finds herself where she is now, following it like that errant sheep. She follows it up along, past the scrubby grass that spills over the path, covering it in places. Further on, furze bushes push into the path and she circumvents them, minding her gown so that it isn't caught by the probing thorns. The path rises gently, and the ash that rim the rise on either side fall away and she emerges into a field. Once inside the field, the call turns into a song. A song that she's missed from deep within the well of her soul. The answering hum within her comes without any thought. They're here. *Beacha.* She scans the field and sees their cone shapes to her right. Up against a south-facing stone wall. Three hives.

Gormlaith's stricken expression confirms what Meadbh knew before she left the castle. As does O'Mathghamhna's stormy one. He gives her barely a glance as Meadbh enters the solar, a fresh jug of water in hand, and he brushes past her on his way out. His men follow in silence, those that are left, their heads down. Feardorcha is among them, his face set, drawn, eyes determined. Except for a brief glance of recognition, he takes no note of her presence. Meadbh feels no distress or any other emotion for the lack of greeting. She spares Gormlaith a sympathetic glance and a brief comforting hand on her arm before heading up the stairs. The tread is so familiar now, she doesn't have to look to avoid the perilous dip of the third one, the narrow ledge of the fifth, the slight bump in the centre of the last one. She reaches the top without a thought to the placement of her feet, and heads to the chamber.

Inside the chamber, the thoughts, the song that have consumed her since finding the *beacha* fill her once more. Infuse her with strength for this task to come. The ritual she will give every care to, for what this poor young girl has endured, and what she never will. She'll take on this ritual to honour Gormlaith as well, because the grief that Meadbh saw shaping Gormlaith's body just now requires that she do so.

The keening surrounds Meadbh. It joins the song inside her, the hum of the *beacha* providing support, strength. A foundation for the keening. It's as though she can feel them over in their field she knows is only a short distance away, and she looks up, expecting to see them flying above, a swarm of hope to meet the swarm of grief below.

Cobhlaigh stands beside Gormlaith, rubbing her back, her keening halfhearted against Gormlaith's. The other women compensate, though. Servant and relatives, these women who are left to gather around the shrouded body that once was Slane all seem to have a genuine grief that infuses the keening. Its sound is lyrical, sweeping through Meadbh, who adds her own special sound to it. It becomes a true *caoine*, one whose sounds become words. Words that lament the time, the events, and most importantly, Slane. The joy of her years on earth, at her mother's side.

There's no priest, but a friar was found and persuaded to come. To say what's necessary. To bless the grave. To give the family, the kin and all who are present, the comfort that they need in such times. Meadbh finds herself glad that they have that much. She thinks of her own father and wonders if a grave can be blessed after the person has been interred. Will God desert his people in such times when these things aren't always possible? It's a question for a priest, but there is no priest. The friar would know only about being humble before God. At least that's what she understands from Teampall Gobnatán.

The food is placed on the trestle table, but there's little heart for it. Those who would eat feel they can't in the face of Gormlaith's grief, and the silence of O'Mathghamhna and Feardorcha. Meadbh sits beside him for the first time in days. It feels strange to be sitting at a table to eat instead of grabbing a hasty bite in passing. She glances over to where Síle sat during the previous occasions, even though she knows she won't find her there. Síle continues in her nursing. The sick can't put their needs aside because of a death. Meadbh knows that soon there will be another. And probably a few more after that. Though the numbers that have fallen ill have only amounted to less than two handfuls, it casts an even greater pall of fear and grief on this gathering.

Cobhlaigh's chatter catches Meadbh's attention when she realises Cobhlaigh is addressing her. She shifts her gaze to fall on Cobhlaigh, assembling her expression into polite interest.

"You must be disappointed about your wedding. Perhaps we should have it sooner, rather than later. It might help lift our spirits."

Her tone is kind, but Meadbh finds it difficult not to shake her head in wonder at this woman's inability to understand how her sentiment is so badly misplaced. For everyone concerned.

Meadbh gives a weak smile instead. "I'm afraid I have much yet to do for the sick. Maybe later, when all this is done." She gives no specifics. For her own sake as much as for everyone in the room.

Cobhlaigh glances around, bewilderment fleeting across her face. Her gaze lands on Gormlaith, whose puffy eyes and frozen look seem to convey that Cobhlaigh has taken a serious misstep. She reddens and looks back at Meadbh.

"Yes of course," she says in a low voice.

"No more talk of this," says O'Mathghamhna. "That's for another time."

Another time. She has no dispute with that sentiment.

"I have found hives," says Meadbh a few moments later. "In the adjacent field."

Gormlaith looks over at Meadbh, her eyes showing a trace of gratitude for the change in subject. "Yes, that's right. Sadbh tends them, when she can. But she does find them too much at times." She gives a fragile smile, full of fondness. "She fears the *beacha* will sting her."

Sadbh. One of the women who now lay sick in the cook

house, and who will likely die. Meadbh brushes the thought aside and smiles. "I'd be happy to tend them, if you'd allow it. Any honey I find I'll be able to use with the sick. It may help."

"Are there still *beacha* there?" asks O'Mathghamhna. "I would think with this cold winter we've had, and the state of the land, there'd be little enough for them around here, even if they have survived the winter. We took the honey, didn't we?"

Gormlaith nods, but her eyes slide away. Meadbh smiles inwardly. She knows the truth of it. The *beacha* had sung that truth.

Chapter Thirty-Two

Meadbh puts a hand on Síle's shoulder. The fatigue is obvious in the way Síle carries her body, and when she turns her face to acknowledge Meadbh's presence, the deep grooves in her face and the strain in her eyes confirm what Meadbh has thought. This woman has done more than enough for people who share no kinship with her.

"Go rest, Síle," says Meadbh. "I'll be fine on my own for a while."

Síle starts to shake her head, but Meadbh tightens the hold on Síle's shoulder and turns her away from her task at the fire.

"Go," says Meadbh.

Meadbh watches Síle's retreating back, and once she's clear of the door and heading towards the castle, Meadbh takes the handle of the spoon Síle was using to stir the broth and lifts to taste it. The herbs it contains blend well with the finely mashed onions, kale and beef bones. It's too early in the season for carrots, and all the turnips had been used in the two feasts. The one that had happened and the one that hadn't. The last of that cooked food was gone.

She glances over at the five people lying on the pallets in the room. Sadbh was in the corner, out of the draught of the door. Meadbh can hear her breathing from here and knows that it won't be long. The man who'd been sick first, Domnall, is already dead. Buried not far from Slane, but without benefit of the friar's words or blessing. The friar had left as soon as his obligation to Slane had been completed.

No one new has succumbed, and Meadbh hopes that it's a sign the pestilence is losing its grip. She can only hope. Tending these sick people has been a distraction, something which gives her a mixture of gratitude and guilt. A blend of emotions that's strange, especially when mixed in with the kernel of fear of falling ill herself. But these emotions are all faint enough that she continues on, the delay in her own circumstances progressing to its inevitable conclusion – only a pause, and its length is beyond her control.

Her other distraction is one whose overriding pleasure leaves her giving no thought to any other emotions that might accompany it. When she's with the *beacha* there's nothing else. There's no one else. What will happen when the pestilence

209

has taken its course is a problem that vanishes in those moments.

The hum is all consuming. It fills her head, her heart and deeper. Its song has words that aren't spoken, just felt. She's lifted off the top of the first hive and notices a loose band that holds the bramble coils in place threatens to come adrift. Perhaps she knocked it accidentally during her last visit, because she knows she went through each coiled bramble, to identify and make any required repairs, not so long ago. She clucks to herself. The chastisement holds no bite, but rather an enjoyment of worrying over such simple events that are part of the pleasure of being among the *beacha*.

Her time with the *beacha* has increased in the past few days, as only two people remain in the cook house. Síle is with them now and Meadbh knows that Síle has sent her here to be with her *beacha* because the two are certain to die by day's end, if not before, and there's nothing much to be done. Síle often tries to spare her the deaths, despite Meadbh's protests that she's immune to them now. Acceptance of the inevitable had long since been achieved, if ever she had a problem with it. She's almost numb to the deaths now. As numb as Gormlaith. As numb as many of the others here in Caisleán na Leachta who have so far survived this terrible disease.

Meadbh continues with her tasks, checking the *beacha* that are gathered inside, busy with their own work, as she locates the queen. Again, she thinks of this *beach* as a queen rather than king. *Cráinbheach*, she decides. She smiles at the thought of a *beach* with a crown on it.

Someone calls her name. At first she doesn't hear, but eventually she realises that someone is there, near enough she can hear them clear their throat. She turns. Feardorcha stands at a careful distance. He studies her, the loosely woven linen cloth covering her head, the leather gloves on her fingers. His expression is one of puzzlement. Uncertainty. Has she spoken her thoughts aloud?

She removes the linen headcovering and looks at him questioningly. A few *beacha* rise from the hive and circle her, a dance of welcome. A dance of possibilities. She feels the response inside her, the humming rising up to greet them, even as Feardorcha speaks.

"It's time, Meadbh. We need to return to Raithlinn."

She regards the *beacha* as more rise up and join the circle, their song filled with promise while her song falls silent.

An extra horse is needed to carry the sacks of food stores, the extra blankets, gowns and *léinte* that Gormlaith and O'Mathghamhna have seen fit to gift them. It seems like a dowry of sorts, only instead of her father providing it, her husband's kin have. The formal marriage ceremony that she once asked for hasn't taken place and she doubts it ever will. There's little heart for it, and these gifts are most likely the compensation. Meadbh knows she should feel grateful for all of it, especially for the finely made gown and mantle they've bestowed on Síle. Síle's expressions of gratitude made up for Meadbh's poor ones. At least Meadbh hopes so. She's uncomfortable with this munificence, as much as she's uncomfortable with the admiring manner with which all regard her now. Even Feardorcha. The arm he'd placed around her the night before as they sat at the table, the meal finished. The smiles he bestowed in her direction, proud, possessive, accepting the compliments given her as though they were directed to him. And that night, in bed, when he stroked her hair, disrobed her and stroked the rest of her body, she felt as if she were a pet dog. That thought had crossed her mind, until he followed his stroking by rutting her until he was spent. Though the rutting reminded her more of animals in the field. But what did she know of such things? All of these actions fuel her discomfort.

A small cart pulls up behind the horse. One of Feardorcha's men holds the shafts. O'Mathghamhna has offered this approach because of the precious cargo in the cart's bed. A hive. Meadbh's gratitude for this gift more than exceeds any she should have felt for the blankets, gowns and *léinte*. It was Gormlaith's doing, although O'Mathghamhna made the formal offer. Feardorcha had only shrugged and deferred to Meadbh, even as she was already issuing her profuse thanks. Her husband's privilege, she thinks, but isn't sure. But surely the *beacha* are hers by right? Whatever the legal answer, she knows the truth of it. And so do the *beacha*. They belong to each other.

The formal goodbyes are done and Meadbh heads to her horse when movement at the back of the procession of horses and the cart catches her eye. Eoin. The sight of him startles her, for she hasn't seen him since Slane fell ill. Eoin gives her a wry smile followed by a slight nod of the head. Meadbh turns to look up at Feardorcha, who has just mounted.

"Eoin is to return with us?"

Feardorcha casts a glance back towards Eoin and nods. "He is, so."

"And Aedh?"

"The lad stays behind. He'll foster with O'Mathghamhna."

Meadbh starts to open her mouth to speak but she's not sure what to say. In some lights it would be considered an honour to foster with the overlord. But Aedh is well past the age when fostering would begin. His battle skills would be well honed by now, his friendships formed. The bond of loyalty with the head of the household was usually formed over the years of boyhood and into early adulthood. There's little doubt that this fosterage label is nothing more than a tool for appearance's sake. His true purpose, the one that brought him here first, has changed little, if at all. She glances at Eoin. Sees the resignation.

"Ah," is all she can manage to say in the end.

Chapter Thirty-Three

They arrive at Raithlinn before the sun has reached its height. Meadbh can feel its heat along her back, and sweat prickles at her neck and gathers at her brow, under her headcloth. Her mantle feels too heavy and unnecessary and she sweeps it aside. She'll wait to take it off. The state of her gown, she's certain, will do little to impress anyone. But who is there to impress? The thought makes her laugh. Her *beacha* will be the last to care. Síle has seen her at her worst. The others are of little matter.

Meadbh slides from her horse without assistance. She's experienced enough now that her gown doesn't catch and she hits the ground with some semblance of grace. Feardorcha is already dismounted, giving orders, and hailing the rest of the men who'd remained at Raithlinn.

Meadbh makes her way back to the cart, Síle at her heels. Síle removes her headcloth and starts to fan her face with it, propriety falling away.

"That heat. *A hiarna.*"

Meadbh smiles at her remark and murmurs agreement. They reach the cart and Meadbh thanks the man who's pulled it since they left Caisleán na Leachta. Though the distance wasn't too great, it was still a heavy task that such a burly man who's doing it would feel the burden of it in this heat. He gently puts down the shafts so that the cart, balanced as it is on two wheels, tilts downward. Meadbh dismisses him to find a cold drink and listens for any change in the sounds from the hives. None greet her to signal concern. She'll get two men to put the hives in position. She knows exactly where they'll go.

"You're here, now. Your new home," she tells them.

Home, she thinks. They will make it their home, and with their presence, she can make Raithlinn her home again.

Meadbh makes her way to the *ráth's* entrance, following Feardorcha. Síle had already entered to ensure that Meadbh and Feardorcha's belongings are stowed in the proper place. She'd framed the words carefully, avoiding the use of chamber or any other word that would indicate or label Meadbh's change in status. Whether it's to spare Meadbh's feelings or Síle's own,

Meadbh wasn't certain, but she appreciates the sentiment, nevertheless. It will take time to become used to the change. Somehow, in a place where everything was different for her as it had been in Caisleán na Leachta, she hadn't felt this change in her situation nearly as much. The pestilence had also played its part in allowing her to forget that she was no longer an unmarried woman. That Feardorcha was her husband now. She gives a moment to a brief time when she'd imagine other outcomes, but the thought is still too raw and she turns her mind to her surroundings.

Light pours in from the opening in the centre of the main chamber, casting a glow over the room, the hearth fire that burns brightly under it extending its range. The sight of it surprises Meadbh. She casts a glance around the room and is surprised to see the chests, polished and neatly arranged. Benches, repaired and lined in place. The trestle table is placed carefully against a wall and the carved chair and stools are in places that recall memories of her father's time.

Eoin enters the chamber. Meadbh catches his bewildered look and gives a slight shrug. Feardorcha gives a grunt of approval. Meadbh too, feels some pleasure, but there's also an unease. Síle's eyes finds hers and Meadbh can see she feels the unease as well.

"Ah, my lord, it's good to see you home again. You've been missed."

Meadbh turns to see her mother standing in the entrance to one of the bed chambers. Her head is covered with a snowy white linen headcloth. Her gown, a golden saffron colour, is edged with fine embroidery. Draped over her shoulders is a closely woven fringed *brat* of blue, secured by a bronze brooch. Even Meadbh remembers the brooch. It used to adorn her father's *brat* when he attended gatherings or held special feasts to host important men, including the overlord.

Meadbh looks over at Feardorcha, who's studying her mother speculatively. Her mother is full of smiles as she speaks about her preparations for his return. That she has sought out his preferences and tried to achieve them in the manner in which the household is arranged. Smiles that invite, placate, supplicate. Smiles that seduce. Meadbh has never seen these smiles on her mother before, except perhaps once, when an important guest with good looks had come. She marvels that her mother possesses such smiles. She takes a moment to feel bemusement and then amusement. A moment only. The motive behind these smiles isn't new. It's part of her oldest and most recent memories.

"I thank you on behalf of myself and my wife," says Feardorcha when her mother has finished speaking.

Her mother's smile falters. "Your wife?"

She scans the room, her eyes flitting over Meadbh to settle on Síle, only to dismiss her a fraction of a moment later and continue her search. After a while, her eyes return to Meadbh. Her gaze is flat. Her expression hardens.

Feardorcha moves over to Meadbh, rests a hand on her shoulder. "You've raised a fine daughter. Worthy of the O'Mathghamhna name."

Meadbh's mother's hands clench into fists. Anger flares in her eyes.

Meadbh can feel Síle's presence behind her as she struggles to secure the *brat* around her shoulders with a knot. Her hands feel clumsy today, as does her body, her eyes bleary with lack of sleep. Feardorcha has had little trouble, collapsing into bed after a busy day, either helping his men work the fields, or tending the cattle and the sheep. Anything that will ensure the prosperity of what is left of this holding. She can admire his ambition, if nothing else. But she tries to spare him little thought, and is grateful that his days are so busy that his nights are solely consumed by sleep. If only the snores weren't so loud.

"Meadbh," says Síle.

Meadbh realises she's let her attention wander, another effect from her sleepless nights. Meadbh sees the look on Síle's face and sighs. "What is it now?"

"The washing."

Meadbh nods for her to continue, but does she really need the full story? The result is the same.

"We'd hung it to dry on the bushes, myself and Úna. I thought to help her. She has enough to do, what with your mother...." Síle clears her throat.

Síle doesn't need to detail the demands her mother makes on Úna and everyone else in this household. And the fact that her mother has so far said nothing to contradict Meadbh's claim of Síle's kinship hangs like a heavy boulder ready to crash down and doesn't help. Her mother is perhaps too caught up in showing her favour to Feardorcha, for whom she has only smiles and consideration. Though she's never overtly mean or overtly derogatory towards Meadbh in front of Feardorcha. She saves that for private conversations, or slyly worded remarks to others.

"So," Síle continues. "I was just returning from the cook house. I thought to bring you..." she waves a hand. "That matters not. On my return I passed the bushes where we'd placed the washing earlier and it was all there, on the ground, muddied and torn."

"The dogs?" Meadbh asks, though she knows better.

Síle gives Meadbh a flat look. "The dogs are shut up. We did that before we began the washing. The men are in the fields."

Meadbh nods. She knows that it's a person behind it. And it was no accident. They both know.

"You must talk to her," says Síle. The words are firm.

Meadbh gives a mirthless laugh. It seems the right path, but Meadbh knows it's a useless one.

"You must," says Síle. "Before she does something worse. Harmful."

The harm they both know would be against Meadbh. To her. Serious harm.

"Feed a portion to the dogs of whatever I don't personally give you, or isn't from a communal plate."

Meadbh nods, understanding. It's a thought that had briefly crossed her mind a few days ago and she'd dismissed it as ludicrous, but now she isn't so sure.

The *beacha* are restless. Some fly out from the hives, perhaps in search of food. Or to get their bearings. Or even to try and fly back to their home. Meadbh isn't certain. She only knows that she understands their restlessness and feels the need to fly away, as they do. But what home would she search for? She shakes her head under her linen cloth. The certainty she'd felt only a few short days ago is gone. The settled feeling, the understanding of how she would go on with her life, the shape it would take, has fizzled under the weight of her mother's glare. Her subtle attempts to sabotage every step Meadbh takes to manage the household. The barrels of oats, the sacks of flour that have either gone missing or been left to damp. The meat that has spoiled. Onions scattered and left for rats. And the washing just this morning. Síle does her best to maintain a watch, as does Meadbh, but they can't be everywhere at once. She's taking Síle's instructions to heart. She'll watch what she eats.

Meadbh listens to the humming as she tries to focus on the buzz, the vibration that would once calm her as much as fill her with joy. She can feel the comfort, but she can find no immediate solution to her mother's actions and potential actions, except for watchfulness and care. Her mother has relinquished her place in the main bedchamber and taken the one nearest without a word. Her presence is there, watchful. There's nothing Meadbh can point to, to admonish or confront. Perhaps she can ask Ita's help. Ita may be able to suggest some way to halt, or at least lessen, her mother's behaviour so that it doesn't take a more dangerous turn. The thought occurs to her as she replaces the lid of the hive. Ita may be naturally protective of Meadbh's mother, but perhaps that can be worked to her advantage. Or, at the very least, Meadbh might add another pair of watchful eyes and listening ears. She thinks of her mother's sparse knowledge of herbs. At least, she recalls it was sparse. Another particular Ita might know.

Meadbh thinks of the hemlock she'd seen just the other day, growing innocently among the cow parsley, the foxglove along the path that goes up to this very field.

Chapter Thirty-Four

Ita walks towards her from her dwelling and greets Meadbh warmly. Traces of worry still cloud Ita's eyes, but there's a faint bounce to her step that shows Eoin's return has helped her spirits. Eoin is attempting to find a place among the men that now crowd Raithlinn. Feardorcha has yet to make it clear if he is still to be head of the *ceithearn tigh,* or have any rank or responsibility beyond the small field attached to his dwelling that belongs to him, which is no rank at all. No status. Not even a *scológ mhaith.* For who could draw a fine living from one field alone? Meadbh wonders at her father, that he never gifted or ensured that his cousin would have more or better land, so that his status reflected his true place and responsibilities after her brother died.

"Did you come to see Eoin?" asks Ita. "I'm sorry, but he isn't here, I'm afraid. He's off with some of the O'Mathghamhna, hunting. He's showing them the best area for deer. Apparently some of the dogs were given the nice haunch of venison we had hanging."

Meadbh frowns at the last words. Recovering, she shakes her head. "No, it's you I came to see. I've hardly had a chance to talk with you since my return."

Ita waves off Meadbh's apology. "There's no need to excuse yourself at all, *bantiarna*, I understand that so many things must take up your time. Your mother was only saying to me how you have so much to learn. So many things you wouldn't understand because you were a nun."

Meadbh strives to digest these words. Words that make her consider that this visit could be futile. She's here, though. She'll make the effort.

She gives Ita a sad smile. "It's true that I have many new responsibilities, but other circumstances have kept me busy as well, otherwise I would have been here sooner. You and Eoin are my kin, Ita. Dearest and closest kin. I would want to see you and spend time with you, above all." She places a hand on Ita's arm. "May I come in and visit with you?"

Ita flushes, her hand flying to her mouth. "Oh, *bantiarna*, I'm so sorry. You must come in, of course."

"Ita, it's me, Meadbh. You must call me Meadbh. I wouldn't have you stand on any ceremony. We're close kin."

Meadbh knows it's a slight stretch, but she hopes by

convincing Ita of this, she may go some way in making progress towards establishing Eoin and his wife as important figures of her *sliocht,* and by that, secure the future for him, Ita and Aedh. And maybe Ita's loyalty in the bargain. She shakes her head as she follows Ita inside. She's so far from the noble and godly image of a nun as anyone can imagine. Just before she enters the dwelling a figure in the distance by the ash catches her eye for a moment. She pauses, but it's gone. She sighs, wondering if it's her mother up to some mischief again.

Meadbh takes the roughhewn three-legged chair that Ita indicates. The same one her mother sat on when Meadbh was here with Diarmuid. She thinks of him and still feels that pain. How different her life is now. She wonders for a moment what might have happened if she'd stayed with him. Would they have made a life there with Desmond? He, Desmond's court *fili,* she, a wife...and a *clairseoir?* Playing a *clairsach* for which she had only rudimentary skills, and that only because she pushed and seized her opportunities when she was young? The thought is laughable, because the skills of a court *clairseoir* are exemplary.

Ita offers Meadbh a cup of watered ale. The cup is an old and battered tin one, but Meadbh knows Ita considers it her best. Ita pours herself a drink in an earthenware cup. A small chip mars the lip and Ita is careful to avoid it as she takes a sip. She takes the low stool opposite Meadbh.

"How are the *beacha?*" Ita asks, her tone careful, considerate.

Meadbh smiles. "They're well, in general. Restless, but it's to be expected, given everything." She realises she's assuring herself as much as Ita. Her *beacha* must make a home here, even as she must.

Ita nods. "It'll be grand to have such access to honey again. Eoin does like honey on his oatcakes."

"There were *beacha* here before?"

Ita looks at her, startled. "Yes. You don't remember?"

Meadbh shakes her head slowly, searching her memories. Memories that are crowded with so many other things she'd rather not recall. But no *beacha*.

"You were young. Too young, I suppose, to remember. Or perhaps you had other interests, concerns back then." Ita gives a small laugh. "What a child you were, though. So curious. So full of life. Always getting into things. Your poor brother, God rest him, could hardly keep up with you."

Meadbh flinches at the mention of her brother. It's the first time anyone has spoken of him. Except for her mother, of course, but they were accusations, flung like daggers with every intention to pierce the most vulnerable parts of her. Ita speaks of memories. Memories of a brother for which, even now, she can feel only mixed emotions.

"We didn't always enjoy each other's company," Meadbh says.

Ita shakes her head and issues another laugh. "Ah, no. You were too different. And I think he was jealous of you."

Meadbh is startled by the words. "Me? No, no. He just liked to find ways to torment me."

Ita shrugs. "All brothers do, but his tormenting was only to try and prove that he was as strong or adventurous as you were."

Meadbh smiled politely. "It's kind of you to say so, but I think my mother would find a different way to express my character and temperament."

Ita reaches out and briefly places a hand on Meadbh's arm. "Don't be so hard on her. She had her own demons to face when she left her home to come to Raithlinn. She was the fourth daughter of Ui Donoghue. Her *sliocht* was once very powerful and your father sought to make a good alliance. But both *sliochts'* fortunes have since fallen. And your father didn't take it well. Your mother was used to more...comfortable surroundings." She grimaces. "There were few servants then, and even fewer now."

"But you're no servant," Meadbh adds. The rest of the thought goes unsaid. That Meadbh's mother treats Ita as though she were a servant.

Ita shrugs. "She found that I could arrange her hair the way she likes it. She takes comfort in my presence."

"She uses you." The words fall out before Meadbh can stop herself.

"No," says Ita. "I don't mind helping her. I understand her."

Meadbh wonders for a moment what Ita's story is that gives her this compassion. She doesn't feel that she can ask, not now. That past might forge the link that Ita shares with Meadbh's mother, though. Her own past is different, but no less troubled, Meadbh thinks.

Meadbh knows Síle is speaking to her, but she's having trouble focusing on the words. Meadbh sits on the small stool in her bedchamber while Síle tends Meadbh's hair, pulling the comb through the strands slowly. The action hypnotises Meadbh, causing her present near-stupor. A stupor that she desires. Síle has done this for her most days, but never now, just after their small meal break at midday. But the men are still hunting, and Meadbh's head pains her, her thoughts crowded. Shoving, pushing, jostling each other, each becoming fiercer, as if a battle is to be won. And perhaps that's the truth of it. What thought, what set of reasoning will triumph? Much that Ita has told her, explained to her about her mother, prods her to compassion, to understanding. But past actions, memories and so much else in her heart war against it. Present actions wage a different battle, one that seems fantastical to contemplate and difficult to understand. "She needs security, now, Meadbh." Ita's closing words as Meadbh rose to leave echo loudly in her mind. The "she" needed no explanation, even though nothing of her mother had been said for a while before that.

"Don't you agree?" asks Síle.

"Of course I agree with you." Meadbh scours the words that had filtered in during the past few moments and recalls none of them.

Síle snorted. "So you do think that the fair folk pulled the washing off the bushes."

Meadbh opened her mouth then shut it. "Maybe." The slight hint of defiance is at odds with the smile on her mouth.

Síle laughed. "Ah, now, see? You actually agree with Fachtna. You can't dislike him so much."

Meadbh grimaces. The man that serves as one of Feardorcha's *ceithearn tigh* is rough and his only good quality is that he fights well. According to Feardorcha. That he's completely lacking in any common sense, and given to superstitions of all kinds, Feardorcha seems to overlook.

Síle patted her shoulder. "There, now. I've done. Let your hair loose for a while, leave off your headcloth and take some air. You'll feel much better after it."

Meadbh sighs and nods absently. Síle might be right. She would go and see her *beacha*. They would certainly help.

The path rises up. To the left is a small wood. It's filled mostly with birch. Young trees. The few oak that were there when she was young are gone. The light bark of the birch, barely embedded with moss, is almost luminescent in the grey light that filters in through the tree canopy where there's a little clearing. Meadbh stops to admire the sight, the breeze stirring her hair, lifting the ends to eddy around her waist. Movement catches her eye over to the far left of the wood. A shadow. She frowns and watches as a mounted figure appears and stops in the clearing. Light pours down on him and he, too, has become luminescent.

Diarmuid.

Meadbh stands there, unmoving.

Chapter Thirty-Five

There are times when Meadbh knows an action shouldn't be taken, or a path she should turn away from. Sound choices should be made instead. Meadbh knows this from her own life. From the paths she followed, but should have refused, from the actions she took, particularly in regard to her mother, and her brother, Felim, that she should have avoided. But Meadbh recognises that her understanding of this part of herself, the part of the past that still causes her pain, changes what she so often does. She chooses poorly.

And Meadbh knows standing here, unmoving, facing the clearing among the birch trees, that another poor choice is in the making.

Diarmuid dismounts and swiftly makes his way to her side. He sweeps her up in his arms, hugs her tightly. Meadbh feels his chest hard against her own, his muscular arms holding her tight, his chin resting on her head. She feels this and more. The "more" is part anger, part wonder, part hurt and part joy. There are so many parts, and they all hold her captive, still. They're battling inside her, and once again she's involved in a warfare of emotions and she isn't certain who she wishes will win.

Diarmuid pulls away a little. Searches her face. Smooths her arms. Takes up her hands. His hair is neatly trimmed, his beard groomed. There's a polish about him that wasn't there before. "You're well. You're unharmed." He places one hand against her cheek. "I'm glad. I was so worried."

Meadbh blinks up at him. The battle being waged inside her is fierce, and these words only add more weapons to all sides.

"Worried?"

The puzzlement is a feeling she can extract from the fight. It's part of the "why" that's played like a counter hum to every dark feeling she's had towards Diarmuid. "Why" goes hand in hand with "betrayal". Two mated swans. Together until death. She would kill this "why" along with the "betrayal".

"Of course I've been worried. You disappeared without a word. I thought something had happened to you. That you'd been taken." He squeezes her arms. "I searched the area, tried to find a trace of you. But there was nothing."

Meadbh thinks of Derbhla, the young woman who helped her at Desmond's castle, and silently thanks her for keeping her secret.

"I even came back here to Raithlinn, to see if you'd returned, or if anyone had word of you. But there was nothing."

Meadbh frowns. "You returned here?"

Diarmuid nods. "Eoin was gone, so I spoke to Ita and your mother."

"You spoke to my mother?" Her tone was incredulous, her thoughts racing more. The battle inside was becoming too much. She puts a hand to her forehead to calm herself. Cool the thoughts raging in her mind.

"Ah, well, it was more to Ita, but your mother was there, adding her usual joyful comments."

The wryness in his tone draws a weak smile from Meadbh for a brief moment. "Of course," she mutters.

"But you're here, now. Unharmed. And I'm thankful for that."

She looks at him, opens her mouth. Closes it. Because his words bring her to the present. And the realisation that no matter what battles are fought inside her, some things are separate, above such battles, and will ultimately triumph. Though that cursed "why" is still lingering persistently, twined like ivy around the oak of "betrayal".

"Yes, Diarmuid," she says calmly. "I'm here, now. With Feardorcha O'Mathghamhna. My husband and lord of Raithlinn."

It's Diarmuid's turn to remain still, cloaked in stunned surprise. Moments pass and then he shakes his head. "No," he says. "You're *my* wife."

Those words they spoke in front of Desmond. Meadbh

thinks of them now and wants to laugh. It's possible they'd be honoured. But what of it?

The distant sound of hoofs ring out, penetrating Meadbh's thoughts and galvanising her into action. She presses her hand on his chest. "You must go. The men are returned."

Diarmuid shakes his head. "We must talk. There's more to be said."

Meadbh looks at him and shakes her head. "It's too dangerous. Feardorcha wouldn't take kindly to your presence. You're only one and they are many. Too many. Leave now, while you can."

He frowns. "I'll go for now. But we must meet. Tonight. In the store house. When everyone is gone to their beds."

She pulls away, turning. Turning her body and her life. She leaves. Resuming the path that was to take her to her *beacha*. That path, at least, isn't ill chosen.

"I don't know," says Meadbh. The phrase is following her around, haunting her like some uneasy spirit. It has joined ranks with the "why" and the "betrayal" that are equally pernicious in their desire to cling like parasites. Only this "I don't know" Meadbh is speaking aloud to Síle. Prompted by the questions Síle has posed after Meadbh recounted the meeting with Diarmuid.

Meadbh had been unable to keep the meeting to herself. Her confusion and battling emotions had arisen even more powerfully when she regained the *ráth* and, after alerting the household to the men's return, she sought refuge in the bedchamber to collect herself before Feardorcha could see her.

231

Síle had followed her in. It only took a little probing before Meadbh spilled it all. It sounded like a bard's tale. Or a *seanchas* from the past, but was so much in Meadbh's present she could find no enjoyment in the telling.

Síle draws her to the sturdy framed bed. They sit next to each other and Síle takes her hand.

The "I don't know" hangs in the air. The words uttered to answer Síle about what Meadbh thinks Diarmuid's intentions are. It's the truth. A truth that speaks of lack of trust. A truth that says there's much about what she feels toward Diarmuid that's confused. It's a confusion she wishes away. But that wish refuses to come true.

"What will you do?" asks Síle. "Will you meet with him?"

The "I don't know" springs to her lips again, but she forces back the phrase. "It's not a wise thing to do." These words she forms carefully and speaks in a neutral tone artfully shaped.

Síle nods. "You're right. And from all you've told me you shouldn't trust him."

"No, I shouldn't trust him." The words she says echo through her head and she frowns hearing them. Understands that their purpose is to try and convince.

Síle studies her carefully. "You're settled now. You're in the home of your birth. You have the *beacha*, too."

Meadbh thinks of the *beacha* and how unsettled they've been.

Feardorcha is in high humour. The hunt was enjoyable, though the deer perhaps not as plentiful as he would have liked. Meadbh sits next to him at the trestle table and flinches

232

slightly when he bangs it in appreciation of a joke Fachtna makes.

The fug that fills the air from the smoke of the hearth fire and the press of too many bodies who have lately exerted themselves nearly makes Meadbh gag. The food in front of her holds no appeal. She catches Síle's frown and pointed glare at her still full trencher. Feardorcha has his own, the one that once belonged to her father, though Feardorcha claims he will have a finer one made when opportunity presents itself.

Laughter breaks around her again and Meadbh realises another joke was made. It's a night of jokes, and many she feels are on her, though their maker isn't even present. She glances over at her mother. Well, perhaps one person who would make jokes on her behalf is here.

Tonight, her mother has chosen to wear a gown that clings tightly to her shape and hugs her arms. The neck is rounded. A kirtle, Meadbh remembers. Over it she wears another, deeply cut, shorter sleeveless gown with deep armholes that extend almost to the waist. A surcoat. At her neck is a ring brooch. Another gift she'd extracted from Meadbh's father. All in all, it's a manner of dress that speaks of Gaill connections and influence. Meadbh can't begin to think how these clothes have been obtained. Or perhaps the poverty of Raithlinn explains it.

"Are you unwell, Meadbh?" her mother asks. Her question appears innocent, but Meadbh can't help but notice the sly look that flashes across her face. "Or is it your courses. I know they always give you trouble." She gives Feardorcha a concerned look. "You shouldn't get your hopes up too quickly. It takes some women time to get a child in their belly. That's what I hear, at least."

All the implications are clear, but Meadbh can only sigh

inwardly. Though no joke, it's most certainly at her expense. And unimaginative. She glances Feardorcha. His momentary puzzlement is clear. He regards Meadbh for a moment. "Are you ill?" A hopeful expression fills his face. He spares a wolfish grin for the rest of the gathered group. "Sometimes a seed can take root quickly, though."

Meadbh finds herself counting the days, unease filling her. Her courses haven't always been regular since she's left Tempeall Gobnatán. She's put it down to anxiety. And she's assinging this current inability to stomach food to the same cause.

"I'm fine, really. There's no reason to think anything but that I'm just not hungry. Most likely because I've been so busy and I'm tired."

Feardorcha frowns, his disappointment clear. Her mother tuts and falls momentarily silent. Until the next barb can come to mind, Meadbh thinks.

Chapter Thirty-Six

Meadbh isn't quite certain how it happens.

She lies there on the bed, clad only in her *léine*, and listens to the soft snores next to her. The night is clammy, heralding midsummer, and even the thin blanket that covers her is too much. Or perhaps it's the earlier exertion, when Feardorcha, no doubt anxious to prove his virility and increase his chances of successfully planting his seed, took her quickly, without bothering to remove her *léine*.

Gratitude for its speed is about all she managed to feel at the time, and even now there's only the urge to wipe herself down.

It might be that urge that gets her up. Galvinises her to don her gown, slip on her leather shoes, knot a brat around her shoulders and tell herself that she must get a bucket of water to cleanse herself properly. She opens the door and wanders out, the stone tread cold even through the leather of her shoes. She enjoys the cold though, lets it seep up her legs.

She makes it to the hall, glances around at the sleeping forms, and threads her way through them, careful of careless limbs and spread cloaks. The light is dim, and she can barely make out where she must and mustn't tread. The hearth fire is smoored for the night, but it still lends itself to the fug that clings to the room, which the breath and sweat do much to enhance.

Meadbh finds herself outside and the breaths she takes are deep and heartfelt. Overhead, stars speckle the sky, shedding light on her. She can see the sky's vastness now. Her head clears, but only insofar as she allows it. She wants no choices offered. She wants no path to select. The destination is only for a pail of water. Water to cleanse herself. She keeps the thought in her mind and heads toward the cook house, where she thinks a bucket may be had. A bucket filled with water, ready for the next day. The spring isn't far, perhaps she might refill the bucket once she's used the water.

Somehow, Meadbh finds herself not in the cook house, but the storehouse.

There are no stars to illuminate her or her surroundings now. The door is closed. There are no windows. Only shadows and shapes. Shapes that tell their story. But she can see nothing of a shape that speaks "bucket". Because only one shape is evident to her now and its story is complex, long, and evokes such emotions in Meadbh she can only inhale sharply with its vastness.

The shape moves forward and embraces her. "Meadbh" comes a soft whisper. A kiss on her forehead, slow, lingering. Meadbh is a startled bird, trembling, afraid to speak. To move.

"You came," he says. "I was afraid for a moment there that you wouldn't."

A hand against her cheek. Another kiss. But this kiss. It's not a forehead kiss. It's not a cheek kiss. Her lips and mouth soften under this kiss. They find ways of feeling and behaving in a manner she's never before experienced.

"Meadbh," comes the whisper again. Only this time the whisper is against her ear and she somehow finds herself caught in closer to him. Her heart nearer to his. How can she manage this? This trembling bird that she's become has no place in this world, in this time. She feels the agony of it all. What must be, what could be, and what mustn't be.

She pulls back. Finds the will to take steps away from him. "No," she says.

In her head the word "no", when she thought it, was firm. Brooking no debate. But all the possibilities for debate and uncertainty are in the word she actually voices. A voice that wobbles. That holds questions. Doubts. So many, many of all these things. That "why" question is among them. And it will hold her up. It will strengthen her.

"You betrayed me." She would put that thought in the front. Her best defence. Strong. Immutable.

"Betrayed you?" The bewilderment in his tone is obvious and it fuels her anger. She's glad of it.

"You said you were taking me to O'Mathghamhna, yet you had no intention of doing that. You led us straight into territory where I'm sure it was no surprise that Desmond's men were lurking. For all I know, you may have even scouted them out before we left and led us right to them."

"What? No."

The force of the "no" halts her for a moment. Shifts her wall of defence off kilter. She gathers herself, brushes his words aside. "Of course you did. What other explanation is there?"

"The truth."

She could hear his heavy breathing. The emotion it contained. His effort to slow it, to calm himself.

"I didn't lead you to Desmond's men," he says finally. "Cast your mind back. I was as surprised as you. And I acted and said things from instinct to protect you. To protect us both."

She frowns. Crosses her arms. More defence. Disbelief is added to the crossed arms. "How do you explain going in the wrong direction? Caisleán na Leachta is not even a day's ride from here. South. Why would you go north?"

Diarmuid steps forward, places his hands on her arms. She feels his touch and tries to discount any pleasure or comfort she might find in them. She keeps her arms crossed.

"I thought to go to Mac Carthaigh, first. I thought O'Math-ghamhna might already be there, pleading his own case to put one of his men in Raithlinn. To finally make it his."

The information throws her off. She's stunned. Suddenly directed onto an entirely different conversation. Her arms drop. "Mac Carthaigh? Why?"

"Mac Carthaigh is O'Mathghamhna's overlord. He would have the last say in this regard."

Meadbh stands silently. She searches her mind, tries to find this piece of knowledge in her memory. She knows she's been absent from Raithlinn for many years, and the early years that she spent here were hardly ones that would have her keenly abreast of all the political nuances of her father's world. That Mac Carthaigh had expanded his territory. But this? Would she have really missed this?"

"Mac Carthaigh is overlord?"

"He is."

"And you knew this? How?"

The words she's uttered remind Meadbh there's so much she doesn't know about this man. His past is as much as a mystery as her lack of knowledge of the reach of Mac Carthaigh's power.

"It's common enough knowledge among those who would know of these things."

She feels his words like a slap. It wakes her from her stupor. "And you're one who would know?" Her tone has bite. She hears it.

"Meadbh." His voice is soft now, pleading. "It's not what you think. There's no betrayal. I wanted to help you."

"Why?" The bite is gone. Puzzlement has returned.

He caresses her cheek. "Can't you guess? I care for you. Deeply."

The words sink into her and part of her welcomes them. It's the part that has held her safe through these days, seasons, years, that flood her now with doubt. "Have you so little that you think a marriage with me would help you make your way in the world? That you would fight to keep my family's holding of Raithinn?"

He answers her with a kiss. It sears her mouth. It's fierce, undeniable in the emotion it conveys. It tell her to listen, to feel, to understand all that he isn't saying, but is surely feeling. But still she's uncertain if she should trust it.

"Trust me," he says.

But whether it's the kiss or him she has to trust, she finds both difficult.

Meadbh shifts her weight. Around her she can hear the sounds of night. An owl. The scuttle of a small nocturnal animal in the underbrush. A breeze ruffling the leaves of a tree branch. They seem both distant and too close. Her senses are adrift, disturbed from their usual place in her body, her mind and her heart. She hasn't quite lost her senses, but they aren't where they should be. How else would it be that she's here, behind Diarmuid, on Fionn's back? Her father would laugh to see that his fine horse is in the possession of this man and has been for some time.

She shakes her head again. What thoughts she's having. Disjointed. Unintelligible. Fionn veers slightly to avoid some obstacle in their path and Meadbh grips Diarmuid's waist tighter. His muscled back ripples with the effort to keep a firm grip on the reins and control the ride. His back feels warm and solid against her chest. She thinks of other journeys and other times when she's felt his back. Admired it. Lain against it.

Why is she here? She pushes that thought forward, ahead of the meanderings on Diarmuid's body. She refuses to meander. She must think. They'll arrive at Mac Carthaigh's tower and she'll do her best for her *sliocht*. For Síle, Eoin, Aedh and Ita. And all of the *sliocht* who dwell in the holding of Raithlinn. That's the only way forward. Especially with the image of her mother, standing at the upper doorway as she watched Diarmuid and Meadbh slip off into the woods. She thinks of her *beacha*, too. The *beacha* that, even now, are unsettled, both inside her and up in the field in their hives.

Chapter Thirty-Seven

The castle impresses Meadbh. It says everything about Mac Carthaigh and the powerful *sliocht* that is Mac Carthaigh. Newly built, it comprises three storeys with at least two towers. A well-tended bawn with several buildings.

Her unease increases when she observes the ease with which Diarmuid dismounts and greets the men who are about in the *bawn*. It tells her much that the men respond with respect. She eyes the mantle Diarmuid wears. It isn't the worn, ill-used one she remembers from before, or the *fallaing*. This one is finely made, and the boots he wears, though perhaps not new, match the mantle in quality. These are not the clothes of a man who labours for nuns at a nunnery. His stance is less quiet. Feet that much wider apart. Shoulders that command respect. His regard is direct when he turns to her. He grips her waist and lifts her down from the horse. Their eyes meet and Meadbh searches Diarmuid's, looking for clues. Who is this man?

Once inside, the castle's interior does little to ease Meadbh's tight chest or anxious thoughts. The entrance is on the ground level, unlike the older castles she's entered, and opens into a large hall, the floor covered with flagstones. Targes, javelins, swords and other battle accoutrements hang on the walls, finely made and ready for use. A few men sit on benches and work on more arms, polishing, sharpening. Bearded, hair shoulder length, their muscles honed, frames wiry and taut. Part of Mac Carthaigh's *ceithearn tigh*, she has no doubt. A few look up at Meadbh as she follows Diarmuid across the hall. Their eyes are neither hostile nor friendly towards her, but their nods to Diarmuid and the few grins some display tell her much about his welcome.

In the face of the obvious power of this *sliocht*, this man Mac Carthaigh, Meadbh tries to bring out the stern words to bolster herself. To infuse her mind and body with the fibre and fabric, as well as the framework, in order to meet all who are concerned with the strength and ability to represent her *sliocht*.

Diarmuid rests a hand on her back. She tries to dismiss the reassurance such a gesture gives her, but it's impossible in the face of all that confronts her, both in her mind and her eye. Mac Carthaigh stands at the end of the hall talking with another man. Two women, one young, linger near him, their fine manner of dressing marking them as close kin. Though she's never seen Mac Carthaigh before in her life, she has no doubt that he's this man. It's not the broad shoulders, the dark hair, now threaded with white, which curls around his neck and bushy beard. She's no idea if that's a trait all those of the Mac Carthaigh *sliocht* share. It's in the drape of his brat, its quality of weave, the brooch that fixes it in place. It's in the fineness of his boots, the snowy white colour of his *léine*. But even without the finery, his posture, his manner, she would know. Everything about him speaks of who he is and the power he holds.

He catches sight of Diarmuid standing beside Meadbh and smiles. He tilts his head, a speculative look on his face.

"Ah, now. You've returned."

There's some humour there. The humour welcomes. The humour meets the rules of hospitality. Sends reassurance of a place at the table. It speaks of familiarity, as well. Of times past when private jokes were enjoyed. It speaks of all that and more. But behind the humour there's a darkening of the eye, a glint that isn't joining in the joyful private joke. A darkness that's akin to wariness. A darkness that roots a coldness deep inside Meadbh. She must use this darkness as a weapon that protects her. Warns her to take more care than before.

"I have, so," says Diarmuid.

He moves forward, leaving Meadbh to remain where she is. She's not annoyed or displeased. No, she's glad that it removes her from the attention of the people in the hall. She notices, then, that the woman and younger woman, whose clothes tell her they are close kin to Mac Carthaigh, regard her curiously, now. Some attention can't be avoided. Another man, the younger one who'd been talking to Mac Carthaigh, still stands by him. More kin? His manner and dress say it might be so. There's something of the warrior about him. His beard is young, but still, it's there. His arms are muscled as if the sword wasn't long from his grasp.

Two other men linger by Mac Carthaigh, their dress and manner more refined in only that they're carefully arranged, as is the hair and beard, which suggests to Meadbh something else. She glances at Diarmuid. Something familiar. There's a cast to the chin and nose in one that is somehow echoed in Diarmuid. The unease inside her grows ever greater.

The eels lay on her plate, succulent in the sauce in which they were cooked. They keep company with the beef. That the eels and meat are on a plate, and that it's made of pewter, is even a marvel to her. Beside her, Diarmuid has added a capon to his eels and beef. There's more than that on offer, too. But no potage. The plenty that's on show on this table is such that she wonders if perhaps it's some religious feast day she's missed, or that the days have passed more quickly than she imagined, and somehow Lughnasadh is upon her.

The solar is very well appointed. Luxury of a sort she's not experienced before surrounds her. Wall hangings, fur covered benches, chairs and chests carved with intricate designs populate the chamber. A fine linen cloth covers the table, with a stitched hem for which even Siúr Máire and Máthairab would find approval. She thinks of the earl Desmond and can only imagine what the castle that his family inhabit is like.

People converse around her. Their names have been spoken, but Meadbh remembers few. She does know that her identification of Mac Carthaigh was correct. She feels no triumph about such acuity. There was no difficulty, no cunning or sharpened wit required for that recognition. No, the real triumph should be assigned to the speculation she formed about the pair who were most certainly not warriors, though power of another sort is clear. Their names are vivid in her mind. Their names rang out when she first heard them, and echo inside her still. Even as she raises food to her mouth and eats it slowly, these names echo through her. Domhnall O'Dalaigh. Gofraidh O'Dalaigh.

It's the surname that rings out loudest. The *sliocht* name that has a pedigree of such importance that many kings have vied for one of that lineage to reside in their court. *Ollamh* of the highest quality. So knowledgeable in their poetry, their composition, that even Meadbh has heard tell of them. Their very words have power. And these two men, with their knowledge and their power, who sit in places of honour on either side of Mac Carthaigh, bear enough of a resemblance to Diarmuid, once she'd seen it, that she can't mistake them as anything but kin.

That recognition and conclusion holds no triumph for her, either. It raises questions, fosters doubts that are so huge it takes her breath away. The manner of these two men towards Diarmuid wouldn't be what she would expect of kin, though. A manner Diarmuid returns in kind. Distant, cool. Meadbh tries to tell herself that she may have made entirely incorrect assumptions. She likes that the word "entirely" has slipped in her thoughts, because it emphasises the absurdity of putting Diarmuid as kin to these men. But then she thinks that some would feel her own mother's manner towards Meadbh wouldn't put the two as kin. It also reminds her that kin fight with one another. A fact as true as any other.

Since she's arrived here, Diarmuid's attention has been engaged with Mac Carthaigh for the most part, so she's had no opportunity to question him about her assumptions, or about the true reason for their presence here in this castle. He has spared her attention from Mac Carthaigh, for which she's grateful. But any conversation among this group consists only of pleasantries. Pleasantries that give her no answers.

The meal is finishing. Smiles continue to appear on the faces as amusing tales are told and a day's activities recounted. Mac Carthaigh's wife, Devorgilla, recounts a mishap with a dye vat and the blue that now adorns the coat of Mac Carthaigh's favourite dog. There's laughter all around and Meadbh finds herself smiling at the image painted.

"What of your journey, then, nephew?" asks Domhnall, the elder O'Dalaigh. "Was it uneventful?"

All eyes turn to Diarmuid. Beside him, Meadbh stills. The words filter through her. Her mind finds it difficult to slot that idea into place, even though she knows it belongs in the full understanding of the man. Of Diarmuid, who is undeniably in some ways, an O'Dalaigh. But is it his *sliocht*? Or is it his mother who was an O'Dalaigh?

She knows in her heart what it must be. Not only from the tension in the room, so heightened now even she feels it wrap around her tightly. The question alone suggests more than the simple journey from Raithlinn to here, though in her mind it was far from simple. It is, in fact, a different set of words that's part of the question that's haunted her for months. Or perhaps longer. From the very first time she saw this man, toiling in the fields of Gort na Tiobratán at Tempeall Gobnatán. The question now raises its voice and echoes through her. Who is this man and what has brought him here?

"Grand enough," says Diarmuid. "As much as I would enjoy regaling you with a tale worthy of any bard, sadly there's nothing that would warrant it."

"Ah, now, you're too modest by far," says Mac Carthaigh. "What of your lady wife? You've yet to recount the tale of meeting her with your uncle and cousin."

The O'Dalaighs turn startled eyes to Meadbh. When Diarmuid had introduced her to the O'Dalaighs, Meadbh had noted that all he'd given was her name with its clear linkage to her father and the Uí Fhlionn *sliocht*. She hadn't minded. It seemed at the time one less complication to explain, to defend. Her presence was not questioned by Mac Carthaigh and that was enough for the O'Dalaigh. Her relationship to Mac Carthaigh wasn't their concern.

This new information brought all into question for the O'Dálaighs now, though. Beside Meadbh, Diarmuid stiffens. He starts to rise, thinks better of it and assembles a pleasant expression on his face. "It is a tale, indeed. One that, for the moment, would take time from the evening's entertainment and I would be loath to do that. Especially when it will be of the highest level."

Domhnall looks over at Mac Carthaigh, raises a brow. Mac Carthaigh nods. "Now, so, nephew. We're at the heart of the matter here. This night's entertainment isn't on my shoulders. Or even Gofraidh, though even at his young age he's well capable." He gives a dramatic pause. Its timing is impeccable, as Meadbh would expect. And though expected, the words that follow the pause still startle her. "You, my nephew, have tonight's entertainment on your shoulders. You'll give us three poems worthy of an *ollamh's* knowledge, now. And compose one this night for tomorrow. That's what you aspire to, isn't it? So if it's *now* your wish to take your rightful place as an *ollamh* from the esteemed lineage that is O'Dalaigh, then you must prove yourself worthy."

His face flushed, Diarmuid casts his glance between Mac Carthaigh and his uncle. Meadbh knows as well as he does that there's no argument to make in this case. She feels only barely able to understand some of the implications of this moment, it's as though she's half blind, scrambling for a foothold on the side of a cliff. How perilous. So perilous. The "why" of it hangs around her like a mist.

A man enters the hall. One of Mac Carthaigh's *ceithearn tigh*. "I beg you excuse me for interrupting, Mac Carthaigh, but O'Mathghamhna and a few of his men have arrived. They've a grave matter to discuss and ask for your welcome."

The familiar words used during a formal arrival of any *slíocht* should have been regarded only with interest. Knowing the *slíocht* in this case is O'Mathghamhna leaves Meadbh cold. There's no doubt in her mind who's with O'Mathghamhna. And no doubt about the nature of his visit.

Chapter Thirty-Eight

Feardorcha and O'Mathghamhna stand before Mac Carthaigh. Their manner is confident. O'Mathghamhna's shoulders are spread out, enhancing the breadth of his chest, his arm muscles bunched. He presents a fine picture of strength. Feardorcha mirrors his actions. O'Mathghamhna and Feardorcha approach Mac Carthaigh, give their greetings and go through the pleasantries quickly. Mac Carthaigh isn't one to rush, at least in this case, and he makes both Feardorcha and Mhaithghamhna endure more pleasantries.

Seats at the table have already been provided for the two men, and the soldiers who have accompanied them are finding their hospitality with the Mac Carthaigh's men below. The seats offered are at the other end to Diarmuid and Meadbh, and for that she's grateful, though Feardorcha's angry glares still find ways to pierce the fragile calm she has pieced together in the time since his arrival was announced.

"O'Mathghamhna, you haven't met some of our guests here," says Mac Carthaigh. "We're most honoured to have Domhnall O'Dalaigh and his son, Gofraidh. That members of such a renown and worthy family, who have so many *ollamhs* among their *fili* that stretch back into the mists of time, and whose very name is synonymous with poetry, should deign to be a guest in my home, is a gift. A blessing. And such blessings must be treated with the utmost respect and reverence." Mac Carthaigh eyes the two men. "Don't you agree?"

The words are clever and the intent clear. There will be no trouble. Feardorcha expression falls into a sulk. Mhaithghamhna gives a curt nod.

Meadbh can only be glad that her mother isn't here, that she somehow hadn't wormed her way into accompanying these men.

The pleasantries begin, any mention of Diarmuid's performance vanished. Meadbh glances at Diarmuid, noting the tense jaw, the measured replies. Even to comments about the number of clouds gathering in the sky. "A storm perhaps?" "Not surprising, but maybe a little early for this time of year to be severe?" "It's not unusual after Lughnasadh and that's only days away." So many words, so little meaning. It matters little who says them, though warnings may be couched inside them. It's hard to say. But if they do contain warnings, they all would issue them.

They all say with these words, "I am here. I am able to meet whatever comes with everything I have."

Meadbh sighs. All these words have little to do with her, though it may appear so when they do come to discussing the matter.

More conversation is made. A few ideas on pasturage are exchanged. Feardorcha does spare a few more glares in Diarmuid and Meadbh's direction, but Meadbh manages to ignore them and feigns interest in the discussion. Everyone in the solar has their attention on the real conversation that isn't spoken. But perhaps Mac Carthaigh has had enough, because he eventually clears his throat to halt conversation.

"We still have our entertainment for the night to come." He looks over at Diarmuid and smiles. "You didn't think we would excuse you on account of our guests? That would be rude, indeed. It's time for you to show off your talents, my lad."

Diarmuid nods slowly. He appears unperturbed, though Meadbh can see tension lines gathering at his eyes. "Of course. I would never be the cause of disappointment for you."

Meadbh refuses to see a different meaning behind his words. There's been too much of that already and her head aches. She must use her energy to find a time to speak and persuade for her cause. She needs to assemble her arguments. It appears no time will be given over to complaints and problems tonight. She'll formulate her thoughts into words in bed.

Diarmuid has already made his way to the centre of the room. Standing there, clad in woolen *truibhas,* a shortened *léine,* as well as his *brat,* he looks more ready to ride than to entertain in a formally. But his posture, his manner, all speak of someone well used to performing, and suddenly, the clothes don't seem so impossible. They're hardly regarded. The moment Diarmuid speaks, only his voice is noticed. It becomes all about the voice and the words it conveys.

A Cholmáin mhóir mheic Léinin, a bhinnegnaidh
bhaisghléimhin,
grádh dhuid as dú d'Ibh Dálaigh, tú ar gcuid dona Colmánaibh.

Atá ann eochaoir leasa, cuimhnigh an gcráoibh gcoibhneasa,
ar léim ná léigsi a chara, dodfhréimh th'éigsi ar n-ealadha.

Túoide an fhileadh ó ttáam, a érlaimh dan hainm Colmán,
as comhrádh as canta amach Colmán dár dhalta Dálach.

Ní bhiadh Dálach ris and dán, mona bheadh re a chois Colmán:
dobhadh léir é ar a oidiocht, sé in gach céim gá chomhaideacht.

Gidh cúich adeir ná badh dleacht ní ar an ndán—dia do
chléireacht—
ní ceard a n-aghaidh Dhéan dán, as é do chabhair Colmán.

253

. . .

Great Colmán son of Léinin, melodious sage of smooth bright hand,
the O'Dalaigh are bound to love thee, thou art our share of the
Colmáns.

Herein is the key of profit, remember the branch of kinship,
suffer thou not, o friend, thy art, our craft, to spring away from
thy stock.

Thou wert the fosterer of the poet from whom we came, thou
patron whose name is Colmán.
Tis a tale that must be told, of Colmáan whose fosterling was
Dálach.

Dálach would not have studied the craft had not Colmán been
by his side.
It was clear from his training that Colmáan was guiding him at
every step.

Whoever says that poetry merits nothing—how clerical!
Poetry is no art opposed to God, it was He who helped Colmán.

. . .

The poem continues on for eleven more quatrains, extolling the virtues of Colmán and the O'Dalaigh, and praising Colmán's legacy to the O'Dalaighs, concluding with the composer invoking Colmán's power at that moment. It's a powerful invocation and praise poem. Clever choice. Wise choice? After a few moments' pause, Diarmuid launches into the next, with only a few words explaining it. It's a poem by his ancestor, Muiread-hach O'Dálaigh, who fled to Scotland after killing someone when they insulted and berated him. Entitled, "An Irritable Genius", it tells the tale by a man, embittered after fifteen years in exile, still hoping his old Irish overlord and patron might help him.

Créd agaibh aoidhigh a gcéin, aghiolla gusan ngaillsgéimh,
a dhream ghaoidhealta ghallda. Naoidheanta sheang
shaorchlannda?

Whence comes it that ye have guests from afar, O youth of
foreign beauty,
O ye who are become Gaelic, yet foreign, young, graceful and
highborn?

He continues on for several quatrains, extolling the virtue of the high lord who he hoped will save him from exile. He explains the triviality of the harm:

Domhnall Doire is Droma Cliabh, ná tréig dhó mé, a mheic
Uilliam;
nach dá mbí go cruaidh ad chionn, an rí thuaidh nocha
tréigeann.

Bea gar bhfala risin bhfear, bachlach do bheith dom chain eadh,
mé do mharbhadh an mhoghadh—a Dhé, an adhbhar
anfholadh?

Domhnall of Derry and Drumcliff, abandon me not to him,
FitzWilliam;
The northern prince does not abandon one who is bold against
thee.

Trifling is our difference with the man: that a churl was abusing
me and that I killed the serf—O God! Is this a ground for
enmity?

The poem continues on for many more quatrains, until finally concluding with a reminder of the gifts he will receive abroad.

Silence reigns higher than any king when Diarmuid finishes. A silence so hushed it speaks of reverence. And something about his performance smacks of holiness, or a magical power of some kind, because the listeners were transported, taken to a different world. A different time.

Meadbh feels this all as the silence stretches, and she wishes that this spell will never be broken. For her, magic is the only possibility, because the holiness she knows comes with obligations, subtle and overt. This is pure. There's nothing but this feeling, this moment, this experience. And she doesn't want it to end.

Meadbh hesitates in the hall. Servants are clearing plates, smooring the fire, taking down the trestle table, moving benches. It's time for sleep, yet Meadbh has no idea where she's to lay her head. She looks at Diarmuid, but he's lost in thought.

Mac Carthaigh comes over to Diarmuid, places a hand on his shoulder. "You, my lad, have a poet's night ahead. Your uncle has requested you be provided with a small windowless room and a pallet, as it would be for any aspiring poet at a school."

Diarmuid grunts and nods. "And what's usually done in nine days must now be contrived in one night."

Mac Carthaigh shrugs. "I'm sure they'll take in consideration your lack of composition time."

Diarmuid gives him a wry smile. "Oh, I'm sure they will."

Mac Carthaigh looks at Meadbh. "Derbhgilla, my wife, will look after you."

As if summoned, Derbhgilla arrives at Mac Carthaigh's side and places an arm around Meadbh. She issues words of welcome and hospitality. Meadbh nods and murmurs the required responses, but her mind is filled with the many questions that have arisen tonight that now join the others that have long remained unanswered.

Chapter Thirty-Nine

The morning air is cool on her face, but Meadbh welcomes this coolness. All night the air in this small chamber has felt close, stuffy, as if no breath were to be had. Sleep had been impossible, and though she should have welcomed the opportunity to calm herself, and assemble the words she knows she has to speak to Mac Carthaigh as soon as she's able, Meadbh found herself wishing for the oblivion that sleep brings. The privacy of the chamber had been as welcome as it was unexpected, though it could barely be called a chamber, rather than more of a store, positioned as it is near the guarderobe.

And now, with the dawn just beginning and no sensible convincing argument formed and stored in her mind, Meadbh rises. A walk may help, she tells herself. To take these last moments in private before the day's events begin. She refuses to contemplate what may happen. Let them unfold as they will, she tells herself. She won't dwell on them. She'll have had her own opportunity to make her case before the official proceedings. She'll make certain of that.

Over her *léine* she dons the simple gown she has worn since leaving Raithlinn. It's far from her best, and is now travel stained and rumpled. It matters little, she tells herself. The discussion, and all the events that may concern her, aren't anything to do with her beauty or lack of it. She winds her plait at the back of her neck and pins it there with the spare wooden hairpin that Mac Carthaigh's wife gave her the night before. Her hair will be tidy, she thinks wryly as she places the simple headcloth on, also provided Mac Carthaigh. She ties the ends at the back. It's enough to cover most of her hair, but stray strands spill out from the sides. She tucks them in, even as she knows in a short while they'll have fallen out. Sighing, she takes up her *brat* and wraps it around her, securing it with a knot.

When she reaches the solar she sees the first sign of stirring. A lone woman tidies her hair while a young boy stirs the fire in the hearth at the room's centre. The woman nods to her, but the boy is too intent on his task to notice Meadbh.

Once outside, Meadbh can hear the distant bellow of a young calf looking for its mother. She hopes that mother tends her calf better than her own did. The thought pulls her up as she recalls Ita's words that gave a different view of her mother.

A view that with any other person she would instantly find sympathy. Her first instinct is to reject such a view again, but she thinks of her own situation. The comparison does little to comfort her or present her a clear picture of any particular view of her mother. Now isn't the time. She must assemble her argument.

A hand grips her arm and she turns to find Diarmuid behind her. His presence takes her by surprise. The warmth of his grip instantly feels more than just a gesture to get her attention. She resists the urge to place her hand over his, to search his eyes and look for some sort of genuine fond feeling to attach to the words that he'd spoken the night before last. After all she's witnessed since she's arrived here, Meadbh knows better than to put any store in that hope.

"Diarmuid," she says in a low voice.

"Come," he says softly. "I would speak with you, if you'll give me the time."

His tone is almost caressing, pleading. It's persuasive and though a small part of her rails against its wisdom, she nods her head in agreement. She'll hear what he has to say.

They find a quiet spot behind the wooden food store shed. He'd taken her hand, led her towards it without hesitation. Noting this familiarity did nothing to calm her thoughts. Instead, they wander in ever more wild directions that have words like "trysting place" among them. It's silly and patently ridiculous, but her mind will not stand correction for a more plausible truth.

He drops her hand and turns her to face him. He briefly

Kristin Gleeson

cups her face in one hand and looks intently into her eyes. "I wanted to explain. I know I haven't been completely truthful to you."

"Completely truthful?" she asks. The fragment of his words emphasise what she desires, rather than what he hasn't been.

He smiles wryly at her reply, acknowledging the underlying meaning. "I'm sorry." He pauses and looks upwards. "There are so many reasons why I haven't explained all to you, but I want you to know that first and foremost in my mind was, and is still, to protect you."

She gives him a doubtful look. "It was to protect me to conceal your *sliocht* from me? To lead me into the hands of Desmond? To lead me here, to Mac Carthaigh and claim me as your wife? You've asked me to trust you and I find I don't even know you."

Silence hangs between them. Diarmuid's eyes are clouded with so many emotions and even as Meadbh studies them she can hardly name them all. Regret, though, has the biggest place. But she detects a hint of fear.

"Who are you, Diarmuid?" she whispers.

Diarmuid bites his lip. Strokes her hair slowly. "I'm a man who loves you, Meadbh inghean Cormac Uí Fhlionn. A man who comes from the esteemed and long line of O'Dálaigh poets. A younger son of a younger son. A man whose father, long dead, was a poet. A man whose older brother became a priest, and so it fell upon the younger son to take up the profession, even though he felt himself more suited to the life of a warrior. And seized every secret opportunity to train, hoping that one day he might prove himself. But this man, who wanted something that no O'Dálaigh should want, had an uncle who refused to listen and ensured that he attend to all his bardic lessons. No punishment was spared when he misbehaved, or failed to achieve what all would expect an O'Dálaigh to achieve.

"When it came time for the final exam where he would be deemed an ollamh and set on the path to become a court *ollamh*, or at the very least an *ollamh* of one of the prominent lords, this man decided that he would demonstrate his determination to follow the path he felt best, and he ran away."

Diarmuid pauses a moment. The pause may initially appear to be made to increase the drama of his words, but in Meadbh's mind, the drama is already present in his words to the fullest degree. Nothing more is needed. But then she sees it is for his own sake that he pauses, so that he can gather himself for the next part of the tale.

He takes it up again, looking into the distance. "This man found a place among the *galloglach* that Mac Carthaigh hired to fight. And it was among them, after many years of fighting, that this man found he'd been mistaken. He wasn't suited for a warrior's life. His was, in fact, a poet. But since he'd foresworn his uncle's home and family, he chose instead to reflect upon what path he'd take, and he found a place as a labourer at Teampall Gobnatán."

Diarmuid returns his gaze to Meadbh. The looks she sees takes her breath away as his words filter through to her mind. "And that's where this regretful, mistaken man first saw a woman. She was tending *beacha,* and the song that came from her mouth was enchanting. Worthy of any bard. This man couldn't take his eyes from her. Sought any sight of her that he could. Wanted to protect her. Found he loved her, as he never loved anyone before. But she hardly knew his name, let alone gave him any notice. And when it came to pass that she needed someone to escort her to her homeplace, this man was so grateful for the opportunity to be close to her, to even have the chance to know her better, that he was willing to risk the pestilence."

Meadbh is so still, caught up in his tale, she hardly lets a breath escape, for fear of missing a word.

"When they arrived at her homeplace and saw the turn of events, his desire to protect her grew thousandfold. And so, he contrived to find a way to get her somewhere safe. Somewhere to give him time to set events into motion that would allow him to take up a place among the O'Dálaigh *ollamhs*, to make her his wife, and give his name and *sliocht* as protection to her and her kin. To return to Mac Carthaigh, who knew him well and liked him, and whose invitation Domhnall O'Dálaigh wouldn't fail to honour." He takes a deep breath. "And as you know, plans are made to only go awry. Just as they have done. But now, I hope that, though delayed, these plans can unfold as originally intended."

He takes up both her hands in his, holds them to his chest. "This man, who stands before you, pledging his love and his life, bears the name Cearbhall mac Diarmuid O'Dálaigh."

Meadbh is stunned. The tale has wrapped her up and held her closely throughout, but his last words have left her speechless. All thoughts that before had crowded her mind, waiting to be uttered are gone. She can only stare. Wonder and feel the anger and hurt that suddenly rises. "Cearbhall? You are called Cearbhall? But why would you give a false one?" The anger taints her tone, but she refuses to disguise it.

Diarmuid sighs. "I have used Diarmuid, my father's name, since I left my uncle's home. I have paired it with O'Donoghue in the past to prevent my family from finding me. And perhaps to spare them the shame should it ever come to light that I was a paid warrior with the *galloglach*. I've learned to trust few, and once I knew you well I couldn't bring myself to tell you the truth, for fear of your reaction."

Meadbh shakes her head, struggling to understand. "You say you care for me. That you love me, yet you couldn't tell me who you really are."

Diarmuid frowns, sorrow joining with the regret in his expression. "I'm sorry. But I would have you know the truth, now. Before this matter with my uncle and Mac Carthaigh is settled. And the matter with O'Mathghamhna. I would know if you would agree to this plan."

Feardorcha. His name comes to her, pushing its way through. There's nothing covert about Feardorcha. He's out in the open, blunt with it. But he's exactly the man he presents to the world. There's no subtlety about Feardorcha. She can value that, but at the same time, she realises, she can see its limitations.

She covers her face with her hands. "I don't know, Diarmuid." She gives a wry laugh. "Cearbhall."

But she does know. And the knowledge makes her afraid.

Chapter Forty

Light shines through the solar window, weak, and a sure signal that the bright summer days are coming to an end. A summer like no other, at least for Meadbh. A summer that followed a spring like no other. Her own awakening, her own rebirth. She's conscious of it now, even as she moves towards Mac Carthaigh, while everyone begins to gather, ready for the day's events.

She knows she must talk to him, even with this new knowledge that lies within her. She's learned so much about herself, and the world she inhabits, and that forces her forward. She must put herself, her *sliocht*, Síle, first. She stops in front of Mac Carthaigh, nods and greets him.

He regards her carefully, a smile playing on his lips. Today, he's dressed formally. His deep blue *brat* sports a knotted fringe that creates an intricate pattern. The brat is fixed in place by a brooch in which an outline of a stag is etched. The brat is full and draped in such a manner that it obscures most of the *ionar* and *léine* he wears. Highly polished boots round off his appearance.

"I hear from Cearbhall that you sing and play the harp to some degree. Or, as he put it, you 'sing in a manner like no other'. I must admit I'm intrigued, and hope you would do us the honour of displaying your talent for us, if not today, perhaps another time."

Meadbh realises much in this conversation. So much that it overwhelms her, but first and foremost, is that this is the first time she's heard Mac Carthaigh name Diarmuid, rather than address him as 'my lad'. That gives rise to the question of whether it was deliberate.

He studies her, waiting carefully, she realises. A reply to his statement falls from her lips almost before she's aware that it's there. "Of course. Whenever it pleases you." She's astonished by the words and hastens to add more. "But I promise you that my talent is very little, and in no way equals ...Cearbhall's." The name still sounds strange upon her ears.

Mac Carthaigh nods, pleased. And for a moment she wonders if she detects humour there. Humour at the ruse that has been played upon her? Or the circumstances that gave rise to it? Either way, it disconcerts her, just as so much has since this morning. Since her arrival yesterday.

He pats her shoulder. "For now, though we must hear Cearbhall's composition." He gestures her to take a seat on the benches that are now placed in rows, facing an empty area in the room. Ready for Cearbhall.

Meadbh begins to open her mouth, to seize the last few moments alone with Mac Carthaigh to make her plea, but his hand is gently ushering her towards a bench and his other hand indicates a place in the front. What can she do but follow her feet and the guidance? A hasty plea before an event such as this is perhaps not the best approach for her cause. At least that's what she tells herself. There will be another time. An additional thing to tell herself. But she must be told. Surely that's something to cling to. In the telling, it shows she hasn't given up.

The room is silent, waiting. The people are also quiet, but emotions hang around them, filling the space, a mix of tensions, patience, curiosity, fear, animosity, warmth, pride, simple interest, plain boredom. The boredom hangs over the dog that lays at Mac Carthaigh's feet, for all he can hear is the droning voice of the older man who holds forth in front of everyone. Or so Meadbh thinks as she listens to Domnall's discourse on the complexities of poetry composition.

"We of course would like to hear Dan Direach form," he says, looking over at Cearbhall who stands beside him, waiting to perform. "Yesterday Cearbhall gave us a sample of one of the earlier forms from long ago. Now, composition has become much more sophisticated, as you saw in the first poem he gave us." Domnall nods to himself, as if to give his personal confirmation of its quality and countenance to the performance. "Today, we'll hear a composition of Cearbhall's own. The final test of anyone aspiring to *ollamh*. I'll judge its quality and whether it complies with the rules of metre and subject matter."

He nods to Cearbhall, takes his seat front and centre and folds his arms over his chest.

Cearbhall steps toward the audience a fraction and fixes his gaze on Meadbh. His stance is confident, but the gaze he fixes on Meadbh is hopeful, loving and a little anxious. She smiles and tries to infuse her own gaze with confidence in his abilities. Of that she has no doubt.

"I've not had the customary nine days, so I can only apologise for its quality. It may not contain all the nuances and fineness of phrase that it should, but it does reflect my feelings for music, and most particularly, the harp. This harp I heard at Knoc I Chosgair."

Cearbhall takes a deep breath and begins:

A chláirsieach Chnuic I Chosgair, chuirios súan síorrosgaibh,
a nuallánach bhinn bhlasda, ghrinn fhuaránach fhlorasda.
A chlár buadha as bláith minlearg, a mhonghárach
mhéirfhiirdhearg
a cheóladhach do chealg sinn, a dhearg leómhanach láinbhinn.

O harp of Chnoc I Chosgair that bringest sleep to eyes long
wakeful
Thou of the sweet and delicate moan, pleasant refreshing, grave.
O choice instrument of the smooth, gentle curve, thou that criest

Under red fingers, musician that has enchanted us, red harp,
high souled, perfect in melody.

Cearbhall continues on, his voice mesmerising, a harp sound of
its own that enchants, just as the harp he describes. He speaks
of its power to lure the bird from its flock, cool the heart, heal
every wounded warrior, charm and beguile women. It's the
favourite of the learned, restless, smooth, sweetly musical,
redstar over elfmounds, breast-jewel of the High Kings. The
poem reaches its culmination in the last few verses before he
brings it to a close.

A fhúaim tráagha ré toinn cciúin, chrann fosgadhghlan fírchiúil,
fleadha 'gá n-ól it fhochair, a ghlór eala ós fhionnshrothaibh,

A núall ban sídhe a Síth Lir,'s gan ceól do chor at aighidh,
ód threóir as téidbhinn gac teach, a chéidrinn cheóil na
gcláirsioch.

O sound of the beach against the gentle wave, shadowy tress of
true melody,
feasts are consumed beside thee, O voice of the swan on bright
streams.

. . .

O cry of the fairy women from the mound of Lear, no music can
match thine;
under thy guidance every house is sweet-stringed, thou pinnacle
of harp-music.

Cearbhall's eyes, still distant and cast above them all, slowly
lower, clear, and gaze out to the group. The room is silent again.
Waiting. Transfixed. But the emotions that hang are one and the
same, focused and wrapped around every person intently. Awe.
Domnall clears his throat, as if he feels it falls upon him to break
the silence. He stands, walks across the room and places a hand
on his nephew's shoulder.

He scans the room, his gaze falling on each individual in the
front. Even Meadbh feels the weight of his regard for a brief
moment.

"I present to you now, this man, Cearbhall mac Diarmuid
O'Dálaigh. A true O'Dálaigh. A true *fili* and *ollamh*."

The words are formal, each of them spoken slowly, with the
fraction of a pause between them. To add to the drama, but also
to add to its weight. Its significance. Joy blossoms inside of
Meadbh and spreads, its petals spreading, opening so wide they
fill her up.

Chapter Forty-One

The air feels fresh on Meadbh's face. The breeze that enters the solar window is just enough to allow her flushed face to calm, even as she feels Cearbhall's hand on her shoulder. She still finds it difficult to get used to this new name.

His hand slips from her shoulder and takes her own hand. "Now, we come to the root of the matter," he says in a low voice.

Behind them, people stand around, while others, O'Mathghamhna's few men and some of Mac Carthaigh's, filter in slowly, seeking out places to squeeze themselves in this increasingly crowded room. Soon O'Mathghamhna and Feardorcha will make their case to Mac Carthaigh. Position and honour are on their side. O'Mathghamhna and his *sliocht's* power and influence may have waned in the decades since his birth, but it's still significant. It's enough. Feardorcha has much to add to the case as well. All in all, they are right to feel as confident as their manner and their expressions convey. Meadbh sees all this when she turns from the window and her heart sinks.

Her heart has told her much in these last moments. These last days. And if she's honest, it's told her much since she first laid eyes on Diarmuid, who is now Cearbhall. That aside, her obligations, her *sliocht* are there in her mind.

Cearbhall squeezes her hand. "Come, it's time."

Meadbh hears Mac Carthaigh speak, but the words won't assemble in their proper order in her mind. The men stand before her as she sits on the bench, alone, except for Derbhgilla who has taken a place beside her, facing forward. There's kindness there in Derbhgilla, but also detachment. This is just another of her husband's judgements, her expression explains. And Meadbh understands that, but at the same time she can't help but feel that she's alone in so many ways. Even with Cearbhall's promises, his hopes. They are his hopes, but at this moment, she's not sure they're hers. She sits here, without a voice. But even if she had one, what would she say?

"Lughnasadh is upon us," says Mac Carthaigh.

O'Mathghamhna, Feardorcha stand on the left and face Cearbhall, his uncle and nephew. Mac Carthaigh is positioned at the head, the *breitheamh* for this case, this dispute that he alone will settle.

"The time of Lughnasadh is when we would have the gathering, where, among other things, we would have the judgements. But because of this time we're in, this time when pestilence sweeps our land, where some of us have had to bear the unbearable," he gives a nod to O'Mathghamhna, acknowledging his particular loss, "and we may yet be asked to bear more, I decided once again that there will be no gathering on this ancient day."

Many cross themselves at his words, offering their own silent hope and prayers that they and their loved ones will be spared. That God shall spare them the punishment that so many speak of. Meadbh even hears a few words of invocation, but at this moment she can only find that lorica she's uttered before and whisper it now. This time she finds she speaks it for Síle, for Eoin, for Ita and Aedh. And even for Cearbhall. She thinks of her mother and finds that she can speak it even for her. Meadbh looks up and finds that Mac Carthaigh is talking again, the moment of silence finished.

"And so this dispute, because of its particulars, will be heard today. This is not a situation for the priests or the bishops however they might feel. We know our heritage, our law. As there's no *breitheambh* available to verify the judgement, I'm taking on that role.

"After both sides have presented their case, I'll pronounce my judgement with the guidance of both God and the Brehon Law custom, as I know it today. I leave it first to you, Feardorcha, to make your case. To present your story as you truthfully witnessed it."

Feardorcha nods, straightens, and clears his throat. His face is flushed. He's a man of action, of battle. He's not a man of words.

"I am cousin to O'Mathghamhna," he begins. "The son of his father's brother. We're like brothers. Closer. I was fostered with him." He looks at O'Mathghamhna and nods. He nods then to Mac Carthaigh, emphasising his words, his connection, his importance and worth. "O'Mathghamhna has long held the lands of Raithlinn, since Ui Fhlionn made pledges of them in return for cattle and goods. These pledges mounted up, until eventually, O'Mathghamhna owned it all." Feardorcha nods again, this time to himself, obviously pleased with the words, the manner of his presentation, so far. "Just this past spring we received word from Raithlinn that Ui Fhlionn was dead of the pestilence." He pauses a moment, allowing a time for comments. Cearbhall's eyes are narrowed, but he holds his silence. Feardorcha takes a breath. "So, hearing that, my cousin asked me to go to Raithlinn and assess the situation. To handle things as I saw fit." He pulls his mouth into a stubborn line. O'Mathghamhna watches him with deep concentration, his expression difficult to read.

"When I arrived, I found it in a terrible state," continues Feardorcha. "Most of the *sliocht* gone or dead. Only three people of the household remained. Ui Fhlionn's wife, a cousin of some sort, and his wife. The fields and cattle were untended. Many lost. How many, well, who can say? Cows were unmilked. The *ráth* wasn't in the best shape, though the wife made it as comfortable as possible. She was most hospitable and helped me understand the extent of the problems at Raithlinn. I resolved to restore things, and began to set my men and myself to gathering up the cattle. It's when I was doing that I came upon the daughter."

275

He nods toward Meadbh and traps her in his gaze. The determination is there. She looks away quickly, afraid to see more.

"It seemed the best plan to make her my wife. To take on Raithlinn for the family. There were no other suitable candidates, and besides, it was time that it was fully made O'Mathghamhna. She's young and will have many years to provide O'Mathghamhna sons to make it so." He looks to O'Mathghamhna. "My foster brother agreed. And so we were married. And so we were bedded." With the last words he looks at Cearbhall, daring him to disagree. "She was untouched, never bedded, before me. And even now, a son may be growing in her belly."

Cearbhall flinches. It's slight, so slight, but Meadbh has seen it. The reaction makes her heart sink. Its truth is undeniable, but will it matter so much?

Meadbh hardly dare look when Cearbhall begins to speak. She finds her hands are the only place she can look. She twines her fingers, making little patterns, overlapping, lacing, weaving. All the threads of her life seem to be in those fingers which are now knotted and nearly painful with their twining. She welcomes this physical pain, because the pain she feels she must bear, the pain that she's now aware of in her heart, is just too sharp. All the emotion she's denied, she tried to reason into something less, something pleasant, has now surfaced and demands to be recognised. The love she has for this man, who perhaps doesn't even deserve it, will no longer be silenced. She nearly groans with the awful truth of it.

"I hear Feardorcha's words." Cearbhall's voice is sonorous. Gravid. "They're full of reason. Full of a purpose that shows a man who is loyal to his *sliocht*. Raithlinn, which has been the holding of Ui Fhlionn for generations, has had to bear the burden of *cuid oidche*, which, as many of you know, demands the host provide entertainment for all when the lord comes to visit. It must be paid for in the cattle slaughtered, ale brewed, deer, fish and fowl caught. Cheese, milk, and other provisions many times over, not to mention the price of a bard, a harper and anyone else who may give the entertainment for the night, or se'en night the lord and his people stay. This is what drove Ui Fhlionn to begin his bargaining, his indebtedness, so that eventually most of the land was more in debt than was not. He was unable to redeem this land in his lifetime, but it can be done."

Cearbhall pauses, scans the room. He fixes his gaze on Meadbh. "I would do this. I would redeem Raithlinn and make it a place for learning. A place where poetry, music and learning can flourish." He looks at Mac Carthaigh. "I would do this in your honour, under your patronage. I would do this with Meadbh, my wife." He shifts his gaze to Feardorcha. "*My* wife. The woman I have known this year and more. The woman I escorted to Raithlinn when her father lay ill. And where I learned of the history, the importance that is Raithlinn. From Eoin, Ui Fhlionn's faithful cousin, head of the *ceithearn tigh* of Ui Fhlionn, and from his wife, Ita. Their own son, Aedh, shows much promise, and is even now in fosterage with O'Mathghamhna." He nods to O'Mathghamhna. He approves of this choice. "At Raithlinn I saw what worth, what character, Meadbh possessed. It's then I knew she would be the worthiest of wives and companions. And with her agreement we decided we would marry, provided we had Mac Carthaigh's approval.

We were on that journey when Desmond's men captured us."
He pauses again, allowing the gasps that echo around the room.
Horror is expressed. Looks exchanged.

"We were taken to Desmond. I gave him a false name, so he
wouldn't suspect my identity. I wasn't certain if he favoured the
O'Dálaighs. But I did declare Meadbh my wife, in public, and
in turn, Meadbh declared me her husband."

Meadbh hears his words and notes the bending of the truth.
There's nothing in his statement that anyone could challenge.
And certainly not his claim about their marriage. Not even
Desmond himself, who was there to hear both declarations. But
the circumstances are what make it not quite what the words
imply. It's what he doesn't say. And his words about establishing
a place of learning? When were they uttered to her? But there's
no one here who'll challenge him on that point either. No one.

"Then, before the next day, after these words were spoken.
Meadbh vanished. Taken by perhaps the very *sídhe* themselves." He gestures out of the window. "For they're everywhere. Even now, they could be outside, looking for any
opportunity to cause mayhem. Trouble. We know what they're
like." He says the words slowly, nodding and in turn, people
mimic the nod. Agreement. They know, they understand what
he means.

"I searched everywhere for her. I returned to her homeplace, to Raithlinn, but no one had seen her." He takes a deep,
emotion-filled breath, looks upward. "I came to Mac Carthaigh,
a friend of old, and the Ui Fhlionn overlord, to ask his help." He
turns to look at Mac Carthaigh, his expression grateful. "And
through his help, we eventually discovered that Meadbh had
finally returned to Raithlinn. But that now, an O'Mathghamhna
had claimed her for his wife, and Raithlinn his holding." He

shook his head slowly, allowing the weight of his words to settle among the listeners. "I journeyed to Raithlinn, to discover the exact nature of these events. And it's there I met with Meadbh, saw the way things were. Her resignation. Her dutifulness. But at the same time, I also saw that, despite all, she still cared for me. And with that knowledge I asked her to come with me. To go to Mac Carthaigh. To establish the legality of our marriage. That being wed to one another should take precedence over her marriage to Feardorcha. That what we talked about, what we hoped to build at Raithlinn was far more important, more worthy, than whatever plans Feardorcha might conceive.

"And that's what I lay before Mac Carthaigh this day. And to you, my listeners. I lay before you my hopes, my dreams that you may deem them noble, worthy. And that Mac Carthaigh, in his infinite wisdom, may deem it so, too."

Cearbhall nods his *sin é*. That's it, indeed. A perfect ending to a perfect speech. Feardorcha, who just an hour ago had appeared more than satisfied that he'd won his case with his reasoned words, now appears flushed again. Angered, and at the same time worried.

Mac Carthaigh nods. He scans the room slowly, considering. His eyes rest on Meadbh. He motions her to follow, his hand gesturing towards her in a curt, sharp manner.

"Come. I would speak with you alone."

Meadbh sits there a moment, paralysed.

Chapter Forty-Two

The chamber is small and dark. It contains a sleep-mussed pallet and nothing else. Was this where Cearbhall spent his night composing? A dark chamber where no light can penetrate? She's heard the stories and can only imagine that it's true. And now she must form her own composition, it seems. One that will determine the rest of her life. Perhaps. She waits for Mac Carthaigh to speak.

"Now so, you've heard the arguments."

"Yes."

He waits for her to say more. There's nothing more. "And what do you think?" He asks finally.

She gathers herself a moment. "I think they both presented very good arguments. Cearbhall's was compelling for the beauty of its presentation, if nothing else."

"And Feardorcha?"

She shrugs. It's an impulse, one that he more than likely couldn't see. "He presented the facts as he saw them very well."

Mac Carthaigh sighed. "I'm asking your opinion, woman, not an account of what I just saw and heard myself. I'm asking you, what do you want?"

Meadbh feels tears prick her eyes. To be asked what she wanted. Was it a trick? She brushes a tear away, determined to meet this challenge head on. To be strong. "I want what's best for my *sliocht*."

"Your *sliocht*, Meadbh, is that of your husband." His tone is kind, now. The earlier impatience, fled. "Would you have one over the other? Or would you favour both? It's a strange arrangement, but one, I'm told by O'Dálaigh that has been done before. We could make that work."

"Both?" The thought astonishes her. She can't imagine it. She doesn't want to imagine it. Even if there is a child growing inside her. She shakes her head. "No. I have a choice." If she must forsake her *sliocht*, there's only one choice. If Mac Carthaigh will allow it.

The hall is silent when the two return and Meadbh returns to her place on the bench. Tension hangs in the air. A tension that buzzes inside Meadbh like a swarm of *beacha*. Her *beacha*. And they will continue to be her *beacha*. At least she hopes so. She can't imagine they would allow otherwise. She takes strength from those *beacha* inside her. They tell her to be hopeful. They sing a song of joy.

Mac Carthaigh stands alone at the centre of the room. "I've heard each party present their facts. Their arguments that would have a judgement in their favour. Both are full of merit. Both men presenting them are indisputably worthy. No one can doubt that." He looks to Cearbhall and then to Feardorcha. "There are two parts to this dispute, as I see it. But the two parts are interlinked. The first part is Raithlinn, and who will have that holding. It's a holding that has long been associated with O'Mathghamhna. That can't be changed. And regardless how Ui Fhlionn came to be indebted, the fact remains is that Raithlinn was the debt. No parcel of land was redeemed. That is truth. And so, in keeping with that understanding, I can only agree that O'Mathghamhna now have that holding in full. It's only a matter of announcing what's already known."

Meadbh's buzzing fades and she wonders at what he's just pronounced. How will her words, her opinion that he asked only moments ago, now be made real? She glances at Cearbhall who stands off to the side as one of the people who await their judgement. He catches her gaze and he forms a smile. It's filled with confidence, but his eyes tell the uncertainty that lurks inside him.

Mac Carthaigh holds up a hand at the murmurings that have broken out. The listeners fall silent. He nods. "As I mentioned, there are two parts. Both intertwined. The second part concerns Meadbh Inghean Cormac Ui Fhlionn. As it stands now she has two husbands. Both recognised under the Brehon Law and the custom of the land. We know this. There are a few options from which to choose. But after discussion and careful thought, as well as understanding the rights of Raithlinn, the reasoned arguments of Feardorcha, and the persuasive words of Cearbhall, I've decided on a slightly different course. I judge it best that Feardorcha and Meadbh divorce and Feardorcha take the widow as his new wife.

"Cearbhall, in the meantime, will keep Meadbh as his wife. This arrangement will allow a fair transition as the formal holder of Raithlinn to O'Mathghamhna. The widow is young enough that she would undoubtedly produce a few sons for Feardorcha. If Meadbh does carry Feardorcha's child, when it's born, it will take its place in Raithlinn's household as an O'Mathghamhna. And until it's certain whether she's carrying a child or not, she'll remain here, separate from Cearbhall as before."

Feardorcha's face is filled with astonishment. His mouth opens, ready to protest. O'Mathghamhna has a pleased grin on his face and he nods. Meadbh can only stare at them as she struggles with the pronouncement she's just heard. She thinks of the child she might be carrying. Already, the thought of giving up the child sends wild uncertainty and loss inside her. And after the time is up, either with an empty womb or until she delivers, where will she go? North to the O'Dálaigh home-place with Cearbhall? Or wander the castles and courts of the Gael lords, or even the Gaill lords? She seeks out Cearbhall and can find only confusion.

Noise fills the air with the discussion that's breaking out around her. Words, fragments of conversation assault her ears and she wants to throw up her hands and cover any possibility of hearing them. She must think. She must think. Eoin. Ita. Aedh. What will happen to them with only her mother there in

Raithlinn? She'll care nothing for them. Nothing. They'll fade into poverty. A family without land, without means to provide for themselves. No need to foster Aedh now O'Mathghamhna has all he wants.

Mac Carthaigh put up his hand once again. "It isn't done. This judgement still has its second part to finish." He turns to Cearbhall. "Your words regarding the need for to create a place of learning were well said. A place, you argued, that would serve the art of music and poetry. There's no such place here in Mac Carthaigh holdings. It would be a grand thing to have that place, would it not O'Mathghamhna?"

O'Mathghamhna nods easily. He's happy now that the judgement has favoured him and his kin so well. "Of course. It would indeed, so."

Mac Carthaigh smiles, satisfied. "Since O'Mathghamhna is so amenable it would be most appropriate, given the circumstances, that he provide a tract of land to establish such a place. A bardic school. One that would bear the O'Dalaigh name." He glances over Domnall and Gofraidh, who'd resumed their place beside Cearbhall. "Wouldn't you agree that would be grand thing all together, Domnall O'Dálaigh? To have the O'Dálaigh name in this part of the land. To have it celebrated, to teach and spread the arts in their name?"

Despite her confusion Meadbh can't help but admire, once again, Mac Carthaigh's cunning. He's a man who is truly worthy of his powerful position. Though she's one of the tools in his political manoeuvering, she finds she can't object to anything he's said, if only for its clever use of words that bring about no offence. At least none that she can see.

"There's nothing at all to object to in that proposition," says Domnall. His eyes glitter with the possibilities, his mind already fashioning the shape of this place of learning. "It should be somewhere remote, removed from the dangers of both war and pestilence." He looks over at O'Mhaithghamnhna. "As much as is possible."

O'Mhathghamhna's pleasure has dimmed. He frowns. Sighs heavily. "Of course," he says finally. "It shall be done."

Meadbh looks over at Cearbhall. She's not certain what she thinks. Except the names and faces of her kin. She knows what she wants regarding them. Cearbhall smiles at her, cocks his head slightly, and nods. He looks over at Mac Carthaigh. "I accept this judgement. And gladly, but I would ask one thing. One addition to the judgement. It's a small matter, one that I'm sure Feardorcha and O'Mathghamhna will find so trivial they'll wonder why I bother with it."

Feardorcha narrows his eyes and Cearbhall gives him an innocent look. "I would ask that the last remaining Ui Fhlionn of the household come with us. Eoin, Ita and their son Aedh. They can serve in our household if they're agreeable."

A bud of joy comes to life inside Meadbh and spreads its petals slowly as she hears agreement from Mac Carthaigh and O'Mathghamhna. Her hopes in that regard are complete. Her family. Herself. They'll be together, now. Safe. And Cearbhall. She'll be his wife and he her husband. And there will be music. And poetry. And all the learning she could wish for. The child that may or may not be in her belly, though. The thought makes her look down and place her hand on her stomach. A tear gathers at her eye. She feels a hand, warm and supportive on her shoulder. She looks up and sees Cearbhall. There's compassion and promise there. A promise that she'll hold on to as they look towards their life together.

Epilogue

Meadbh stands on *drom an fhéich*, the hill of the debt, overlooking the large bay and the small islands in it, and the other peninsula across from it. The day is clear and she can see the edges of the land as it curves around, its hills and valleys undulating. A breeze catches her plait and whips it around so that it hangs along her chest. She's left off her headcovering today. No one will see her. The lads are in their rooms studying, learning the 300 poems that is their goal. Some, the advanced ones, are composing, lying in their dark chamber for the requisite nine days before they're examined. It's nearly Bealtaine, the time when the school will break up for the year. For summer. She's glad for that. Though she enjoys the boys, the sound of their joyful voices and often rambunctious behaviour gladdens her, this time she knows her husband needs his rest. He's worked non-stop since they established this school. Every day is precious to him for what can be accomplished. But she knows, this next month he'll take a short rest. A rest while her child is born. He did that when she gave birth to their son, scarcely a year after they moved here. And he did that for their daughter, too, only two years before. He'll do it now. Síle will be there, too, though her limbs are stiff and she's able for little more than encouraging smiles. Ita will assist, of course, for she's just as key in Meadbh's household as she could ever wish. As are Eoin and Aedh in the management of the lands. They lands are extensive, and though some O'Mathghamhna and other labourers give their toil, it still takes up much of Eoin and Aedh's time. Now Aedh's new wife's belly will soon begin to swell and there will be more Uí Fhlionns, a thought that gladdens Meadbh's heart.

She catches sight of the field nearest their home. She has yet to visit her *beacha* today. It's a task, no, a pleasure that she saves for the quietest time of day. She has three hives, now. Enough for her to tend on her own, for that's how it must be for her. Until her daughter is of an age, she amends to herself. She knows her daughter will share her affinity for the *beacha*. How could she not, when the *beacha* had sung to her all the while she was in Meadbh's belly? She smiles at the memory.

The *beacha* call her even now, their song sinking deep inside her. She begins her own song in response, one that she's perfected both with the *beacha* and on her harp. The harp that gives her and Cearbhall pleasure. She's composed a few simple pieces with the *beacha's* voice inside her. One is a *suantraí*, a lullaby, for her children. The other is a love song, the words it contains formed with the help of Cearbhall. The words are about love of a person, a family, a *sliocht*, a home. Her home.

HISTORICAL NOTES

I had intended to write another novel set in Medieval Munster after publishing *In Praise of the Bees*, featuring the descendants of the main characters, and this novel turned out to be just that. It started out as a short story for an anthology with stories centred around the plague, *We All Fall Down*, published in 2020. I wrote the story in 2018, well before the Covid pandemic and one of the elements that fascinated me was Ireland's experience of plague compared to the rest of Europe. When the plague arrived in the autumn of 1348, Ireland was suffering from cycles of famine and deprivation brought on by the wars a few decades before and a few bouts of drought. It was also a time of great power struggles. The Anglo Irish, the English rulers who were absent, were fighting amongst themselves as well as fighting the Gaelic Irish. The Gaelic Irish were also fighting amongst themselves. Borders shifted along with loyalties. Gaelic Irish and Anglo Irish lords rose in prominence or declined, either from losing lands through battles, or, in the case of Anglo Irish because the king took away their power, or, in the Gaelic Irish case, the convoluted customs and system of obligations and requirements to overlords impoverished some lords, or enriched others. The division between the Gaelic Irish and the Anglo Irish was still evident in so many aspects of society and politics, even though it had been over two centuries since the arrival of the Norman and Welsh in 1169. And despite the fact that many of the Anglo Irish lords had Gaelic Irish mothers and grandmothers. The Gaelic Irish still followed a revised version of the Brehon laws, though that was fading by this time and some of the English system was either being enforced or loosely adapted. Clothes were distinctive between the two societies, but there was some cross adaptation.

One clear distinction was the settlement patterns of the two different societies. The Anglo Irish settled primarily in the cities and some towns that were mostly of their creation or by the Norse some centuries previously. The densely settled communities provided optimal conditions for the rapid spread of the plague when it arrived. And the use of wheat, stored in a manner that attracted rats carrying fleas was also a factor. The wattle and daub huts and timber framed dwellings they inhabited allowed rats to find their way into dwellings or storage areas. The more well-to-do nobles had stone buildings and castles and so their homes weren't as easily penetrated – and as a consequence they didn't suffer the plague as much.

The Gaelic Irish, on the other hand, settled in small, scattered communities within clans, called clachans. Many lived on isolated farms, and their manner of trade wasn't centred around towns or cities, for the most part. There were no major roads for travellers to move with ease and frequent access. The plague spread slowly, mostly along rivers where goods were transported. Its toll is difficult to know, because few records are available, unlike Britain or the rest of Europe. A famous account was recorded by Friar John Clyn, whose friary in Kilkenny was struck in 1350 and most of the inhabitants, including him, died. But in close quarters such as the friary, the outcome isn't surprising. The percentage of dead there shouldn't be used as a representation of the percentages across Ireland. Given what is known, the numbers estimated are a lot more conservative. That said, Dublin suffered severely and a significant number of the population died.

What is known is that Ireland suffered from both bubonic

plague and pneumonic plague. It's surmised that bubonic (spread by fleas on rats) rarely spreads directly between humans. Pneumonic infects the lungs and is caused by direct transmission of the bacilli from infected humans, primarily through airborne droplets or inhaling faeces of infected fleas.

The knowledge of its cause and treatment was very minimal to none at all. One belief is that it was spread by a miasma and it could enter through mouth, nose, eyes and ears. That's the reason I had Diarmuid and, later, Meadbh cover up their faces. This is purely my own speculation as to what an individual might think to do and not what was the general practice.

Another difference between the Anglo Irish society and Gaelic Irish was the status and treatment of women. Neither were outstanding when it came to women's agency. I try to be historically accurate, so Meadbh and the female characters I have portrayed are more reflective of my research rather than any attempt to create a story that would show women with any kind of agency/power they might have today. It is tough to uncover women's stories and experience, especially the Gaelic Irish, because the sources are fewer. Recent work with wills, judgements and other records have uncovered a small amount. Enough to indicate that there were some differences between a Gaelic woman's experience and an Anglo Irish woman's experience. At this time, a lot of the important Anglo Irish were marrying Gaelic Irish women so the cultures were starting to blend, though. Anglo Irish men sometimes employed/honoured Brehon laws and sometimes not. Gaelic women could divorce and marry easily, as could the men. Marriage rarely took place in front of a priest but with the stated words of intent. Children out of wedlock enjoyed the same status as those born in wedlock. Gaelic women, however, were always in the care/wardship of either their husband, father, brother – or if they were all dead, the closest male kin. Anglo Irish women had a few more acknowledged rights. For example, when it came to land or, if middle class, conducting trade on their own if they were widowed, they would be allowed to administer the land or conduct the business. Divorce, however, was not an option among Anglo Irish women, only annulment, and that was at the mercy of the ecclesiastical courts.

As mentioned above, the shifting power and control among the Gaelic Irish clans and their overlords can make for some confusing history. I did my best to sort through the various allegiances at that time for the MacCarthy, O'Mahony and O'Flynn clans that were influential and powerful in the area of County Cork, mostly in the West Cork area. It was in flux at that time, with MacCarthy and O'Mahony vying for power. In addition, there were a few branches of MacCarthy who weren't always on the best of terms with each other and constantly challenged each other for optimum supremacy, that added to the confusion. O'Flynn had been important in the Bandon and Macroom area back in the early Medieval period and had once established a castle in Macroom. But by the time of the novel the clan's power had declined, and O'Mahony was the area overlord, though it was difficult to really trace when exactly the clan collapsed, so I took a little license with that. I may even be right!

The O'Dalaigh/O'Daly clan were, as indicated in the novel, an important clan whose members were poets, some very famous ones, including Gofraidh, who appears in the novel as a young man. The poems in this novel are actual poems either by Gofraidh himself, (primarily the ones claimed for Cearbhall). A man called Cearbhall is reputed to have been a poet that oversaw the bardic school Muintir Bháire, the Sheep's Head Peninsula, in the early years. According to a few obscure sources, the bardic school was well established by about 1300. It continued until around the 1600s and the ruins are still there today. There are conflicting accounts about how the O'Dalys came to settle there. One claim is that the land was O'Mahony's who gave it, and another states it was the allies of MacCarthy. It's clear, though, that O'Dalys were particularly successful at bedding themselves into new positions and consolidating hereditary claims to their ollamhships in lordships such as Carbery and Duhallow.

The reference to "castles" in this novel could mean a varying type of building and in no way should the reader imagine a classic castle found in Britain or the continent. It was the term employed at the time – and now, for the most part, these structures are called "tower houses" which better reflects what they looked like. There are plenty of examples and detailed descriptions online about their construction in different time periods. I am fortunate to have access to many examples that are still in fairly good shape, to imagine what it would have been like to inhabit.

RESOURCES

Art Cosgrove, ed. - A New History of Ireland Vol. II

Sean Duffy ed. - Medieval Ireland: an encyclopedia

Sean Duffy ed. - Princes, Prelates and Poets in Medieval Ireland

Finbar Dwyer - Medieval Ireland

Finbar Dwyer - 1348

Finbar Bergin - Irish Bardic Poetry

Kenneth Nicholls - Gaelic and Gaelicized Ireland in the Middle Ages

Maria Kelly - A History of the Black Death in Ireland

Gillian Kenny - Anglo-Irish and Gaelic women in Ireland 1170-1540

Tracy Collins - Female Monasticism in Medieval Ireland

A.J. Olway-Ruthven - A History of Medieval Ireland

Osbern Bergin - Irish Bardic Poetry

Claudia Kinmouth - Irish Country Furniture 1750-1950

J.E. Caerwyn Williams - The Court Poet in Medieval Ireland

Pat Herlihy - Ballyvourney 3501

CD

Preab Meadar - Lorcán Mac Mathúna, Daire Bracken

Acknowledgments

As usual I owe a great debt of thanks to my alpha team of readers, especially Jean, Jane, Claire and Babs, who gave a great fresh perspective. I also would like to give a special thanks to librarian extraordinaire Paula Walker at Bandon library and the Louise Mackey in the Heritage Studies department of the Cork County Council Library who were so helpful in helping me track down clan heads and overlords in the Bandon area during a very chaotic time period in Ireland's history. Thanks also to Lorcán Mac Mathúna and Daire Bracken for their fine talk about early Irish poetry and their creative talent to set music and dance to it. And answering my questions so graciously. And again, I owe a debt of gratitude to Áine Uí Cuill for reviewing the Irish and ensuring that it was accurate.

Also I want to thank my fantastic editor, Sandra Mangan, and my amazing cover designer, Jane Dixon-Smith whose creative genius has gone a long way to help make my books a success.

And most of all, I want to thank my brilliant readers, whose support down the years has helped to make my writing such a wonderful experience.

ABOUT THE AUTHOR

Originally from Philadelphia, Kristin Gleeson lives in Ireland, in the West Cork Gaeltacht, where she teaches art classes, plays harp, sings in a choir and runs two book clubs for the village library. She holds a Masters in Library Science and a Ph.D. in history and for a time was an administrator of a large archives, library and museum in America. She also served as a public librarian in America and in Ireland.

Kristin Gleeson has also published The Celtic Knot Series, The Renaissance Sojourner Series, the Rise of the Celtic Gods Series and the Highland Ballad Series. In addition to her novels, a biography on a First Nations Canadian woman, *Anahareo, A Wilderness Spirit*, is also available.

If you have enjoyed this book please post a review. It helps so much towards getting the book noticed.

If you go to the author website and join the mailing list to receive news of forthcoming releases, special offers and events, you'll receive an e novelette *A Treasure Beyond Worth,* a FREE prequel novelette and its ebook novel *Along the Far Shores* at www.krisgleeson.com

Music is a big part of Kristin's life and many of the books have music connected to them. Listen to the music while you read—go to www.krisgleeson.com/music and download the files. Keep checking back, as more pieces will be added to the library in the course of time.

Made in the USA
Las Vegas, NV
07 September 2025

27524975R00174